ABOUT THE AUTHOR

GB Williams specialises in complex, fast-paced crime novels. Born and bred in Kent, GB moved to South Wales as a supposedly first step on a year around the world. Then she met a guy. Kept the guy, kissed the travel goodbye.

Since then, she's worked, married, had two great kids – the usual. Now working as a freelance editor and writer, she lives with her family and the world's most demanding cat. And she hates every photo ever taken of her. Find out more at www.gailbwilliams.co.uk.

Published in Great Britain in 2022
By Diamond Crime

ISBN 978-1-7397448-6-1

Book design: jacksonbone.co.uk
Cover photograph: Dimitry Anikin/Unsplash

Printed and bound by
Ashford Colour Press Ltd, Gosport, Hants PO13 0FW

DIAMOND BOOKS

Diamond Crime is an imprint of Diamond Books Ltd.

Coming soon to Diamond Books
from GB Williams:

Play the Game

For Bobby and Queen

BREAKING FREE

[signature]

GB WILLIAMS

CHAPTER ONE

"So, what you're saying is that you've been helping my husband lie to me. For twenty-five years."

Twenty-five years. A quarter of a century. A lifetime. The lifetime of their friendship. Much of what she had listened to this afternoon made no sense. Yet, simultaneously, it was the keystone, the puzzle-piece that made everything else fit.

Elaine scrutinised the two women at the table with her. A corner table in a wine bar, the three of them occupied a small round table. Unnoticed by Elaine, they had positioned themselves such that if she made a move, they could stop her relatively easily. She hoped they wouldn't try because while she might be able to keep control of her voice, her ability to control her temper if one of them got in her way right now was less certain.

Keira sat directly opposite. Keira — her supposed best friend. The only friend she had after twenty-five years with a man she wasn't sure she knew anymore — if indeed, she'd ever known him. The blonde wasn't as blonde as she pretended, and the svelte body came from rarely eating and hours in the gym. Hours which resulted in a too low body fat ratio. Every vein and sinew showed in Keira's hands, in her scrawny neck. Snappable. Elaine clenched her hands under the table.

Do not show emotion, it's too messy.

Jason's words, not hers.

Jason. Her husband. Eight days ago, he'd headed out of the house for a three-week assignment in Prague, after that a visit to some conferences in Germany; he'd be home in six weeks.

Only he wouldn't be.

The IT team he had been part of had disappeared five days ago. Just gone. Five missing Englishmen missed the headlines. No kidnapper threats, no ransom demands. Nothing worthy of a headline, so no headline. And now, if she believed these two, no Jason. Or Steve. Or the other three.

How did Keira sit so calmly amidst all this? Say her own husband, Steve, was dead and act like it didn't matter? Easy. She's had two decades to get used to the possibility. I've had ten minutes.

"Elaine," Keira said softly, "you have to understand…"

"Oh, I understand." How she managed the reasonable tone, she wasn't sure. "You're my best friend, but you consider me an idiot."

At least Keira had the good grace to drop her gaze. The other woman didn't. Elaine now realised they hadn't been introduced, no names exchanged. Like Elaine and Keira, the woman was in her forties, but at the higher end, she looked tired, careworn. Every concern and responsibility had etched deep lines on her face.

"You don't have the clearance."

Even the woman's flat voice was devoid of emotion, as if all expression had been ground out of her. Elaine was more than a little familiar with that feeling, that numbness. Though she suspected it was an affectation in this woman.

"But she does?" Elaine tipped her head towards Keira.

"It's different."

"Really?"

"Complicated."

"And you think I'm simple."

This time she saw Keira swallow.

This wine bar was the best in town, but Elaine rarely came in. She loved wine but resented paying as much for a glass in a bar as she did for a whole bottle from the supermarket. A glass sat before her, spotted with beads of condensation. One spot grew so heavy it overcame the water tension and slipped down the curve from rim to stem. Instinct told Elaine this was the closest to tears she would get today.

She stared at the wine. Perfectly chilled. Warmer than the atmosphere at the table. How it tasted remained a mystery. The conversation left a bitter enough flavour. She didn't want a drink.

That wasn't true. She desperately wanted a drink, to go home and drink a full bottle, possibly two. She'd have to stop and shop on the way home.

"Are you in love with him?"

Elaine's attention snapped back to the women. "What?"

"Do you love Jason?"

"We've been married nearly twenty-four years." Marry in haste, repent at leisure. She sighed. "Not that it's relevant in this case. The man I've spent all those years with is the man I married, but if I believe you, he never really existed."

Was it possible? What if everything that these two had just told her was true? What if everything up to this point had been a construct, a lie? What if Jason lied to her about everything? Outright lies and lies of omission. And even if she had known, would it have made a difference?

3

Again, she looked around her. Everything seemed so normal.

The other woman frowned, her lips pursed. Lines deepened around her mouth, between her unplucked eyebrows. "Do you understand what we have said?"

The facts had been laid out clearly and logically. Only an imbecile wouldn't have understood. "Yes."

"And you understand the need for discretion?"

Of course she did. Heat rose through Elaine. Her cheeks burned, tension pulled in every fibre. Apparently, she'd been being treated like a child her entire adult life. If they were going to be stupid, she might as well be.

"No." The steady, reasonable tone surprised even her. Usually, when her belly knotted and her face burned like this, her tone dripped sarcasm. One messy emotion she couldn't always contain. "Why should I be discreet? Why shouldn't I go to the papers with what you've told me?"

"Elaine."

"No." She scowled at Keira but kept her voice controlled. "It's not like I've got anything left to lose. No family, no more kids, no husband." Her eyes grazed over Keira, who wasn't just her friend, but her boss in the pension and insurance company they both worked for. "Shitty job."

"That would be unwise," the other woman said.

"Really?" This time the sarcasm resounded. "If I go to the papers, tell all; I'd get paid a wodge of cash and be out of the country before you'd even see the headline."

The two women glared at each other.

"How much?"

Elaine didn't even blink. Stupid question. Right now, getting away from these two to process what she'd heard would be payment enough. But if the scrawny bitch was going to be ridiculous, so was she. "Half a million."

She grabbed her bag and without a word, ignoring Keira's call of her name, she deliberately and unnecessarily pushed past the unnamed woman, who needed to grab the table to stay upright on the chair. Elaine strode from the building.

CHAPTER TWO

"This woman has to be the most boring person in the world — ever."

"I'll take your word for it," the voice in his earpiece murmured. "You've met her."

"Years ago, and not as me."

"Her being boring is why Jason was allowed to marry her. She's not a security risk."

The only risk anyone could attach to Elaine Annie Blake was the risk of being bored to death. Though in fairness, in that one long ago meeting, he'd thought her actually quite nice. Bland but nice.

"Besides," the voice in his ear said, "you're looking for the evidence, not the woman. We know where she is."

He hoped she was having more fun than him. "I'm looking for evidence there is no evidence of." He looked into the drawer as he returned it to the bedside cabinet. He'd taken it out to check for anything taped inside or underneath. For a one moment, he'd felt tape and hope, only to pull it off and find he had a manufacturer's label in his hand. This drawer, like all the others he had gone through, was obsessively tidy. Elaine must have some form of OCD.

As he stood, he looked around. No more drawers, cupboards, shelves, or boxes to check. He'd gone over every inch of the house, looked in places normal people didn't even think they had places. And he hadn't encountered one single dust bunny.

On the neatly made bed, the pristine duvet had developed a dimple where he'd leant against the side there; he smoothed the dimple out. A covert mission; search – leave no trace. The overly clean house helped with that, no dust to disturb, no mess to drag out from under beds, chairs, tables, sofas, or other furniture. On the other hand, organised drawers meant any movement would be as obvious as if he had just tipped them out.

"There's nothing here."

"There must be."

The growl rumbled deep in his throat. "I'm telling you, there's nothing."

"Time to start pulling up the floorboards?"

He looked down. "Not much point." It wasn't dejection, it was realism. "Every room is floored with laminate. You can't get this stuff up without it becoming obvious, so if Jason was hiding anything under them, then it would be visible, and believe me I have looked closely."

"The woman must have it on her then," the voice in his ear said. "Set the bugs."

Had they found what they sought, there would be no need for further surveillance, but the item remained missing. He reached into the pocket of the plain blue boiler suit he wore to appear to be another anonymous workman. Each no bigger than a watch battery, seven bugs sat easily in the palm of his hand. Eight remained in the pocket. Normally he'd have no qualms about slipping these anywhere, but a woman who cleaned under every piece of furniture every time meant extreme care had to be taken, which meant deep consideration of placement. Mostly because there wasn't one obvious place. The perfectly hung curtains had an inch deep hem under the lining. Thick, possibly blackout lining.

To check, he slipped a bug in. The extra weight did not show.

Other bugs he slipped into more curtain hems upstairs.

Downstairs proved more difficult. In the kitchen, he managed to fix one into the mixer, under a cover that his earlier search told him there was no attachment for.

The sitting room became the next challenge. The curtains here were voiles only, no hem. The vertical blinds offered nothing. The array of family pictures offered nothing. It was just a display. Mother love. The only sign of anyone alive here. The knickknacks were all dust free, so under one wasn't an option, if he slipped one inside the china, it would likely rattle, and the bug would be quickly found. He knelt to test the corner joints of the coffee table. Not a speck of dust in any. That wouldn't work then. The well-watered pot plant sat too snug to the outer pot to put the bug between the two. The compost was soft, the finger hole simple to make. He slipped the mike in. A light cover of soil should still allow the bug to pick up sufficient sound, and more watering seemed unlikely for a couple of days.

"Shit."

At the word in his ear, he looked at his finger. "Not quite."

"What?" the voice demanded. "Whatever! Number Two called. The mark is away. You need to get out of there."

He gave the okay. That they still called Number Two, Number Two always struck him as odd. He remembered the insult that had started the nickname, but remained more shocked that Number Two had let it go, and even taken ownership of it. It was by no means an official title or rank, but somehow, she had made it work.

Thinking of work, he only had one place left to bug. The hallway. The only option was inside the fire alarm. Jason had rigged the house years ago with a security system that seemed to be only an alarm and exterior lights, but actually offered visuals without sound, of inside and outside. He had already tapped into that system.

Last bug set, ready to leave, he turned at the door to look back over the house. As pristine as a show house, only the family photographs assured him someone actually lived here. After more years investigating people than he wanted to think about, he'd never gone through anyone else's home in such detail, and yet gained so little insight into who the person was.

It was clear what belonged to Jason Blake, or at least to the construct used here. Yet Elaine Blake remained a shadow, a will-o'-the-wisp, nothing to reveal who she was. Not even her clothes, she had fewer clothes than any woman he had ever known, and almost all of it was office wear. One pair of designer jeans, seemingly unworn. One pair of sweatpants, black, and one hoodie, grey marl, might be worn with the one pair of trainers he found with tread barely worn. A pair of hardly used hiking boots sat near an outdoor outfit. Good names, quality goods, minimal evidence of use. This Jason didn't hike, which apparently meant Elaine wasn't allowed to.

One last glance assured him everything was as it had been when he'd walked in that morning. He left wondering how any person could be so dull.

Settled into the van, he checked the equipment was working, making sure the receiver volumes were audible not loud, as the mark's Ford Fiesta rounded the corner. A well-kept, if not entirely clean, 2014 model in grey. That didn't tell him anything either. She pulled up to the curb a little fast, but not dangerously so. She got out, did not slam the car door. She carried a bag, seemed to have something heavy in it. Her journey up the path was rapid, but no stomping to the door. All so very normal.

The headphones were comfortable, but even when he adjusted the volume, there seemed to be nothing to hear. He turned to the bank of monitors and moved the mouse, reactivating the screens to show the Blake's security system. He concentrated on the hall camera, the one fixed inside the smoke detector. Elaine stood with her forehead against the closed front door. Without movement, he guessed she might be crying, but he couldn't be sure. Lack of sound didn't really tell him anything. She was a ghost, but dead enough not to cry over a lost husband?

There was no sign of tears as she moved into the sitting room and paused, scanning the immaculate room. Had he left something out of place? Her handbag got slung to the sofa as she kicked off her shoes, leaving them where they fell with a curl of her lip.

As she entered the kitchen, he changed the camera feed. She pulled wine from the bag and slipped it into the freezer to chill faster. Again, she looked around. Did she have a hiding place he'd missed? Was that possible? That room was virtually sterile. He'd been in dirtier hospitals, and not all of them overseas.

"Like no one actually lives here."

He heard her words but struggled to find the inflexion.

"But there again, no one actually does."

There it was, the only tell in her voice. Lugubrious. She was Eeyore, without the personality. More interestingly, if even she thought no one lived there; where did she live? He grabbed his mobile and pushed back one earphone.

CHAPTER THREE

Today hadn't been anything Elaine would ever have expected. Uncertain, she passed back through the living room, ignoring the shoes, to go up to the bedroom. Her bedroom. The second bedroom. Whatever the truth about Jason, one thing was certain: he wasn't coming home tonight. She removed her skirt, shirt and tights, leaving them where they dropped. Next, the pins from her hair, those were placed carefully onto the dressing table — she had experienced how painful stepping on hairpins was — and having her hair down and free came as such a relief. A glance in the mirror showed a few greys in the dull brown, but not enough to bother dying it. Yet. Not until Jason saw it and complained. If he ever did. Sweatpants and hoodie tonight, pulled from the depths of the wardrobe, hidden where Jason wouldn't find them, so no more retrieving them from the bin. Of course, he wouldn't look anymore, he didn't need to. Holding them before her, the indifference was hers not his. Two more of Jason's pet hates. But they were comfortable.

Sod his opinion, he's not here.

She turned to leave and slipped on the discarded tights.

With a tut, she leant down and picked everything up. Rebellion without purpose was pointless, especially when it annoyed her. She dumped it all in the nearby empty washing basket in the bathroom.

Back down in the kitchen, she opened the fridge. The bottle of wine from two days ago awaited. She liked to drink, but not usually to excess. She emptied the bottle into a single glass. Well over 250 ml, but she was the only one to judge. She left the glass on the counter as she nipped out the back to put the bottle in the recycling. She stopped a step away from the glass box. *What am I doing? I could have left it on the side for the night.* She dropped it in the box; recycling mattered more than the habit. More than a pointless rebellion.

Back inside, she locked up, then spotted the glass, condensation beading. Her memory flashed up the image of the earlier untouched glass. New questions came to mind. Why tell her in a wine bar? Come to that, why tell her at all? She stepped over and took up the glass, sipping the chilled wine.

There had to be some rational explanation. She just had to figure it out.

In the sitting room, she switched on the television, selected a news channel. *Why tell me?* That question repeated in her head. She replayed the conversation. Either she'd missed something or there was something they hadn't said before she'd walked out. But what? She sipped more of the wine and ignored the news story about yet more tension in Eastern Europe. It made a change from the usual political idiocy.

If they had to tell her, they had to want something. But that begged the questions of what they wanted, and why tell her in a wine bar?

To keep me out of the house.

The glass stopped halfway to her lips. Statue still, her eyes swept the room. They took her to the wine bar to keep her out of the house. They'd gone straight from work, which meant someone could have been here all day. Jason had trusted Steve with a spare key to the house years ago, so it wasn't like they'd have to break in, and they'd left no mess. Not that they'd need to — Jason's constant demands for the place to be spotless meant she kept it so clean as to be devoid of mess and personality. Everything had a place and was in it. Books and CDs strictly alphabetised, artist, then title. Anything that didn't look good was hidden in a box or a drawer, and drawers had to be tidy. Everything dusted so there would be no trail marks. If someone had been in looking for something, they'd cleaned up after themselves. She had nothing to hide, not even the lacy lingerie she'd once brought to try to zest up their sex life. Jason had taken one glance at her in it and sneered that she needed to lose at least a stone before wearing that again. She'd slept in the spare room since that night; the lingerie had gone. She had binned it along with any hope of a loving old age. Now they had his and hers rooms. She didn't even miss it anymore.

With effort, she dragged her mind back to the present. Whatever they were looking for, they must have found it.

She jumped at the knock. She switched off the TV, uncurling from the sofa, and headed to the door, flicking on the outside light as she passed the switch. Keira. With a sigh, Elaine opened the door.

"Yes?"

Keira smiled and moved to step in. Elaine crossed her arms but didn't move back.

"Can I come in?"

"I usually only let people I trust come in. Who did you let in earlier?"

Keira sighed. "Why are you being like this?"

Elaine felt her eyebrows rise. "Why am I being distrustful of a woman who's been lying to me for over two decades? Oh, I can't imagine. What do you want?"

Keira's features pinched. A part of Elaine wanted Keira to suffer. Part wanted her friend back. When Keira looked to the side, Elaine looked out, too. She spotted various cars and two vans she didn't recognise, but that didn't mean much. She stood straight and sighed, stepped back, obviously allowing Keira in.

"If you want a drink, I'm sure you know where everything is," she said, closing the door after Keira stepped past. "Help yourself."

Keira headed straight to the sitting room. Somehow Elaine wasn't surprised that the blonde paused at the sight of shoes strewn across the carpet. Keira deliberately stepped over one of the offending items to sit down. Elaine sat opposite, curling her legs up under her.

"So, what are they after?"

"Who?"

"The people outside who told you to come speak to me."

Keira made noises, as if she were being strangled. Thankfully, other noises caught her attention.

"What on earth is that?"

Unlike Keira, Elaine didn't need to search the ceiling for the source of that dreadful rattle. It sounded like someone was taking a hammer to the pipework.

"It's an audio illusion. The central heating just came on. One of the bands holding the lagging on the hot water tank is loose, eventually the thing twists and the metal catch shifts so that if the pipes vibrate, which they sometimes do when the heating pump first comes on, the metal clasp rattles against the pipework. It sounds worse down here than it does in the airing cupboard. Jace keeps promising to sort it."

Keira watched her and offered a sad smile. "He hated being called Jace."

"Oh, he wouldn't get past the shoes on the floor, my hair being loose, the slob-out gear, or the fact that I've put a glass on the coffee table without a coaster." As she listed Jason's pet hates, she noticed Keira's frown increasing.

"I thought you hated all that."

Elaine scowled. "Some friend you are, if that's what you saw. I pick up after everyone because Jason does his nut if I don't. He complains if I don't dress the way he likes, do my hair the way he likes. He'd hate this, too. Back chat." She sighed and slumped back, tipped her head against the sofa to stare at the ceiling. "Used to be that I'd let it all slip if he wasn't here. Have my little rebellion, let the place get messy. Then he came home early a couple of times and soon beat that habit out of me."

"You can't break someone else's habits."

Elaine raised her head, looked at Keira. The woman understood nothing. "I didn't say he broke the habit. I said he beat it out of me. At first it was shouting, a total hissy fit, a slap across the face, a split lip. A while later, it an actual full-on beating. I wasn't stupid enough to let it happen a third time at that rate of escalation." She shouldn't have been stupid enough to stay either, but she'd been too scared to face the world outside. Still was. "Well, that's not entirely true. There were several small incidents between. Pinches, painful holds, punches. Hair pulls. Even full-on spanking, painful, not playful. Though admittedly, most of them did turn into rough sex. Jason always wanted to be in control."

Keira's mouth was slack, her head slightly shaking. Suddenly, it didn't matter that the woman didn't believe. It was all true, and it all showed how pathetic a wife she had been. Elaine let her head go to the back of the sofa and she studied the ceiling. The rattle calmed and stopped.

"I didn't realise." Keira's voice was small, barely there.

Elaine shrugged. "It was my fault. I understood the rules. And I get how stupid that sounds. A man raising his fists to a woman is always his choice, and it should take more than what I did to drive him to it. But it didn't." She shrugged. "And of course, you don't know me. I've spent a long time in hiding."

"What do you mean?"

The whirls in the ceiling Artex swam nonsensically tonight. Elaine had never liked that finish. "Some... stuff happened when I was a teenager. Not good stuff. After that I started trying to conform, but I've never found that too easy. We met in what? Freshers' week? Barely 18 years old, out in the wider world of university. Babies, thinking we were all grown up." With another sigh, she pushed herself back upright, leaned forward and picked up the wine glass, taking a big glug before looking at Keira again. "What are they looking for?"

"Who?" The way the word drifted off told Elaine there was someone. Keira sighed. "They're looking for some evidence Jason had."

So, this is going to be like pulling teeth, then. "What evidence?"

Keira looked away, sucked on her lip.

"Oh, for God's sake, don't tell me then. Carry on playing your stupid spy games. But go play elsewhere. I can't help you if I don't know what you're looking for or why."

It was childish, but she wasn't in the best of moods.

"The spy games aren't mine. I'm an actuary, remember?"

"Oh, I remember. I remember getting the higher-class degree than you too, but you're the ambitious one, the one who did everything necessary to get promoted. And you're the one playing with the spies. I just unwittingly married one."

The look she got could sour milk. "Treachery," Keira said. "Apparently there is some evidence of it, and they're looking for that evidence."

"Oh, I really must be out of touch." Elaine frowned. "The only treachery I'm aware of is that from you and Jace." Keira's slight flinch told her she hit the bullseye. "Right, let me get this straight. Earlier you said Jason's a spy, a secret agent, now he's a traitor? But if he's dead, so what? Dead double-agent, treachery over, surely?"

"No," Keira tutted. "Jason's not a traitor, but he had evidence of who was."

"Oh." Elaine sipped again. "Why didn't he give it straight to his superiors?"

Keira shrugged.

"Maybe his superior is the spy." Elaine laughed at her own stupidity. "No, wait, they're all spies. That's the problem." She focused on Keira again. "Why are you telling me?"

This time, Keira looked uncomfortable. Perhaps she shouldn't be telling her. But that was Keira's problem, not Elaine's.

"Do you have anything in storage?"

Elaine considered not answering, but if they were any good as spies, they'd already know she paid a monthly fee for a small storage unit. What was in there was private, personal, hers. Letting someone go through that was letting them riffling through her memories. But they were her memories, no one looking on would ever see the real meaning. She nodded. "It's all mine though, not Jason's. It's where I keep the things Jason won't let me keep in the house. Mostly stuff from my childhood." She tried not to think of that disaster, nor the fact that she could no more get rid of the detritus than she could the scars on her psyche. "Did they check the lofts? I never go up on account of the spiders, the place I won't go would be a good starting point for Jason to hide stuff."

"I believe so."

"Both of them?"

Keira was frowning again. "Pardon?"

"The main access is through the hatch on the landing, but the back of the house is an extension, that part of the loft you get to through a hatch in Jason's study. I struggle to see it when I'm looking for it. Anyone unaware of it might not spot it."

"These guys spot everything."

"Bold statement." And not one Elaine believed. Even when known about, that hatch was hard to spot. And therefore, made a great hiding place. "Ask them. If they did, great. If not, tell them to come again tomorrow." She sipped more wine before contemplating the dwindling liquid. She'd drunk about a third, she'd expected it to be more. There would definitely be more later. "Preferably not too early."

"I can try, but they'll do what they want."

"Typical men." Elaine sipped some more.

Keira stood up. "I think I'll leave you to wallow in self-pity."

"You do that." *So good to have a sympathetic friend.* "Doesn't it bother you?"

"What?" Keira snapped.

"Losing Steven?" Elaine saw no reaction to the name. "You've been married twenty-two years, and you've just been told to consider him dead. But you don't seem bothered. Or is he not really dead? Have they told you something that they won't tell me?"

Keira sighed. "Now you're seeing conspiracy where none exists."

"Really? Do you want to know what I see? Or more to the point, what I'm failing to see? What I don't see is one half of the most loving couple I've ever known reacting to the loss of the other half."

"You're not exactly in floods of tears over Jason's loss."

"I'm dressed like a slob and crawling into a bottle. Neither of which is like me. It's called acting out. Tears may come later, once I start believing he's actually dead, and I need a bit more than some stranger's say so for that."

Keira sighed. Elaine recognised it as one of those long-suffering, why-do-I-put-up-with-this-crap sighs. "They have no reason to lie to you."

"Then why have they been lying to me for twenty-five years?"

Apparently, Keira had no answer for that. Or if she did, she clamped her jaw on it. The truth seemed to be that neither of them really knew the other; certainly not the real other. Keira held out her hand.

"Keys?"

Elaine frowned.

"For the lockup."

Elaine moved to the console table in the hallway, pulled out her keys, and removed one. Then passed it to Keira.

"If it is true," she said as Keira stepped to the front door. "I really am sorry for your loss."

Keira was holding herself tight, but Elaine saw the painful gulp as she nodded. "What about your loss?"

Elaine shrugged. Keira stepped out, only turning at the last second.

"Was marriage just a word to you?"

Elaine closed the door.

CHAPTER FOUR

"No."

He heard the softly spoken word as Elaine locked the door behind Keira.

"Marriage isn't a word. It was never just a word. It was a sentence."

He continued wondering about that while watching the woman in the monitors return to the sitting room. She picked up the wine glass. He heard that pipe tapping again. This time she frowned up at the ceiling. With a sigh, she put the glass down and grabbed her handbag.

In the hall, she retried her car keys, then headed out. He moved to the front of the van, his partner in the second van had already left and he had to be ready to move is she did. Elaine locked the door, then reversed the car from the drive. He waited until she was at the junction of the road before he started the van and followed her.

B&Q? Really?

Ten minutes after parking, she was back out with a new hot water storage jacket. Back to the house.

A small flurry of activity as she carried the purchase into the house, then…

Wow, shocker.

In the living room, she grabbed the wine, must have warmed by now, finished it in one. In the kitchen, she took the bottle from the freezer and poured a very generous measure. Returning to the sitting room, she sat in the middle of the sofa. Sat properly, the wine held by the stem and rested on her knee so as not to warm it with her body heat. She stared straight ahead. No watching TV, no reading, just sitting.

After a quarter of an hour, he began to wonder if she was real or a mannequin. Just to make sure that the screens were refreshing, he switched to others in the house, when he scrolled back to the sitting room camera, the movement of her drink reassured him that she was a living human being.

In the uncomfortable confines of the back of the van, he watched her. She didn't make any sense.

The file on her had nothing. He didn't have to look to see, he had had a good memory and had read it through. Elaine Underwood had gone from a council estate in the Southeast to a suburban wife in Cardiff. Great grades in school. Phenomenal grades in university. Average job, little ambition. This was not a stupid woman, so why be what she was? How could someone that intelligent live like they were nothing? A life only to serve a husband and children, was that her view? She didn't even have any children. Not really. Though there were pictures of twenty-one children in the house, mostly clustered in pride of place in the sitting room, but they had only ever been fostered. Lasting from as little as three weeks up to ten years. All reports said she was the perfect mother. But they hadn't fostered in over two years. So, what was she now?

An empty-nester with nothing to do but clean?

Watching her, he wondered if unnecessary movement was forbidden in her world. What was going on inside her head?

How could someone sit so still for so long?

She finished the wine.

He checked his watch. 21:52.

It had been a very long few hours. Long and boring.

She wasn't moving.

Unmoving, he sat and watched.

She jolted to her feet. Then stopped.

What now? He wondered. *More wine? A bathroom break – I need one.*

The monitors showed her go to the kitchen. She reached for the door to the dishwasher, it was only open an inch when she let go and the glass slapped heavily down beside the sink. She turned determinedly away. Everything about her demeanour screamed that this was an act of rebellion. She'd told Keira that Jason was the neat-freak, only he knew that wasn't true. Jason could be a total slob. He hadn't had to work with the man often, which was a bonus, he'd never especially liked him, but the fact remained, Jason Blake was not a tidy individual. That house was immaculate. The Jason Blake he knew also didn't hit women, yet Elaine said he'd literally beaten her, and apparently got some gratification out of the experience as well. There again, the Jason Blake he and the rest of the organisation thought they knew wouldn't withhold evidence either, and that was why he was here.

Bathroom break next, one he matched, to great relief, thanks to bringing an empty bottle on stakeout. Then she entered the second bedroom, the one he had assumed would be a guest bedroom until he'd looked around it. It struck him as odd that the Blakes kept separate rooms, but he'd never been married, so his view might be outdated, or simply wrong. She undressed, folded her clothes, and put them away. She had a nice body. Plump. Round in all the right places and a few extra ones. Very nice breasts. He'd always appreciated a nice pair of breasts.

Then she slipped under the covers and switched off the lights.

He could wait and see if anything happened, but that seemed unlikely, and they'd be back in the morning, anyway. They hadn't known about the second loft space.

Besides, he had a lock up to go search.

The lockup had 24/7 access and getting into the small unit was simple. He wasn't surprised to find that everything was stored in labelled durable plastic boxes. What did surprise him was the labels. He reached for the first box.

Sketch books and dry art supplies

The click closures snapped open, and he looked in. Yep, sketch books, and dry art supplies, various tins, boxes of pencils, sketching and coloured, chalks and pastels. He picked up a sketch pad and flicked it open. Where he had expected ugly, disproportionate scribbles, he saw practised, talented tableaus. The more he flicked through, the more surprised he was. This sketch book was full of anatomical studies, some body parts, some whole figures. Towards the back he saw fantasy creatures. Lots of dragons, a few fairies, mostly monsters. He looked closely at one, a chilling werewolf snarling at the viewer. The next was a vampire, something looked familiar. He checked back to the werewolf. The eyes were the same. So was the head shape, except for the ears. She must have modelled the images on someone she knew back then.

With a shake of the head, he put that away and flicked through the next. The evidence could be anything and he had to be thorough. A sketchbook of landscapes. He recognised Big Ben, saw a castle, but not one he recognised. Again, he saw the progression of work, the landscapes changed from real to imaginary. Fantasy places like he'd seen on book covers, one had dragons too. She'd even given this one a title. *Dragon Attack.*

He searched through the next box. *Acrylics and Oils.* Nothing.

The next box was larger, canvases. He pulled a couple out. This made no sense, Elaine had been a maths nerd, all numbers and logic. These paintings weren't by the number, they were by a very talented, emotional, and imaginative artist. He turned the canvas over. There was a date, a quick calculation, he realised Elaine had painted this when she was sixteen.

SIXTEEN!

He turned it around and scanned the image again. The breath-taking beauty, the harshness and yet realism of the fantasy landscape drew the eye subtly to the centre, the tiny figure standing there, sword drawn but down. The last one left, the sole survivor of a pyrrhic victory.

Her artwork wasn't flat, but full of movement and texture. Her talent was something rare, especially from someone so young. She'd displayed life and emotion, captured something dynamic in all the images, even the landscapes. This level of connection with a subject demonstrated a sensitivity to the world, an understanding of spirit. This was an artist easily hurt. As he moved through the boxes, he saw more sketch books, small ones, easy to keep in a handbag. The sort of thing she could keep hidden. The talent hadn't faded with age, though the subjects had grown darker and, conversely, blander. The mystery and magic had been replaced by real life. The still life of fruit was excellent, though the fruit was literally rotten. The damage done.

How did someone who could do this, become the drudge he'd seen in Elaine Blake? The woman made no sense.

It was gone three in the morning before he'd left. He'd gone through every box, every book, and there were many of those, every trinket and treasure. He'd found nothing of interest to his investigation, but a whole new mystery.

Who was Elaine Annie Blake?

CHAPTER FIVE

Special Agent Turner knew something was wrong. Part of the work of an analyst was to know instinctively when something needed analysing, and this was something. Five missing men, two of them undercover British Agents and not a single headline?

Okay, there were no recent worrying political or antisocial breakouts between the Czech Republic and the UK, which didn't mean the missing men didn't matter.

The bosses could point out all they wanted, that the matter was for the UK services to worry about not the American, but that couldn't stop this one American worrying.

There was an undeniable and well recorded connection between Special Agent Turner and one of the missing agents. A fact that had been pointed out as making her less impartial in the case, and therefore less suitable to investigate. Not, they underlined more times and with more force than was necessary, that there was anything for the CIA to investigate. The question as to whether they knew something they weren't saying was paramount in Turner's mind. But they were adamant that this was not something for them, or anyone who wanted to stay a Special Agent, to investigate.

The secret part of their service came from not saying too much. Security often took the same route. But mistrust opted for that same path too.

What weren't they telling her?

Didn't they trust her?

Did Turner trust them?

Maybe they had a point about proximity to the case causing issues. Given the circumstances, perhaps that was understandable. But there was no way of letting go this time, Turner would have to fight from the inside.

Even their service had heard rumours about just what these particular agents had been running with, and if those rumours were even half true, those men had something that could blow a huge gaping hole in UK security. If UK security was weakened, by extension that weakened US security. So why weren't the bosses interested? They weren't idiots; when the issue had been raised and the report discussed, it was clear that they had understood. They might even have agreed. But they'd ordered Turner to shut it down anyway.

It made no sense.

If there really was evidence of a UK agent giving, well, selling information to Russian authorities, or mafia, that didn't spell anything good for anyone on the right side of the political divide. Unlike many, Turner realised that in choosing a side, there was a chance of somehow being wrong. This was based on understanding that neither side actually had the monopoly on right or wrong. But the belief in truth, justice and the American way, while a terrible quote and a worse cliché, was something that was as integral to Agent Turner as a heartbeat. The choice had been made and every action would be taken to support that belief and that way of life.

Even from the wrong side of The Pond. But there again, they had a special relationship with the UK. Turner's relationship with the country was a useful support system.

The personal relationship with Agent Jason Blake, if not a special one, ensured that this matter wasn't going to be dropped. Not even in the stonewall face of her superior's orders.

The problem with those orders, was one specific order. There was a phone call that could not be made. It probably wouldn't help much, except on a personal level. Only, making that call had been vetoed. They had even given strict instructions on what could or couldn't be said should the call be made to Turner. Disobeying that order was possible, but it was more than likely to be picked up instantly and a charge of such direct insubordination would be impossible to avoid.

They wanted a job done, situations monitored, analysed. That was Turner's speciality. If there was one more situation to monitor and analyse, then so be it. And if not reporting that analysis proved problematic, then that too would be dealt with when the problem arose.

There were plenty of computer records to search, but that was Monday to Friday's constant grind. Though she had the access from home, Turner was well aware that using that access would be logged and she understood that every electronic touch left a trace. So, time to go old school, she fetched a pad and pen. At the dining room table, rather than the desk, Turner wrote down everything known about Jason and Elaine Blake.

Married aged 29 and 19 respectively, they had been married now twenty-five years. The house they lived in was the one they brought just before marrying, it was in Cardiff because that was where Elaine had been studying at the time. They had never moved. With a large four-bedroom house, why would they have needed to? Jason's work was officially in London, and Elaine didn't seem to mind his long absences from the home. What that said about their marriage could be anything from complete trust to complete uninterest.

Jason's apparently double life was the opposite end of the scale to the extraordinarily bland life his wife led. She worked but devoted herself to the children and housework. She wasn't a member of any society or club, not even really online. She had a Facebook account but used it only as a method of communication with a few of their fostered children.

Noting everything that Turner had discovered about their children, was going to take some time, but it was important, so that was fine.

Though Elaine was unable to have children of her own, she had been more than willing to take in other peoples. Turner knew that twenty-one foster children in twenty-five years was a lot. Some had stayed with the Blakes for years, others, just a few weeks, but Elaine remembered each of them and stayed in touch with as many as she could.

Looking down the list Turner was also able to identify another issue. Jason knew the truth, but did Elaine? Reading all those names, knowing the things that weren't written down, Turner had to wonder if Elaine was aware of the facts or not. She guessed not.

Every one of the children Jason had taken into his home, was either the child of an agent, British or Allied, mostly friendly states, but some neutral, and one verging on hostile. If not that, then they were the innocent victims who survived a case Jason had worked on. This was a fact hidden from most, probably including Elaine who, from what Turner could see, had been kept in the dark on pretty much everything.

The first foster child taken in by the Blakes, had been the daughter of two married CIA agents who had been killed in what was reported as a simple car accident. Turner's more recent investigations of that incident revealed that it was, in fact, a staged murder. At the time, the daughter had been in a UK safe house, for her own protection. Jason Blake had been one of those assigned to protect her. When word had come of the agents' deaths, and in the following week, Jason had persuaded his bosses to be allowed to take the girl to his home. He had argued that in some part this would act as 'continuity of care,' which would ease the transition, he also heavily hinted that it would be good for his wife, taking care of other people's children in the absence of being able to have her own.

Looking at that argument in the cold light of day, Turner realised how unfeeling that could actually have been. How having other people's children foisted upon her might have done actual psychological harm to Elaine. To Turner's knowledge, it hadn't, but was that Jason knowing his wife, a tribute to Elaine's inner strength, or just dumb luck?

Turner selected Elaine's inner strength as the answer, trying not to paint Jason unnecessarily black for internal reasons rather than analysis of cold hard facts.

Of course, one thing that was known to Turner, but wasn't in the files, was that Jason had been trying to seduce the girl's mother despite the presence of the husband/father. And the girl was the spitting image of that now dead CIA agent. In fact, now the daughter was grown up, photos of the two were indistinguishable. If it weren't for the fashions worn, there would be no telling them apart.

The real question to Turner's mind, was why had Jason's bosses allowed the practice to start, let alone continue? Maybe persuading them once was a blip that could be explained away as expedience. But a further twenty times? They had to have had a plan.

Yet, whatever way Turner tried to bring that plan into focus, it wasn't obvious. The best, most viable explanation, was simply that Elaine was very good with children. Maybe it helped that most of the children were from London and the southeast, several were non-British citizens, and getting them away to the quiet suburbs of Cardiff was putting a useful distance between the action and children without sending them so far away that they were beyond easy reach. Relatively easy reach. But Turner believed that Elaine's quiet, loving strength was what had actually helped all those lost and frightened children.

Several of those children had themselves grown up to join the security services. The security services famously liking where possible to employ those without living family ties. Three, including the first girl, had done so to follow in the footsteps of lost parents, not to fulfil any obligation Jason might otherwise have pressed upon them. There were two further fosters whom Jason had recruited, and one of those was now dead. Dead in suspicious if unprovable circumstances.

And now Jason was missing. Possibly dead.

Did Elaine Blake know?

What about the children, most of whom were admittedly not children anymore, did they know?

The Blakes had never been a picture-perfect couple, but they were real, and they, especially Elaine, had been really important to the people they had helped. So, what was the reality of the Blake marriage and why was it only now occurring to Turner to wonder?

CHAPTER SIX

Elaine barely slept, just lay in the dark thinking. Overthinking. It wasn't unusual and it didn't do any good, so she got up, made the bed and was downstairs drinking coffee when someone knocked the door. She didn't rush to answer, it would be the men from Jason's work here to search the loft, so hardly a friendly visit. The door opened easily. The sun tried to climb over the horizon and the general grey cloud cover did nothing to help it on its way. Wondering if she should have put the outside light on, she was surprised to look down at the man facing her, the small step up from the pavers outside meant that at five four that hardly ever happened to her. Another man shadowed the first; he stood a little taller, but otherwise as average to look at. The obvious difference was that the second man carried a short triple layer ladder.

"Yes?"

"We've come to inspect the loft, Mrs Blake."

Of course they had, only she wasn't giving way that easy. "Got ID?"

He looked at her, his head tipped, eyebrows raised.

"How am I supposed to know you are who you claim to be?"

"I haven't claimed to be anyone."

"Then you've no right to come in."

One surprise shove and he simply pushed past her; she tried to block his path, but it wasn't happening. As she watched him head for the stairs, she called out, but a shadow fell over her. The other man had stepped in and closed the door behind his back as the first man headed upstairs.

"Do you want to show us where the hatch is?"

She turned to the second man, since he had spoken. She scowled up at him, through the ladder he carried. As she stood barefoot, she looked up ten to fifteen centimetres. He had conservatively cut blond hair and clear grey eyes that didn't look at her like she was an idiot. She'd forgotten how that felt.

"No. I want you to prove who you are."

His gaze was impenetrable. Since she'd heard the front door catch click, she huffed, and headed up the stairs, overly aware that the man behind her would have a clear view of her rump. The one Jason said should come with warnings of 'a wide load.' She pulled the back of her jumper right down, thankful that the shapeless thing covered so much. The first man stood on the landing, looking around.

"Where?"

"If you can't find the room, how do you hope to find whatever you're looking for?"

A phone appeared by Elaine's elbow. A cheap Nokia like no one used anymore. Was this what they called a burner phone? She saw it was connected and heard a voice. She took the phone and put it to her ear.

"Hello?"

"Elaine?" She recognised Keira's voice. "Why are you calling from a withheld number?"

Her eyes slid backward, but Elaine didn't see the man behind her. "I didn't call. One of the men who's come this morning did. Do you know who they are?"

"No idea. Just let them in and let them get on."

Keira ended the call. For all Elaine knew, one or both of these two men were the traitor they sought evidence of. There again, she'd spent more than half her life living with a man who she probably couldn't identify from an accurate description. She was hardly a good judge of character. She passed the phone back to ladder man.

"That door." Elaine pointed to the second door on their right.

"What's that?" The first man asked.

Elaine turned to the tall round bundle leaning at an angle in the corner of the hallway in front of the bathroom door. Covered in transparent plastic it was clearly marked Water Tank Jacket. She turned back to the pushy man. "Can't you read?"

She squeezed past him and into Jason's study. It was supposed to be the fourth bedroom. When they'd bought the house, she'd had hopes of a big family, but that hadn't exactly worked out. Something else that was her fault, and Jason had the medical evidence to prove it. *In the past.* She had to deal with the here and now. She held the door and used the doorstop to keep it open. Once that was secure, she looked up and pointed to the interior corner of the ceiling.

"Hatch is there. See that slight finger mark? Push that and it'll open for you."

Resigned to their intrusion, Elaine left them to it and headed down to finish her coffee. She wasn't interested in them or what they might find. She sat and sipped.

"I was wrong," she said softly to herself. "I lied when I said I loved Jason. I shouldn't despise myself for not grieving, I don't feel anything because I simply don't care. Haven't for a while. And exactly when did I start talking to myself?" Exasperated, she stood, hating the knowledge that she'd been talking to herself for years to avoid having a home as silent as a mausoleum.

Keep busy.

That was the answer — had almost always been the answer. Activity to avoid stagnation. She washed her coffee mug and left it upside down on the drainer, then fetched the toolbox from the garage and headed back up to the airing cupboard.

After pulling out the summer duvets she'd changed for the winter ones last week, she took the Stanley knife and pulled out the lowest strap. It didn't move far, only enough to let her slip the blade behind. It took several sawing motions, but eventually the plastic webbing gave way. The next proved no easier and Elaine realised her mistake when the loose strap at the top allowed the separate parts of the jacket to fall partway down the tank. With a huff, she moved the loose strap and noticed a tear in one of the back segments. Perhaps it was as well she'd decided to replace the whole jacket rather than only the straps. The front segment proved obstinate, she smacked her elbow on the door jamb when her hand slipped off it, so she slashed the strap and chucked each segment behind her onto the landing. Working towards the back, she pulled the torn segment towards her, and it made an odd crackling sound. Like dried leaves.

Or paper.

She leant back to look towards Jason's study. Whatever they were up to, the men remained out of sight. With one hand holding the segment against the cupboard wall, she pushed her other hand against it and down. A couple of inches below the tear, the crackle happened again, and she felt a lump beneath that. The tear was too small for her to reach easily down, so she ripped the top layer and out fell a fold of paper. Still stuck in the fibres of the lagging hung a small key. She disentangled the key from the fibres and turned it over in her hand.

It wasn't a key she recognised. To insubstantial to be a door key. Too big to be something like a box key. It seemed more like a locker key; it even had a number etched into the side – 862.

As she reached for the fallen fold of paper, she slipped the key into the back pocket of her jeans. The dried and yellowed paper curved, probably more the result of being next to the boiler heat rather than age. Though folded into quarters, she realised from the size and two rounded corners that it was a page from the notebooks Jason preferred. She unfolded it to reveal a page of incoherent letters.

Spies and codes.

She should give this straight to the anonymous men in her loft. With a sigh, she shifted to do so.

NO!

The silent scream came from deep inside. Somewhere so deep inside her she'd forgotten it existed. With Jason gone, she could kick her shoes off, get sarcastic to strangers in her own home, change the lagging because the clip rattled, and keep anything she found in this house to herself for as long as she wanted.

The paper slipped easily into her back pocket too.

She might pass the paper and key on later, if she felt like it, but not just yet.

She made sure her jumper covered everything again. Knowing she dare not risk looking closer at the paper until the men were gone, she concentrated on replacing the boiler jacket.

Once done, she stepped out.

"Aaugh!"

Her heart was jumping like someone had electrocuted her. Her hand covered the offending organ as she scowled up at the man stood in front of her. The ladder man. "What the hell!"

"What happened?"

"Heart attack! You scared me half to death. Do you always creep up on people? Is it part of the job description?"

"What happened—" His tone suggested he spoke to a recalcitrant five-year-old. "—to that?" He pointed to the torn lagging.

It was a good thing her heart hadn't calmed down because that question ramped it right back up again. She stared at the limp item on the floor. The patch of fibre more yellowed than the rest, the neighbouring patch of white on show.

She shrugged. "It had ripped somehow and when I pulled it from around the back of the tank, I ripped it more. Does it matter?" Her heart was calmer now, not normal, but calmer. Her hand dropped away.

"Depends on what you found."

"Found?"

"Inside the lagging."

She managed to maintain eye contact, but she couldn't hide her surprise. She could only hope that he thought she was surprised by the question. "Erm, more lagging. What did you expect?"

His eyes narrowed, drilling into her.

"Do I have to frisk you?"

This time her brows shot up. She didn't want that, but there were limits to what she could do. Were there limits to what he would do? "Go on then." She put her arms out to the side. "Who knows, I might enjoy being touched after so many years."

He didn't react, but she was horrified by what she'd let slip. Without another word, he turned and walked away.

Heart rate still elevated, Elaine closed the cupboard door and gathered the rubbish together, stuffing the old lagging into the bag for the new. She dragged it to the top of the stairs before she moved to the door of the study. The loft hatch hung open, the ladder propped into it. Ladder man sat at Jason's desk, using a jacked-up laptop that she hadn't seen before. He must have gone back out to their van at some point. She assumed that the other guy remained in the loft.

"Is there really that much to go through up there?"

The man didn't even glance up. "Obviously."

Cold shoulder much?

"Fine. How long do you reckon you'll be?"

"As long as it takes."

She scowled at the back of his head. "Well thank you for that oh so helpful response."

His hands stilled over the keypad and several heartbeats passed before he turned to her. "What did you expect?"

"Some respect in my own home would be nice." *Be a bloody miracle, but it'd be nice.*

His eyes raked over her, she glared back. That was when she noticed.

"You're wearing a wig." She looked closer. "Makeup too." That didn't make sense. "What for?" Suddenly it made more sense. "Is this so I can't identify you? Have we met and you don't want me to realise?" She didn't recognise his accent, but that didn't necessarily mean anything. Voices could be controlled.

His lack of expression gave nothing away. "We'll be as long as we need to be."

"Fine. I'm going out."

"Where?"

"It's a beautiful day, I just thought I'd go out. Move your van." Their van blocked her car in.

His voice measured and dark he asked, "Where are you going?"

"Where do you get off speaking to me like I'm an idiot?"

"Where you go get off acting like one?"

Natural instinct had her desperately searching for a comeback, but Jason had taught her not to push too far for fear of retaliation. "Tip. I'm going to the tip." *I'm going to Hell for being a coward.*

"Why?"

She couldn't quite believe that question. "Military intelligence really is an oxymoron."

"I'm not military."

"You're not denying being a moron then."

She saw the muscle in his jaw clench.

"What are you taking to the tip?"

"Plastics, glass, newspapers and tins. The usual stuff. And that lagging. You have an issue with recycling?"

This time he simply shook his head and turned back to the computer.

"So, are you going to move the van now?"

"No."

"Move the bloody van!"

The second face appeared upside down in the hatch, Elaine jumped, having forgotten about the guy in the loft.

"Don't let him wind you up," the head indicated the other man. "He's being pedantic. He won't move the van now, because you need time to fill the car, he'll move the van when you're ready to go."

The head disappeared, and she looked back to the other. If only she had Superman's laser eyes to burn out his brain. "So, you're not going to stop me?"

"No."

Relieved, she started to turn away. Then she realised something. "Why aren't you demanding to go through it all?" He didn't pause what he was doing. "You've already gone through it all haven't you? Well, I hope you found the smell disgusting." She often did. "Cos it was a total waste of time, Jason doesn't touch the recycling, nor the bins, in fact, he barely even goes into the garage. Is there any part of the house you haven't gone through?"

"Nope."

He was still concentrating on the computer screen.

"Including my underwear drawer?" *Oh my God.*

"It's not the first vibrator I've ever seen."

Face burning, Elaine turned, grabbed the rubbish, and ran from the house.

CHAPTER SEVEN

He waited in the lounge. The empty personality-absent lounge. He heard the car draw up and moved to the doorway to the hall.

Elaine stepped in, her head down, carrying nothing. She turned and closed the door. He stepped up.

She sprung round, eyes wide, punched out.

He grabbed her wrist, the bones delicate under his tight grip. He forced her back as she punched out again; grabbing that wrist too. Her head butted forward, slamming into his chest, forcing air and a grunt of pain from him. She tried to wriggle, but he pushed forward, crushing her body between him and the wall. Her foot stamped on his toes. Another involuntary grunt.

"What is wrong with you, woman?"

She stilled at the words and looked up. Her eyes wide. "Ladder Man?"

He reared at the name. *Too close.*

"The van's gone. What are you still doing here?"

Some tension drained from her body. He eased his grip on her wrists, but wouldn't let go, or move away.

"We're not finished."

"Oh, okay. Do you think you might finish with the pressing me against the wall now?"

"Why? You enjoying it?" He shouldn't be but was, couldn't help it. How long had it been?

"Not really; the harder you press, the more my bladder screams."

He let go and stepped away. She rushed into the cloakroom. Sound proved the need.

He needed something, but not necessarily the coffee he headed into the kitchen for. The milk come from the fridge, but once the lid came off, he took his coffee black. Finally, she appeared and pointed at the milk on the side.

"That gone off?"

He nodded.

"Sorry, I don't drink it, so I don't always notice." She took the other mug that he had left out. "Where's your mate gone?"

"Elsewhere."

Her lips compressed, but she said nothing. He sensed she had something to say, but she kept quiet. Then she turned towards the lounge, he shifted slightly, she stopped. Observation and sensitivity. He liked that. She was a smart woman.

"Where are you going?"

"Elsewhere."

Smart mouth, too.

"Ha-ha."

"What does it matter?" she asked. "You're still searching the house, aren't you?"

"Not so much. I want you to look at something."

Indicating that she should precede him, he put his coffee aside, but she took hers into the hall.

She only half turned to ask, "In the study?"

"Yes."

The study was empty, the hatch closed, and the ladder, like his colleague, was gone. The laptop sat open on the desk, the screen blank. He moved past her, putting his back between her and the screen to enter the twenty-character password. He stood back, indicated she should take the seat, and she did, even though he pushed the chair back to position her. Her eyes on the screen, which had sprung to life with a colourful picture, the image expanded to fill the screen.

"Tell me about this."

As he spoke, his hand moved under her hair. She tensed. Her hair was thick and heavy, surprisingly silky as his fingers glided over smooth skin until his hand settled over her neck. The tips of his fingers on her artery measured her pulse, which jumped. Had it really been that long since a man touched her? He used light pressure to assure her that if he needed to, he could snap her spine without difficulty.

"Really?" she asked.

"Yes." Clearly, she would resist in every small way. "And don't tell me it's a photograph of your fifteenth wedding anniversary party."

"Okay, but it is. What do you want to know?"

"Who are all these people?" He already knew, it was just a test.

She started at the left of the screen, under the edge of the 'Happy 15th Wedding Anniversary' banner, pointing to an older couple. "That's Peter and Nicola Smart, they live two doors down, the house with the For Sale sign? That's them. He's in banking, she's on the admin side of the NHS. They're downsizing now their kids have left home." She pointed to a couple who would have been mid-twenties at the time. "That's Utku and Madison. They were both emergency foster care placements with me and Jace. First two, actually. They stayed here together for a few of years, always got on. They keep in touch with us and each other. At the party it kind of looked like they might have a thing, but I don't believe they did. Madison came to us when she was eleven, going on twelve, stayed with us for years. American family had moved to the UK, then her parents died in a car crash, we took her in. Nearly broke my heart when she left. She's something big in the city now, business analyst." She sighed, communicating a pain or regret. Given some of the other photos, if she knew about them, there should be a lot – of both. "Utku is a doctor now. A surgeon. He joined Médecins Sans Frontières a few years ago. We don't talk as often as I'd like. Letters sometimes, cards for occasions. He moves around a lot, he's busy."

She was making excuses for the younger man, or was she hiding from the truth? Or hiding from the likely reality she could work out for herself if she had the courage, that the man wasn't interested in staying in touch. Her neck felt warm beneath his fingers, and her heart rate was a little rapid. Was she afraid of him? In poorer health than she should be? Did she find the contact as affecting as he did?

He heard her swallow.

"You miss them?"

A nod now. "Miss all of them."

The pointing finger moved across the picture, she pointed to each person, named each and gave a potted history. Then there was five more of no interest, then standing with her, was Lazlo, who was, unusually, smiling.

She pointed to the man on the extreme right. It was clear from his features that he had Arabic blood. "I think his name was Talek, something like that. I only met him the once, but I remember he said he lived in Paris, certainly had a French accent. I remember telling him that I really wanted to visit

Paris, to go up the Eiffel Tower. Think he said he lived near there."

She had the name wrong, but the rest left him curious. "Why haven't you been to Paris?"

Her heart rate skittered. Something had bothered her, and he didn't expect her to answer.

"I don't travel well."

"Why?" The question slipped out. The answer didn't.

"I get headaches. Do, say, the wrong thing. Upset people. Embarrass Jason."

Somehow, he suspected all of those things were about Jason, not her. That was how abusive relationships worked, the abuser made the victim shoulder the responsible. While he hadn't found what he'd been looking for, he'd found other things, things that illuminated Jason Blake's character to an unpleasant degree. Did Elaine know? Was she part of it, or just another victim?

"What about these four?"

He pointed to what at first glance looked like a family grouping.

"Well, given that those are Steve and Keira Southgate, I assumed that you'd recognise them."

Of course he did, but he couldn't give away too much. As he pulled his hand from the screen, he moved it to her shoulder, now he had a hand on each. "The kids?"

"Jessica, their daughter, and LaTrice." She didn't need to point out which was which, given that LaTrice was half Swahili and skin tone made that obvious. "LaTrice always got on well with Steve and Jessica, but Keira never took to her. LaTrice was another of our foster kids, she stayed with us about six months. I tried to keep in touch, but… They move on, you know, better things to do."

"How many kids have you taken in over the years?"

"Twenty-one."

"You didn't even stop to think about that."

"Didn't need to. You want me to run through their names?"

"No." The office had already given him the list. "Why didn't you have kids of your own?"

Tension bunched under his hands. A reflex reaction, self-defence. Now he felt her force her muscles to relax. The more she felt under pressure, the better, it made her more likely to tell the truth, though he had no reason to believe she'd lied to him yet.

"I can't."

The difficulty of the admission clawed at his heart. Her breath juddered in before she could speak again.

"We tried, but… we got tested. Jason arranged for it all to be done privately, and that's not cheap. Those things are easier for men than women. He's fine, so it must be me. Something the doctors confirmed."

That must have hurt someone as good with kids as her. He'd seen it for himself. He ignored the image of him in her garden, but on that day, a day for her celebration, he's seen her put everyone, children and guests alike, before herself.

"Was it all worth it?"

"Taking in other peoples' kids?"

Now she looked up at him, and he tried to keep his own expression neutral as he read the happiness in hers. Tinged happiness, but happiness all the same.

"Oh yeah, it's very rewarding." She nodded, looking back to the picture. "But painful." She huffed at herself. "See what a fool I've been?"

Not really.

The shaking breath pulled her back into self-control. "Any chance you can leave me copies of these photos? Haven't seen them for years. That's the problem with all this digital photography. Pictures don't get printed anymore and we forget about them. Out of sight, out of mind."

A motto for his life, but she wasn't finished.

"Out of touch. Untouched."

That last said so quietly he doubted she meant to say it. Is that why she reacted to him earlier, why her heart rate skittered beneath his fingers even now? He'd seen all the other photographs on that pen drive. He should take it away. Some things, some people, were beyond saving.

"Is Jason really dead?"

"Yes."

"I don't believe you."

Smart lady, but for once I'm telling the truth as I know it. "Why not?"

"No evidence," she said. "Have you seen his body?"

"No, he died overseas."

"Bodies can be returned."

True, but apparently not in this case.

"I've not even got a death certificate."

And she would need one to do all the things one did when a spouse died. He realised she was looking up at him.

"Is there anything else?"

Lots of things. However boring he had originally considered this woman, he realised he was wrong, there was more than he'd seen. The sarcasm showed that. She didn't deserve what had happened. Or what was going to happen. He moved his hands away. She should be untouched.

CHAPTER EIGHT

Elaine sat alone. The men were long gone. The concentration required to read had deserted her, so she put things aside, switched on the TV for company, and sat as she always did, even though she felt the chill a bit. September had been nicely mild, but October had come in with an awesome chill, especially at night. Perhaps she should turn up the heating. Tensing to rise and do so, she heard the central heating switch on, the boiler start up. And this time there was no rattle of the clasp on the pipe. I did that.

Didn't know I had it in me.

The world had shifted; in twenty-six hours, everything had skewed. It was impossible to ignore the things that were wrong anymore. Her marriage had been a joke, she'd been taught that wedding vows were binding and unbreakable. She'd been bound by them; had Jason? It seemed unlikely.

Unlikely? Don't kid yourself, no way he was faithful, and in all honestly, that doesn't bother you either.

She was just another nobody. Bland. Conventional. Caged. If the men had found anything, she wasn't aware of it. Apparently, there were a lot of things she hadn't been aware of. *Change bland to blind. Wilfully blind.*

Perhaps that was why she hadn't told the men what she'd found. Some small stupid act of rebellion. The key was in her purse and the page of letters sat at her side. As did the pen drive Ladderman gave her before he left. Images. Photos. She didn't want to look at those; everything felt too raw at the moment. At some point she would have to start wilfully seeing the truth, but she wasn't sure she was ready just yet. So, she studied the curled page. What did it mean?

Clearly it was a cypher of some kind, but what kind? She could look it up on the internet. Her eyes slid over to the laptop in its case, hidden beside the sofa. The case now faced the opposite direction to when she'd put it there. She could tell by the strap hook, one would never hang straight and she always hid that at the back, now it was on display. They'd been through her laptop. It wouldn't take a genius to figure out her password, she'd long since been thinking of changing it, but again there was nothing on her browser history to be fearful or ashamed of. Researching how to solve a cypher, however, might just ring a few alarm bells, and if they'd broken her password, then they'd probably installed spyware, a key-logger.

Did it matter?

Even if she cracked the code, what was she going to do other than hand it over to the professionals? Depended on what the cypher told her, probably.

Decode it and find out.

That pushy little voice from the depths was starting to sound a lot like teenage her.

Oh God, teenage her.

Closed eyes helped to fight the rising fear. It was a long time ago; she wasn't that person anymore. Then who was she?

Decode the cypher and find out.

Or be a total coward and just hand it over and stay chained.

There wasn't much other choice. She had to find out what the cypher said. Her eyes slid across the room again. She needed a new laptop.

Could she afford one?

She could. She had no debt and higher credit limits on cards than she wanted to think about and never wanted to go near. She always paid her statements in full, but she didn't have to. She could have a proper splurge if she wanted. She didn't want to. The biggest problem with a new laptop would be setting it up. She did, however, already have a tab. If she switched off the wireless, they wouldn't be able to do much to get into that, and it had been in her handbag the whole time, so they wouldn't have been through it.

But even that only helped her if she knew how to deal with the cypher. If she couldn't Google it, there had to be another way. She padded to the hall and stared at the thermostat. Jason wouldn't allow it above 15 degrees until December. She twisted it up to 20. Then back down to 17; she wanted a warm house not a sauna.

She stepped into the lounge, closed the doors and looked around her. In the tall bookcases, though at the bottom, were her pride and joy, the Encyclopaedia Britannica. Two hours later she was reasonably sure that the paper held a Vigenère cypher. Still not sure how to solve it, at least she now understood it needed a keyword she didn't possess.

What she did possess was a good knowledge of maths and an abundance of logic, she could code a solution until the only thing she had to do was plug in the keyword and set a macro running. There again, if she could do that, she was willing to bet that someone else had already done it and put it on the internet.

She returned the books to the shelf, then fetched a glass of wine. And her tab.

* * *

"You're sure?" The voice of MI6 Chief Intelligence Officer Smith was cold and demanding.

"As sure as I can be," he said. He wasn't sure why they had started calling her Number Two, but that was, for good or bad, how everyone knew her.

The voice at the other end of the line made a noise of indignant annoyance.

"I've been through every square inch of the place, and the lock up. I've been through his computer and hers. If Jason Blake had any evidence, it is not in his home, nor with his wife." He took a breath. "I'm not now convinced he ever even had anything."

"Oh, he had it," the emotionless Number Two assured him. "And I want it."

"It's not here."

"It must be. Do you have any idea what that data could tell us?"

Scandal? No, he'd already sent in the pictures of that. So, since he really didn't, he kept quiet. Not that she gave him the chance to speak.

"Not only will we know who's selling secrets from our side, but we'll be able to cut several smuggling routes and have the evidence to support at least four extradition requests. And that's just what we know is in there."

"What we've been told is in there," he argued. "We don't know what it actually is."

"Hmm."

He clearly wasn't impressing anyone. "I searched every byte of that computer. The only evidence I found is in the photographic files I sent you." He'd also given them to Elaine, and he was waiting for the fall out from that.

"We need the other evidence."

Thank God she couldn't hear an eye roll. "Yes, ma'am."

"Given the nature of said evidence…"

He didn't like what he was hearing, but it was all too predictable. As far as Number Two was concerned, that traitor might even be him, since he hadn't passed anything on. As she ran through all the lowlights of his career, the length of her memory was only out-striped by the dread of the instructions she dispensed.

"Understand?"

"Yes, ma'am." The phone call ended.

He understood, but didn't appreciate. Silent running. Find the evidence, don't come back without it. He was on his own.

CHAPTER NINE

Sunday morning. Elaine had arrived at the library before it had opened, so she sat in her car and played games on her unconnected tab. Not that it mattered now. She'd fished out an unused pen drive, and saved the cypher on that rather than storing it on the tab. Thank God she'd brought the adaptor with the tab. Another thing Jason called a waste of money because God forbid, she defy him and go on social media or any other site he didn't approve of. Though in all honesty, she'd only ever social media in years other than for communication with some of the children.

Sod him.

The lights came on in the library, so she headed inside where she asked about the log in codes for the computers. She sanitised her hands, then she went to work. Once Google found a site able to decode a Vigenère cypher. She copied in the coded text; she opened the pad with the list of words that she thought Jason might use as a keyword and started.

Two hours later, nothing was resolved. Slumping and pushing her hair back, Elaine supposed it wasn't that surprising she failed to find the right keyword. She simply didn't know Jason well enough. She wondered if Jason was even his real name. Overthinking had a lot to answer for.

She tried his name. Nothing.

Her name. Nothing.

The names of twenty-one children, which only served to remind her how many people she missed and who she should be calling to advise of Jason's demise. Nothing.

Steve. Nothing.

Hell, she might as well try, she typed Keira in as the key. Hit return. And it suddenly made sense.

The words seemed incoherent. Even as she starred at the screen, Elaine couldn't process what she was seeing, she couldn't register the words. Mechanically, she noted them down. Pen and paper couldn't be hacked. She copied the answer, verbatim. Without once realising what any of it meant.

Keira.

Elaine didn't want to believe it.

Keira!

She was the code key.

There simply wasn't enough hand sanitiser in the world for this.

Mouth dry and eyes damp, Elaine logged out of the computer and gathered her belongings. The sharpness of the wind outside cut through her jumper, but at least it made her feel, even if all she felt was cold.

She walked the length of town, till the only thing her brain registered was the blister forming on her heel. *Should have worn thicker socks.* This pair of walking boots always did that, they weren't yet probably walked in, and she hadn't expected to walk far today. She turned around and headed for the car. As she passed a travel agent a poster for Paris caught her eye, an advert for a weekend break. Beside it, the dunes of Tunisia looked impossibly inviting. The bright lights of Times Square at Christmas suggested a joy of shopping. All the things that people should do when young and able.

Lost opportunity. *You're not a good traveller.* Yes, she got headaches; Jason forever telling her what to do; what she mustn't forget; how she should be careful; the dangers out there; where she shouldn't go; what she couldn't eat; how she shouldn't waste money. She pushed Jason's scalding voice away and moved on.

Move on. I really should move on.

But the problem was, where to move on to? Right now, the knowledge that Jason used Keira's name for a cypher key bothered her. What did that mean? That he found his friend's wife more memorable her? Keira had known about what Jason and Steve did for a living, maybe she was part of it. What if Keira had the evidence of treachery? What if Keira was — what did they call it — a sleeper agent? Elaine told herself she was taking it all too far, yet the idea tortured her all that way back to the car.

She vaguely remembered the girl she was in her teens. She understood why she'd decided to change. The image she'd presented when she'd met Keira was everything Keira was naturally, what Elaine had so work hard at being. Her choice, but Elaine had had to shackle her true nature to become what others considered acceptable. One mistake to pay for, for the rest of her life.

One damn big mistake. Total disaster in fact.

All the self-hatred rose like a zombie to eat her soul, or at least her peace of mind. *Stop overthinking.* It happened. Over. Case closed. *Forgive yourself and move on. The case might be closed, but the truth isn't out.*

Shut up. Shut up! SHUT UP!

* * *

Lunch was light. Scrambled egg on toast. At home. Alone. She should be more used to this.

The name Keira kept laughing in her head. Keira who she had worked so hard to emulate, whom apparently Jason had preferred. She focused on remembering the good times when they were all young. When she and Keira had been friends. When Jason loved her.

Did he ever love me?

Growling in frustration, Elaine dumped the dirty dish in the sink and turned away. Pausing at the door, she considered going back.

No. It's one small pan, a single dish, one knife, one fork. The washing up can wait until there's enough to do. Jason is not coming home to complain.

Her laptop case being turned around still bothered her. Yes, she could go buy a new one, but why bother? There was nothing she was worried about anyone seeing. Besides, she wanted to look through the pictures.

Soon enough that anniversary picture filled the screen. That had been a good day. Friends and family. Not that she had family anymore, they'd passed. But the kids had made it worthwhile. Of the twenty-one she was still in touch with sixteen. Jason said that defined her problem, she couldn't let go, too needy, too clingy.

Blinking, she looked slightly off screen, pushing down the sickness that rose every time she remembered she had chosen the restrictions in her life. Her choice, and a tough choice it was.

Her peripheral vision noticed what she hadn't. In the corner of the purple banner, was a blue spot. She rubbed her eyes and shook her head to clear her vision, she looked again, probably just her imagination. Or her eyesight going.

Oh, the joys of middle age. She looked more closely. Yes, there was definitely a blue spot. She zoomed into that spot. Definitely something wrong there. She kept zooming in until the area became pixilated, she had to blink again to be sure she was seeing what she was seeing.

A series of tiny characters inscribed within the dot. Elaine had no idea how that was even possible. But she wasn't imagining it. She grabbed her handbag, found her notebook, and copied out the code. Twenty-two characters; two letters, two numbers, four letters, fourteen numbers. They didn't mean anything to her. She zoomed back out.

Had the men who'd seen this photo, seen that? *Bound to.* They were better trained to spot such things than she was. Closing the file, Elaine was again faced with the file explorer. Right now, it was just a list of auto-generated numbers and dates, she'd been able to find the anniversary one first because she'd known the date it had been taken.

What else had Jason been hiding from her? She turned the 'details' view into 'large icon' view. Her heart stopped. Then it started to hammer. Never mind the party shots, these shots that proved Jason liked to party and clearly not with her.

Just looking at the icons dried out her throat, she couldn't face the pictures in full detail. One of her many regrets was having done some glamour modelling before she was legal. So, she recognised the poses, knew the set-up, understood it was always seedy even when the pictures weren't. Only these were. Keira just about wearing some royal blue lace undies and contorted into shapes men might want to look at but could give a woman serious back problems. There was no point denying it.

Much as she hated to, she opened them and started scrolling. Nausea took hold of her stomach, not because she was a prude, she could look at porn and get turned on like anyone else. It was the knowledge that these photographs had been taken by her husband and all were of people she knew.

In one, Elaine wasn't sure if she should be impressed or disgusted at the size of the black dildo which had been inserted for the picture. Given the pleasure on Keira's face in the shot, she assumed it wasn't painful. Perhaps post-childbirth it wouldn't be. And these were definitely post childbirth, she recognised the bed, it was one Keira and Steve had brought the year Jessica started boarding school. The image name, the date and time reference just confirmed it.

Elaine moved through the images, a mishmash of the innocuous and the obscene. Aside from the few of their anniversary at the start of the drive, there were none with her in. The ones of Madison were more tasteful, but the fact that Jason had them at all was disturbing. The first few she saw were tasteful, artsy and appealing. Madison had a beautiful body, checking the file title, she would have been seventeen in these pictures. Beautiful, alluring. These were gentle, sexy, nothing to be ashamed of. In the next she was more sultry, dark eyes looking at the camera, mouth slightly open, her hand on her own sex, fingers slipping inside. Elaine flicked to the next image. Madison with her head back, clearly having a good time alone. Madison was healthy and young and though the taking of the photographs was questionable, there was nothing wrong with a young woman enjoying her own body. Elaine clicked the next picture – seeing Madison being roughly fucked by Jason was a different matter. Not that Jason's face was pictured, but she recognised him all the same. Twenty-five years of marriage ensured that.

She squeezed her eyes shut. Bile rose in throat. The idea of seeing more revolted her, just how far would Jason go?

She opened her eyes and shifted to the next picture.

Images of Colin and Lazlo came next. The two boys, both young, about eleven and twelve, give or take. They were in trunks in the garden, a sweltering summer by the looks, innocent images of children at play. She breathed a sigh of relief. Clicked on the next image. Same boys, same Speedos, inside this time. The boys were on the bed. The spare bed where she slept, her stomach clenched. She opened the next one. Colin's hand on Lazlo's crotch. Next photo. The Speedos gone, the boys knelt opposite one another —

Bastard.

She couldn't see any more.

Tears ran hot down her cheeks as she turned and saw Colin bent over the edge of the bed, Lazlo buried to the cods in his backside. Still so many photos to go.

She screamed and threw the whole laptop at the wall, not caring that it, like her life, shattered into a thousand pieces.

Her whole life had been a lie. She never knew Jason at all. Suddenly she was surprised any of the children had stayed in touch. How had she lived so long with a man she knew so little about? Was there anyone in her life who hadn't betrayed her?

Sobs rent from her, unable to do anything else, she curled up in ball and cried.

* * *

Silent running.

Radio silence.

Do what he had to do, just without any back up, no

support. The fail-and-don't-come-back wasn't even implied — it was blatantly stated.

He moved money from various easy access accounts. He checked his passports. One day he'd travel under his own name. Just for the hell of it. He only had to pack now.

While pulling the case from beneath the bed he reviewed the situation. Jason missing, evidence missing, Steve missing. Keira carrying on. He wasn't sure about Elaine The Boring. At least he now understood the link between Jason and Lazlo. Not quite what he'd been expecting when he'd found those pictures, but it explained a lot.

And he'd given those photographs to Elaine.

With a sharp, harsh movement, he had zipped the bag then taken it with him to the car. Not his car, not a company car. A cheap rental he'd used someone else's details to hire. An ex-neighbour who had pissed him off too often.

He reached the street where Elaine lived and parked a few doors down. Easily tuning into the bugs, he couldn't hear anything. A glance reassured him that Elaine's car stood on the drive, so she was likely there too. But she wasn't making any sound. No TV, no radio. The only way he'd know what she was up to was to have a look. It took longer to hack into the cameras, but not as long as the first time.

There she was, in the living room, curled up on the sofa. Was she crying? If she so, she was doing it silently. A glance around the room showed him the mess on the floor. It took a moment, but among the detritus, he saw a pen drive. A double check showed a new dent in the wall plaster. He guessed the main part of the laptop was hidden by the sofa.

So, she hadn't known what was in those photographs before.

CHAPTER TEN

Her arm was numb, her neck cricked. Blinking, Elaine found herself in a dark room with only the lights of the Wi-Fi hub and the DVD clock to show her the way. 05:46.

The usual Monday morning dread overcame her. She didn't have to get up and go to work for an hour yet, but she'd clearly cried herself to sleep on the sofa and every part of her body ached; head, throat, eyes. She spotted the smashed mess of the laptop and groaned. And felt... nothing.

She should feel something. Even if it was only the urge to clean up. But no. All the same, she got up. Time to tidy. Jason or no, she wouldn't leave that mess around. Most of it just got thrown into the bin. Then at the last moment, she reached back in and retrieved the pen drive.

The room spick and span again, she wondered if she'd imagined it. There was nothing left to — she picked a tiny piece of screen glass from the edge of the carpet — now there was nothing left to suggest any kind of trouble. She stretched her neck, it clicked. Okay, there was a dent in the wall, filler and paint would solve that. Or not. Maybe she should redecorate completely. Maybe she should sell the house. It had never really felt like home to her. Maybe she should just burn it to the ground and leave it in the ashes like everything else in her life.

Maybe she should stop thinking like a petulant child.

Maybe a hot shower would help.

It didn't.

Work had become mechanical years ago, she sat at her desk, but those pictures she could never unsee played across her vision. Still, she carried on. That was what she always did. Keep going. Slog through it. Jane in accounts had told Elaine that her mantra was 'mortgage, two kids,' only Elaine didn't have a mortgage or two kids. Jason made the mortgage repayments, but she'd been careful with their money and saved, paying off additional amounts so they had cleared the mortgage five years early. Eighteen months ago.

Keep going.

Another email request for information. She could just send the required data, but, having checked her sent box and got the exact time, she responded to Giles-the-oh-so-wonderful that perhaps he should read his emails, most specifically the one she had sent the previous Thursday at 15:06 that contained all the requested information. Just to be spiteful, she copied in Patrick Makepeace, her line manager, since Giles had copied in his.

That was going to come back to bite her on the arse, but in that moment she didn't care.

* * *

Every agency was a hive of rumour and gossip. It was what espionage thrived on. The total lack of either in this case worried Agent Turner. As far as it was possible to tell, no side was talking about this. Not one. Not even the British. Which was odd, given that they were the ones who'd lost men. And what about the ones who weren't agents? Didn't those men matter? Didn't they have families who deserved to know what was really going on?

Analysis often took unexpected twists and turns. Direct routes could be dead ends; alleyways that seemed to lead nowhere could prove to be back routes to many a nugget of value.

Only not this time. The frustration was more than palpable. It was a headset being thrown across the office. The resulting clatter drawing unnecessary and unwanted attention.

"Did the headset do something to upset you?" the next analyst over asked.

"Pinched my ear." With that snap Agent Turner, forced back the chair and stomped over to reclaim the headset. It seemed perfectly intact. Which drew out an internal swear word.

The other analyst stood, halting Turner's progress back to the desk.

"Take a break." It was less a suggestion than an order, not that an analyst of equal rank could give such an order. But the headset was taken from Turner's hand all the same. "Your tension is rubbing off on me and I don't need that much stress in my life. You were bad enough last week, I thought the weekend might see you more bearable today, but clearly, I was wrong. Go get yourself a pretzel and a coffee. And you can bring me one too by way of apologising for being so dang irritating."

* * *

More meaningless business data analysis, but the only analysis that really occupied Elaine's mind revolved around the images Ladderman had given her. He'd passed her the drive of photographs, so he had have known what was on it, the likely impact it would have on her. While she didn't actually expect him to care, some general consideration would have been nice. He was also the only one she'd mentioned a death certificate to. Had he requested that?

"Elaine, are you okay?"

Blinking, she struggled to focus on Patrick, as he looked at her over their desk divider. There was a deep frown on his forehead.

"Sorry?" She had completely lost track of everything that was going on around her.

"I asked if you are okay."

She had no idea why he thought she wouldn't be okay. "Is this about that email to Giles?" she asked.

"No, the man deserved that. Are you okay? I don't suppose you would be, really."

She could only stare at him. She suspected her jaw was slack; she probably looked like a halfwit. She felt like one. "What?"

"Well, you and Keira are close friends."

She still didn't understand what he was talking about.

"With her being on compassionate leave, I guess you're affected too."

"Compassionate leave?" Elaine's brain seemed to misfire.

Now the frown grew a lot deeper. "You're not okay at all, are you? I know the accident was a shock to Keira, losing Steve that way is such a blow. But of course, you knew him too. It would affect you."

She swallowed and looked down at the keyboard. Keira hadn't been working, and she hadn't noticed. She focused back on Patrick. He was a good man, way better at the politics of management than she, but he wasn't as good as he thought he was.

"Did you know my husband worked with Steve?"

His look was sympathetic. "No, he must be feeling it dreadfully too."

"Not really." Elaine decided it was time to take the plunge. "He was in the same accident."

Patrick paled unhealthily. "He's… he's… too?"

Unable to bring herself to say the word, Elaine could only nod. She heard the drip and looked down. Apparently, she was crying. The tears were hot and heavy, but without sobs, just burning tears.

Patrick mumbled apologies for not realising. He shifted agitatedly in his chair. Like he wanted to do something but didn't know what.

"How could you?" she tried to absolve his apparent guilt. "I didn't say."

"Right, from now on you are on compassionate leave. Put your out of office on and go…" He floundered. "Go do whatever you need to go do, forget about work. We'll cope."

Grateful for his concern, she offered him a watery smile. "I'll do that. And thank you."

* * *

The envelope was obvious as Elaine opened the door. A plain brown envelope, typed and franked, but the franking gave nothing away except that it had been sent from London. It looked both official and not. Curious, she pushed the door closed and moved into the living room. she turned it over and ripped the flap open.

A death certificate.

Stumbling back, she sat unsteadily on to sofa.

Jason's death certificate.

Death by misadventure.

She pushed the misadventures of his photographic career aside.

This didn't really tell her anything, a government-backed cover-up.

She stared at the certificate, checked the envelope for any note that came with it – nothing. She carefully put the certificate back into the envelope, stood and placed it in the slim letter rack on the hallway console table. It was the only letter there, all the bills were paid by direct debit and, as a rule, she dealt with mail as it arrived. She couldn't deal with that piece of mail. Not right now.

Food.

She should eat. But the thought of food churned her stomach in all the wrong ways. Instead, she reached for the phone.

"Hi Madison."

"Mom?"

That simple word made her close her eyes and hold back tears. That Madison called her 'Mom' was both blessing and curse. She tried not to see the sexualised young woman in Jason's pictures.

"Yeah, it's me; just checking you're okay."

"I'm fine, why wouldn't I be?"

Elaine frowned. *Because Jason's gone and you two were close? Close? Ha!* There again, she hadn't told Madison yet. Besides there was a strain to the younger woman's voice. "I don't know, Madison, why aren't you okay? I can tell when the jollity is forced, you know."

She heard the sighed. "Sorry, Mom. It's been a stressful day. I was just trying to hide that."

"Okay. Anything you want to talk about?"

"No. Thanks, but no. It's just work stuff. You know how that can be. Besides, it's not why you called. Why did you call?"

Elaine thought she heard a note of hope, of interest. Clearly Madison needed some cheering up, and the news she had at the moment was the exact opposite of cheery. "No reason actually. I just miss my little girl, that's all."

Madison laughed. "Mom, I'm thirty-two. What? Ten years younger than you, I'm hardly a little girl."

Elaine smiled down the line. "True. Doesn't mean I don't care any—" She cut herself off, tears threatening again. "Anyway, you're fine, that's what I called to find out, guess I'd better let you go again."

"If I weren't due to go into an important meeting, you wouldn't get away with that. I'll call you later."

* * *

Sometimes it wasn't easy to just sit back and watch, listen. Though in fairness, right now that was exactly all he could do. The wind was picking up, it buffeted the car. It was oddly like being rocked to sleep.

Knowing there was more to Elaine Blake than she let on didn't make a cohesive whole with the woman he was watching and listening to. She woke up, prepared for the day, commuted to the office and worked.

She could, and did, sit still for hours seemingly doing nothing. He wondered where her mind wondered to when she did that. His mind recalled all that incredible artwork in the lockup. Did she paint those images in her mind? Escape to new worlds? Or was that world plagued by the monsters she drew?

Was what she'd said about Jason true? Did he hit her?

Given his pre-existing low opinion of Jason, it was easy to believe he was a wife beater. What else could deaden a woman's personality so completely? Then there were the photographs, Jason had been abusing a lot of people for a long time. The only reason he had given Elaine those photographs was to gauge her reaction. Her throwing the laptop around and crying herself to sleep were strong arguments that she had not known about the abuse.

It had also added to the stress she was under. She suffered it. That she broke down and cried in work was understandable. Not that she'd actually broken down, just cried.

Bad as that was for her, it was good for him. Stressed people made poor choices. Her sarcasm when they'd turned up on Saturday had been a reaction, striking out at them because she had no one else to strike at.

If she had any knowledge of the evidence they were looking for, he just had to keep pushing her until she led him to it.

From the office he'd followed her back home. There was no notable change of pace. No rush, no delay. A steady, normal pace. In the house, she simply sat back down like a robot in need of charging.

With a move so sudden it almost made Mac jump, Elaine grabbed the shoulder bag she kept behind the sofa. She grabbed car keys from the drawer in the console table, and her coat from the hook by the door.

He put his own equipment to the side and started the car. Only when she left the house did he slip the laptop safely under the front passenger footwell.

CHAPTER ELEVEN

Elaine needed answers and there was only one place she could think to get them.

This was probably a bad idea.

But she was already parked outside Keira's house.

Once she and Keira had, she thought, been good friends, and she missed that. Despite what she now knew had been going on behind her back, she still cared about her friend. And if Keira was grieving for Steve, Elaine wanted to be there for her. Not knowing if Keira would want her to visit or sympathise kept her in the car wondering what to do for the best; frozen in analysis paralysis.

Jessica coming out of the front door and heading straight for Elaine's car surprised Elaine. Now fourteen years old, and looking way more mature, Jessica was already taller than Elaine, and years of dance classes had kept her thin and fit. With long blond hair and perfect teeth, she was an enviably attractive young girl. Elaine wound down the window.

"Hey Jess."

"Hi Aunt E." Jess had never called her by her full name. "Aren't you coming in?"

Elaine swallowed, not knowing what to say. "Last time I spoke to your mum, it didn't exactly end well."

"Yeah well, with everything that's happened..." Jessica shrugged. "Guess neither of you will be at your best, but you've been friends like forever. You should come in."

Since Jessica opened the car door, Elaine didn't really have much choice, so she waited until the electric window wound all the way back up then turned the electrics off, released her seatbelt and stepped out. She walked up the drive with Jessica.

"How are you?" she asked the young girl.

Jessica hugged herself as they walked. The cold air was partly an excuse given the bulk of the jumper she wore, and the light was already dimming for evening. "Oh, I'm okay." Now she pushed her hair back. "It's not like I got to see him often. Being away all the time."

Steve, like Jason, was away for work a lot and with Jessica often away for dance competitions, they were ships in the night. They had reached the house and stepped through the double doors into a massive foyer area.

"It's almost like it's not real and any minute now he's going to walk back in."

"I feel exactly the same," Elaine admitted. "I hear a noise and automatically think Jason's back." She tensed every time which she supposed was a very different reaction. "Then I remember."

"I feel…" Jessica nodded.

"Yeah." Elaine reached out and hugged the girl.

Jessica hugged Elaine back, burying her face on Elaine's shoulder. Jessica's trembling turned to shaking. The girl burst into tears, clinging onto Elaine, sobbing her heart out. Unable to hold back, Elaine's own tears started.

Keira appeared in the sitting room doorway. She wore a tracksuit and no makeup, her hair unbrushed and her eyes red. She was hugging herself, and a white tissue was crumpled in one hand, held to her mouth. Elaine had never seen her in such a state. One arm still around Jessica, Elaine held her arm out to Keira. Like a lost little girl, Keira ran to join the hug, the two adults sandwiching the teenager in a confluence of tears.

The weight of the other two women started to strain Elaine, and Jessica's sobs calmed. She shifted her head and suggested they move into the sitting room. With nods and general inarticulate agreement, they parted. Jessica used the cuff of her jumper to dry her eyes and said she'd go up to her room to let them talk.

"You don't have to run away because of me."

"I'm not. I just want to be on my own for a bit."

Elaine nodded and watched as the girl ran upstairs.

"I think she needed that," Keira said, her voice still shaking from her own tears.

"I think we all did."

When Elaine turned back, Keira was nodding. Still a little uncertain, Elaine waited for the silent indication that they should move to the sitting room. When they did, she sat first, and Keira took the seat opposite. Elaine swallowed the lump in her throat; they usually sat together, always had. Words deserted her.

"So," Keira said. "I hear you've been working."

Elaine wondered how she heard, who from? "It was a distraction."

Keira nodded.

Elaine was lost for what to say. Nothing felt right. *Facts. If you can't do the emotional, stick to the facts.*

"Well, I guess you won't need to anymore."

"Won't need to what?"

"Work."

Elaine frowned at Keira. "Why not?"

"Well, you don't have a mortgage and with the money, well…"

Her head started aching from the depth of the frown ploughing itself so deeply on her forehead. "What money?"

"You asked for money to keep quiet, they paid it. All you have to do is keep schtum now."

For a second that made little sense. Elaine hadn't checked her bank account. She didn't until payday, ready to make sure that all the direct debits were covered and shift what money she could into saving accounts. "I…" the word ended on an expulsion of confused air. "Are you sure?"

Keira nodded. "That's what I was told."

It didn't compute. "I didn't mean it. She was annoying me, so I said something stupid."

"Stupidly lucky."

"Maybe, but why? Why would they just give me that kind of cash?"

"Hush money?"

Elaine didn't believe it. "But that doesn't make sense. If they wanted me hushed, there are cheaper and easier ways to do it. Trump up some charge, get me locked up. Discredit me. Hell, even pump me full of psychotropics and have me carted away to a mental institution. Half a million is a hefty price to pay and not even get me to sign an NDA."

"A what?"

"Non-disclosure agreement?"

Keira shook her head and sighed. "Of course. Not on point at the moment."

At least that seemed understandable. The most explainable Keira had been since the news of what happened in Prague. That didn't make the payment any more explainable. What were they thinking? What was she meant to think? It didn't seem any more real than Jason's death. Which took her to the reason she had come here.

"I got something in the post this morning, and I'm not sure what to do about it."

"What was it?"

Actually, saying the words out loud was harder than she had expected, so had to take a deep fortifying breath. "Jason's—" her voice cracked. She swallowed and tried again. "Jason's death certificate."

Keira looked away, sucking her lips, hugging herself. "I got Steve's too."

"I told Patrick about Jason today."

Keira picked her head up to look at her; Elaine wasn't sure what to read in that expression.

"Had to, really. I was just sitting there. Crying. He sent me home."

"Is that why you're here now?"

Elaine nodded.

"And not over the weekend?"

Was the pain she heard in Keira's voice real or just the need Elaine felt she needed to hear. It was difficult to answer, but she had to tell the truth. "I wasn't sure I'd be welcome."

With a keen that echoed pain, Keira left her seat and moved over to sit next to Elaine. Hugged her. Elaine hugged back.

"I didn't think you'd want to see me," Keira admitted. "I feared I'd ruined our friendship."

As Keira sat back, Elaine shifted to see her better.

"Nearly did," she admitted. "I really didn't – don't like that you've lied to me for so long. You betrayed me." And in ways she wasn't strong enough to expose, but bitterness flavoured her heart, making her hate herself as much as Keira.

"It wasn't my choice."

Elaine reckoned it was Keira's choice to sleep with Jason and let him take those photos. But all Elaine did was shrug. Now wasn't the time. She doubted there would ever be a time. Did it matter anymore? "Well… I guess… friends will be friends. Just promise you won't lie to me again."

* * *

Why would Elaine go to Keira now?

He sat down the street from the Southgate home and waited. He'd managed to put a tracker on Elaine's car, but not a bug in her handbag, he therefore couldn't listen in to what was being said. Not that a bug in her handbag would do him that much good right now, she hadn't taken it with her. He'd have to think again about the best way to get a bug on Elaine herself.

That was a worry for another time, right now he had to ask why she came here to see her husband's mistress. *Bitch fight?* Somehow, he doubted that.

He didn't think Elaine had seen those pictures before he passed them on, but he shouldn't discount the possibility. Was she part of it? Part of child abuse?

No one could be as dull as Elaine Blake appeared, the artwork and the thousands of books he'd found in her storage unit proved there was more to her. So why couldn't he find anything?

Not even a speeding ticket. Who the hell got through over twenty years of driving with no speeding tickets? Okay his record showed none but mostly because he'd had them expunged. Or given false identities. Could she have done the same?

Jason had lied to her about who he was and what he did. Had Elaine done the same? If so, why? Was she a sleeper agent? Could she be someone other the girl born Elaine Annie Underwood? From the history and photographs he'd seen, it couldn't be. Not unless they found a total doppelgänger.

Great, now I'm so bored I'm making things up.

* * *

The call had been a double-edged sword. Agent Madison Turner took the phone from her ear and stared at it. Until she cancelled it would continue to show caller ID. Elaine Blake. The woman she was banned from calling, the one she couldn't say anything to.

But why hadn't Elaine said anything?

Was that her fault? Clearly Elaine had picked up on her stress. It would be just like Elaine to consider that and keep information to herself not to cause additional upset.

Madison was well aware that Elaine had been told that Jason would be away for six weeks, they'd chatted about it in a call before Jason left. They were only about halfway through that window. Was Elaine not saying anything because she was still hopeful Jason would be back? Madison doubted it. While she couldn't fault Elaine on being a foster mother, there had always been something weird about the marriage between her and Jason.

Madison had long worked on the principle of what Mom didn't know, wouldn't hurt her. It was a guiding light for most teenagers when living at home, and Madison would never have wanted to hurt Elaine. But she wondered now if there were some hurts that were necessary. Cruel to be kind?

How would Elaine react if Madison were cruel enough to tell her the truth? The risk of losing the only Mom she had was too great. She couldn't do that. She cancelled the caller screen and turned back to her computer.

What Elaine hadn't said was as interesting as what she had said. Jason was missing. Why hadn't she told Madison that? Did she not know? Did she know what Madison couldn't find any evidence of, that the Brits were planning retrieval and return?

It was a conundrum, and one Madison set to work on.

"Don't work too late."

Madison looked up to see her neighbour standing and pulling his coat on.

"And for God's sake, have a restful evening."

A glance around showed the room had already emptied. Eyes flicked to the large clock on the wall. Ten past nine. It was solidly dark outside. She'd been working at least five hours and come up with nothing. No missing person's report, even the original one had been redacted. Nothing. This was the very definition of frustrating. It was also too late to call Mom back.

She offered a smile. "I'll try, sorry I've been annoying you. I hadn't realised the time. I'll log out now. Night."

CHAPTER TWELVE

Circuitous thoughts dripped poison into Elaine's mind as she returned home. Those pictures. Being too weak to confront Keira. What that bastard had done to her children. Those images burned in her soul like the brand from hell. How could he? How dare he? She had to remind herself over and over to push past the images and find a way to function.

Patrick called around seven, apologised for calling so late, but he asked if she was okay, told her she had the standard ten days compassionate leave, but if she needed more time, that would was fine, he'd call next week.

He's being nice.

He doesn't need me.

She laughed at that thought. He *didn't* need her, she had set up all reports to run automatically; as long as someone checked the input, the output was guaranteed. She'd made it so easy; she'd made herself the loser in the end. But then that was her life story.

She pulled her notebook from her bag. The one containing all the cyphers. A number she didn't understand, names that meant nothing. Perhaps she should send it all to the men who searched her house, but she had no idea how to contact them. Through Keira probably. That idea sent her thoughts spiralling again. She couldn't face talking to Keira about what she knew. The dissociation she felt with the house was only clarified by the lack of violation she had experienced since the search. People who had been burgled were said to feel violated, but she felt nothing. She needed no privacy because there was nothing here worth hiding, not even her vibrator, apparently. She was nothing. Just being seen would be nice. She hadn't vacuumed properly all week. It wouldn't matter, no one visited. Jason wouldn't be back. She wasn't bothered. She would just sit like this forever and let the spiders build their webs and cover her once pristine home in gossamer. Like Miss Havisham, with opposite reasoning.

That this house had been invaded and searched should upset her. It didn't. A shift of her head showed light reflecting off some small shard of broken laptop. That could haunt the place for a long time. But not her. She broke that laptop for a reason, a reason she had sobbed for, the violation of others. It didn't touch her now. Was she as broken as the machine?

Her eye line moved up, to the one photograph in the room. A posed studio portrait Jason had wanted done about twenty years ago. He was most prominent, promoting him as head of the household, his idea of an ideal husband. A constant reminder of his dominance, and a hindrance to making this a home. Little wonder she and the kids had always spent more time in the kitchen diner. In that image, she stood subservient. She looked closer and finally noticed quite how blank she appeared. Her mouth tipped up, but she wasn't smiling, there was no warmth in her eyes. It was just a mask not an expression. She wasn't really there at all. The real her was hidden, caged. Trapped. But that was then, what about now?

You're still hiding.

The damn voice again.

You've been hiding a long time. Too long.

True. Hide the truth, have a normal life. She'd done it. Only this normal life never satisfied. Wanting more had always been problematic. She considered the only available facsimile she had of Jason to hand. *I certainly want to break free from your lies.* Freddy Mercury singing those famous lines in her head was almost funny, and the lyrics carried inappropriately on.

His lies or yours?

The ringing mobile made her jump, but thankfully not spill any of the wine she was drinking. She answered.

"Hello?"

"Mum, thank God," the voice came breathy and nervous.

"Lazlo?" The sense of urgency echoed her rapid heartbeat as she sat up, spine straight, and placed the wine glass carefully on the coffee table. It didn't matter what she'd seen, this was one of her babies and he needed her. "What's wrong?"

"Look, you have to listen."

Stomach knotting, Elaine couldn't do much else.

"Mum, they're going to hurt me and Dad if you don't do what I ask."

She thought about the certificate in the drawer and her fearful conviction that Jason wasn't really dead. Heart thumping, she sat still, the phone clamped to her ear.

"Jason had something," Lazlo said. "Some evidence. They say if you can get it, give it to them, they'll let us go."

Elaine struggled to assimilate this. "Jason's dead."

"No. Mum you have to listen. You have to give them the evidence."

Her throat was dry, she had to lick her lips. "Wh-what evidence?"

"I don't know."

If he didn't know, how she was supposed to? But she sort of did know. How much should she reveal? "How will I recognise it?"

"Jason said he hid it where no one would think to look."

"People have been looking," she admitted. "I have no idea if they found anything or not. I didn't see anything." Except those damning photos.

"Jason said that they would search but wouldn't find it. You would."

"I'll look."

"Hurry. I'll call you again."

The line went dead. Calling his name did no good. Her hand trembled as she lowered the phone. Ladderman and his mate had been through the house, Jason's computers, everything. If there was anything here, they would have found it. She stared at the notepad, the key.

They didn't find that.

* * *

Lazlo?

He took the headphones from his ears and hung them around his neck.

Why would the boy call now? Why would he tell Elaine that Jason was alive?

Was it possible?

This job had long since taught him that everyone lied.

If Jason was alive, the bosses had lied to him. Or had they themselves been lied to? Certainty was impossible. He reached for his phone. Let it drop back to the car seat.

Silent running.

Elaine's questions came back to him. *Have you seen the body?* No, and he'd had to ask about the death certificates too. Why had they been issued? Because Jason was dead or because he was beyond retrieval? Was Jason the traitor? If he wasn't, and there was a traitor in their midst, how high up did it go?

He tried to stretch his legs out, but there wasn't as much room in this car as the company van. He'd been lucky enough to have got into a position to be able to pick up the signal from the bugs he'd left in the Blake house. But all he picked up were more silence which led to more questions. Sometimes cases were like that.

And what did Elaine mean, she'd look? She knew that he'd looked, he'd definitely looked in places she never would. She had sounded so certain, but what good was certainty when there was nothing to find?

There again, they hadn't started pulling up floor boards, though he had pulled out the bath panel and checked under there. That was the only place in the entire house he'd found dirt. Apparently even Elaine didn't clean under there.

And if she intended to look, why was she still sitting still in the living room?

Or was she lying about that too?

She stared up at the picture on the wall. Though he couldn't see it from the camera, he knew it was a picture of Jason and Elaine. When he'd looked at it, it was like looking at a man and a mannequin. Nothing about that image of Elaine looked alive. He'd taken that picture down, just as Elaine now did. In fact, as he watched, she did exactly what he'd done.

She looked closely at the image. She turned it over and ran a hand around the frame, testing for inserts as he had. Then, going further than he had, she started picking at the tape that held the image in the frame. They hadn't done that as such tampering would have been too obvious. The rest of the pictures, yes, they were mostly photographs of the foster children in reusable frames, there were several with Jason in, but none of Elaine. He watched closely as she examined the portrait.

The tape tore repeatedly as she pulled it away. She had an awkward moment when the frame and print on canvas finally parted company. She glanced over the frame, then threw it on the sofa. She reviewed the picture from the back. He assumed she didn't see anything as she turned it to face her. The clock ticked as she kept her attention on the image stretched across the frame. What was she seeing?

With a sharp movement, she split the picture over her knee.

He blinked in surprise at the image from the camera.

Elaine nearly smiled before she dropped the picture and disappeared. He followed her on camera until she entered the back garden, and his visuals couldn't follow her anymore. A few moments later she was back. With a bucket. A beat-up metal bucket.

In the lounge, she picked up the remnants of canvas and cheap pine and put them in the bucket.

He frowned as she also broke up the frame. Stamping viciously on it.

She took both to the kitchen door, where she poured oil over the canvas. From a drawer she found some slim wooden skewers and broke them into the bucket. Another drawer provided a tea light and a cigarette lighter. She used one to light the other. Which she dropped into the bucket. Elaine's body language indicated triumph as she grabbed oven gloves and she picked up the bucket to take it out back.

The camera flare as she disappeared into the garden suggested the gloves were a good idea.

What was that all about? If there was anything in the

picture, which he'd seen no evidence of, it was gone now.

She came back, locked up and returned to the sitting room to sit.

Was that it for looking?

An hour later, she hadn't moved. Had she lied to Lazlo? Or had she already found something?

He sighed and leant back against the head rest. In a world of liars, he was a liar, he worked with liars, everyone lied. What kind of a life was this?

CHAPTER THIRTEEN

Elaine waited in line, her stomach cramping. This was an insane idea, but the only idea she had, and she's spent a lot of time thinking about it the previous night. This was still stone cold crazy. *What am I doing?*

Saving my son.

Things weren't simple, but that was what it came back to. She would do anything for her children. Fostered or not, they were her children, and she would do whatever she could to help them. There was no evidence in the house. If there had been, Ladderman and his mate would have found it. Unless Jason hid something under the floorboards, but with every floor covered with laminate that would have been very difficult without kicking up some dust at least – never mind the need to remove skirting. No. She cleaned like a dervish most days, if he'd done something like that, she would have noticed. The only out of place thing was the cypher and the key. That was all there was, that had to be the thing. The solution to the cypher didn't make much sense to her, but it might to Lazlo, and if he was alive, it would to Jason.

This was the best way she could help.

After rising ridiculously early, she had gathered everything she figured she might need. There were no new cars she could see in the street, but even she realised that she might not know one way or another, she didn't actually take that much notice of her neighbours these days, what vehicles they drove was of supreme indifference to her. Then she'd left.

Now she waited in the line at the bank to withdraw the money she would need to help Lazlo. Not being first was her own fault for sitting in a coffee shop drinking an Americano and two rounds of toast to start the day. Only she couldn't face actually eating the toast once it was before her. How many times had she lectured the children about making sure they ate breakfast? How often had Lazlo just rolled his eyes at the admonishment?

Even then she'd been thinking, debating with herself if she could do this. The plan was half baked, nuts, but it was the right thing to do. It was entirely possible that she was also deluding herself. This was exactly the kind of thing she had never done. Had never before even contemplated doing. Should probably never do. Probably couldn't do. She'd be lucky to get through this without throwing up.

Her dry eyes stared at the number board that would tell her which position was open. Only when she heard the tut from behind, did she realise she was next up and that she had to go to position pedwar – number four. The young man behind the glass wore a badge declaring him to be Sikandar, he was very presentable and clearly of Indian descent, so much so that the strong Birmingham accent nearly floored her.

"It's okay, it surprises a lot of non-Brummies."

Elaine momentarily hung her head, ashamed that she'd been so easily read. "It would in Cardiff. Sorry. I didn't mean to be insulting."

He shrugged. "Hey, anything's better the 'go home, Paki'." He leaned slightly forward, a play smile. "I mean my family aren't even from Pakistan."

She offered a small uncomfortable laugh and Sikandar asked how he could help. When she told him what she wanted he looked surprised, shocked even. Thankfully, he covered well and started to take care of the transaction.

"I'm sorry to do this, but because of the level of the transaction, I need to ask you for additional identification and I'm going to have to get me manager to sign the transaction off."

Elaine's mouth dried out. "I have to jump through hoops to get my own money?"

Sikandar looked uncomfortable. "Sorry."

"So do you want to go get your manager?"

"I'll take you through to one of the offices. Hold on, I'll be out in a mo."

Sikandar swivelled on his chair behind the counter. Fear washed through Elaine, which was dumb, whatever else it was, it was her money, and she wasn't leaving without it. She followed Sikandar to a small office with a tiny table and a computer terminal.

"If you wouldn't mind waiting in here."

"No problem," she said with a smile. "But I am in a hurry. Why don't you tell your manager that if I have to wait more than—" She deliberately checked her watch. "—five minutes, I won't be asking for ten grand, I'll be closing my account taking the full half million." She carefully increased her volume on the last amount and saw Sikandar pale and other customers who had heard perk up. They probably thought she was a right twonk. She would in their position. "Now run along, you wouldn't want to waste any of those valuable minutes now, would you?"

Head held up and imperious, Elaine sat, knowing that Sikandar, poor man, was clearly surprised by her behaviour.

She wasn't overly surprised when the female supervisor came in only four minutes later.

"Good morning, Mrs Blake, sorry for keeping you waiting." The woman smiled as she came in and sat down.

Elaine's smile was tight. Guilt ran bitterly through her veins. She had to remind herself that she wasn't doing anything wrong. To be fair neither was the woman she faced, except for being way too young. Elaine realised she was probably old enough to be this woman's mother, and that just darkened her mood. She read the badge on the woman's navy lapel. "Hayleigh." Apparently, they were too hip and modern for the respect of surnames. Elaine felt every muscle fibre clench. Modern life in general, and officious people thinking they were funky, in particular, just made her want to punch something. Still, she'd had over twenty years to contain that rage. Which was why she suspected it was written clearly on her face right now. That worried her. So far, she hadn't actually done anything to help Lazlo, if she was this nervous just retrieving her own money, how was she ever going to take the next steps?

One at a time. Take each step in turn until you get there.

"I understand that you want to make a significant withdrawal from our bank."

"Of *my* money, yes. Is that a problem?"

"Well, usually we like twenty-four hours' notice."

"And how much time do you want for a bank draft of four hundred and fifty thousand, Miss-?" she realised she didn't know the woman's name. "You do have a surname?"

"Navarro," Hayleigh said, finally recovering from the surprise of the amount stated. "Hayleigh Navarro."

Elaine gave her credit for staying cool.

"Of course, we can sort this out, but because of the magnitude of the transaction, I will need two additional forms of identification, one of which needs to be photographic ID."

"I have both my driver's licence and my passport. Will those do?"

"That would be fine."

Elaine dragged her bag up by its shoulder strap, unzipped the outer fastening and then the security pocket inside to find the passport which she lay on the table, several inches from the edge, but deliberately closer to her than Hayleigh, who could easily reach it. Next Elaine retrieved her purse and pulled out her driver's licence, which she set on top of the passport. Ignoring both items she took her time to close up her purse, return it to her bag, then place that on the floor. When she looked back Hayleigh hadn't reached for the identification. She faced the woman. When Hayleigh still didn't move, she tipped her head inspecting the woman.

"There doesn't appear to be anything wrong with your arms."

Hayleigh's eyes narrowed and her nostrils flared as she reached the short distance to take and inspect the two pieces of ID. Carefully inspecting them and taking her own sweet time about it. The spike of annoyance quickly fell under the amused realisation that Hayleigh was conducting a little rebellion of her own.

"Seems to be in order."

"Of course, now let's get down to business. I would, as you know, very much like to take ten thousand pounds in cash away with me now, along with a bank draft for four hundred and fifty thousand. How do you think you can facilitate that?"

Hayleigh didn't immediately answer.

Elaine tried to keep the annoyance out of her tone. "I understand that you are desperately trying to find a reason to refuse me because I've already shown that I can be an awkward customer and often people in positions of power such as yours want to be shown some deference. But here's the thing, Hayleigh, I have been with this bank probably longer than you've been alive, and while I appreciate that such loyalty won't mean much to most people of your generation, I don't know you well enough to know if that includes you. I can, however, tell you that it still means something to people of my generation. And which generation do you think makes up the majority of your bosses? And believe it or not I know several of them." She leant forward and spoke quietly as if letting Hayleigh into a secret. "In fact, Peter Smart lives two doors up from me." She wasn't about to say that the banks manager had the largest style of house on the development, and the one with the biggest plot. Or that her house while large in itself, was the smallest that had been on offer. The way Hayleigh blanched, she didn't have to say anything at all. "Now, are you going to force a smile and be nice?"

"Are you?"

Elaine allowed her smile to broaden, and she genuinely laughed as she sat back. "Oh, you'll go far, but sort my money out first, eh?" She'd never been a demanding customer before and she liked it, odd that she wasn't being as nice as normal yet was getting more respect. Even that push back was delivered more timidly than it could have been.

Hayleigh took a breath and checked the ID. Then she nudged her mouse and moved to log on. "Are you off somewhere nice?" she asked they waited for the machine to catch up.

"Just trying to help someone I care about."

Hayleigh looked at her. "That's a lot of help. Look, I realise you're about to tell me to wind my neck in, but I feel I have to ask, you're not being coerced into this pay-out, are you?"

"No, but actually, thank you for asking. It's good to know you do care about your customers. It's just that for once, I'm just in a position to do something good for someone I care about."

Hayleigh reached under the counter for a card reader. "Would you mind slotting your debit card in there?"

To get the cash took some time. The sum was too high to be kept in the cashier's drawers, in case of a raid, so Hayleigh had to go out to the back safes to fetch the money.

When she came back, she sat back down before she counted out the bundles ready for Elaine. "And make sure you keep this very safe."

"Oh, I will." Elaine smiled as she reached out and took the last piece of paper, the bank draft, zipping it carefully into her bag before she distributed the cash though the various pockets. She stood, thanked Hayleigh, and left.

* * *

He hadn't found sleeping in the car pleasant, but it was a necessity he couldn't forego. The parabolic listening device wasn't much use when he couldn't get a decent position to use it and the battery power on the bugs had run out. He woke up desperate for a pee and starving hungry. He'd filled his waste bottle, so he risked a drive to the nearest McDonalds, used the facilities and ordered breakfast to go.

Thankfully, the grey Fiesta remained on the drive when he returned. Elaine wasn't working at the moment, so this was both a relief and no great surprise. With fewer cars around now that the commuters had started to head to work, he was able to get the spot opposite the house.

He sat for a while eating the McMuffin. It had cooled, the egg had congealed and tasted like rubber. But he needed sustenance. He studied the house. It was impossible to know if the bedroom curtains were still closed, because Elaine's room was at the back, but all the other curtains were open.

He frowned as he washed the last bite away with tepid coffee.

Had those curtains been open last night?

He tried to think back. They'd been open when Elaine took the call from Lazlo. And when she'd burnt that picture. They'd been open for him to see her fill up another glass of wine and head for bed, so yes, those curtains had been open all night.

That was a relief, he hadn't missed her then.

So, he sat. And waited.

He waited another hour.

Frowned.

This wasn't right.

He waited while he debated the possibility that she was sleeping off a hangover. She had had two glasses of wine, large glasses yes, but only two. And that seemed to be the usual for her. So, a hangover didn't seem likely. Without a power source, he couldn't use the laptop to see the security feed.

From the glove compartment, he took the spare key Keira had given him, and left the car. No one on the street paid him any attention, he walked up to the house as if he owned it and the door gave him entry easily. No deadlock, just on the Yale. Not a good sign.

"Elaine?" he called out. "Elaine!"

Nothing.

He ran up the stairs two steps at a time. Her bedroom door was open, he didn't have to go in to see that the bed was made, but he stepped in all the same. He looked around. No signs of a struggle, everything where it should be. Except there was no hairbrush laying neatly in front of the mirror.

He moved over and checked the drawers. A fair bit of her underwear was gone.

The wardrobe doors slid open easily. Only a few items missing, but enough to confirm his fear. She'd done a bunk, and he'd missed it.

"Fuck."

* * *

"Actually, I spoke to her yesterday, early afternoon," Madison told her supervisor's supervisor. She was good at her job, and she wanted to work directly to this man, so she needed to impress him, or at least not disappoint him. "And as I reported then, she didn't mention Jason."

"And you haven't called her back?"

"No, sir. You told me not to make contact."

The description 'poker-faced' could have been created for Alan Bromstad. His expression gave nothing away, totally unreadable. He asked again if Elaine Blake had mentioned Jason's disappearance, and again, Madison truthfully denied it.

"Any theory on why?"

The very question she didn't even want to ask herself again. "I wish I knew, sir." She kept her voice calm. "All I can think is that Elaine has been told Jason is missing, but that she doesn't want to worry me. She may well believe that he'll be back. We are still within the six-week time frame that she was told he would be away for."

"How far in?"

Madison had to think about it. "Thirteen days."

Time stretched as he watched her. Silence remained her best option. While she continued to keep an eye on the situation, to follow his orders not to contact Elaine, she couldn't let it go completely. Eventually her nerves stretched too far, she had to ask.

"Sir, what's changed?"

"What do you mean?"

If was clear to Madison that he knew precisely what she meant, but she was an analyst, and she had to prove her analysis in this case.

"Last week when I presented the case for watching developments in this situation, including noting my own connection, you stated clearly that you felt it was not an issue which we needed to be concerned about, and that you didn't feel it was advisable for me, as a representative of the company, to be seen questioning it. I understand and respect that decision, even if I don't entirely like it. But you called me to this meeting, and I've not been able to give you any more information than I had last week. So, I'm just wondering, what is it that's changed?"

Again, nothing was said.

"Shall I take that to mean whatever it is, it's above my clearance level?"

The wall of silence was granite and not to be breeched.

"Is there anything else I can do to support you today, sir?"

He seemed to consider that before he spoke. "The embargo on your talking to Mrs Blake is in relation to the case you seem to think so important. It is a matter of security and secrecy. You do understand that?"

She nodded. "Of course, sir. I trust you understand that there is no question as my loyalty to my job or my country?"

"No, of course not, Agent Turner. That's never been in doubt." Then he sat forward with what he probably considered an avuncular attitude, but was ever so slightly and totally unwittingly, threatening. "As a son with an ailing mother, and a father who has faced his own tribulations with the support of his children, I have to tell you that I see no reason why you shouldn't call the woman who is, effectively, your mother should you feel that she might need the support. Given the… sensitivity of the current situation, I would however like to be kept informed of any communications you have with Mrs Blake. While I don't wish to intrude upon your private life, this matter may impact upon other areas of my concern."

In truth, if he wanted to intrude on her private life, he was pretty much at liberty to do so. "Thank you, sir. I should very much like to speak to Mom, so I appreciate the freedom to do so. I also appreciate your position and will report any matters of concern beyond the immediate family issues."

He nodded and she offered a small smile of acknowledgement before she stood. As she turned towards the door, his call turned her back.

"Agent Turner?"

"Yes, sir?"

"Report directly to me on this matter, please."

Unusual, but not unreasonable. Also, potentially good for her future. "Yes, sir."

That he raised an arm and held out a business card surprised her. She took it and saw nothing more than his name, without title or job, and mobile number. His personal mobile number. This was not information he readily gave out.

"Family chats tend to be outside of business hours, and I'm not always in this office. Call me if something comes up. Whenever it comes up."

CHAPTER FOURTEEN

Bile burned in Elaine's throat as she sat in the train. Now five minutes since they had come to a juddering halt within sight of Paddington Station. Many of the passengers who had stood up preparing for the whole London scene, now huffed their annoyance, some had slumped back down in their seats. Mutterings about the people running the rail company lacking paternity, had a rehearsed tone suggesting the insults were time honoured more than felt in the moment. Acceptance sat beneath the annoyance. Elaine didn't share that sense as she remained seated. She glanced down at the sketch pad on her lap. She'd picked up the sketch book at the station in Cardiff, along with a small set of drawing pencils. It was hard-backed, spiral bound and at only six inches square it fit easily in her bag. Then again, it was a big bag. On the way she had been idly sketching, in this case, the face of Lazlo, as she remembered him the day he'd come into her care. He'd been a lost kid then, what was he now? From where she stood, he was still a lost kid.

Out of the window, the tracks seemed wobbly through the distortion of the rain pouring down the windows. She hadn't been alone on a train in more years than she could count. Come to that, she hadn't even been on a train.

Why not?

Because Jason made you think you couldn't cope.

The problem was that her twisted guts were now saying the same thing. *They're lying to you.* She glared down at her grumbling belly. *Liar.* That didn't exactly help.

She could do this. She was on a train she'd boarded in Cardiff, and technically in London even if still stuck on said train. Step one complete. A big step. Part of what she had to do. If the next bit proved too much, turning tail, to run back home remained possible. *And leave Lazlo stranded?* No, she wouldn't do that. The mere idea twisted her guts. Guts that rumbled badly. Since that fateful phone call, food hadn't been easy to swallow. She checked her watch. Unbelievable. Not even been 24 hours yet.

The lurch as the train started forward surprised her, she automatically grabbed the seat arm. *You used to love roller coasters, remember?* She had, but one go on the Octopus at a fair with Jason while dating and he put a stop to such silliness. She hadn't been on a coaster since.

Another jolt rocked her as the train stopped. The carriage started emptying. Now there was space, Elaine stood, struggled to reach up and pull down the small wheeled holdall she had packed that morning, and left as the last straggler from that carriage.

On the platform she pulled up the handle of the wheeled case and began to drag it along behind her. The case ground and clicked over the joints in the concourse. Footfalls marked a staccato beat that Elaine found herself rushing to follow. Harried, breathless, she realised she had no need to rush. Let the people from carriages further back overtake her, it made no difference. She wasn't expected and wasn't sure what kind of reception she'd get by turning up out of the blue. She slowed to a more comfortable pace.

Her inner voice listed all the reasons why she should take the next train home. There were too many ways she could fail Lazlo, and they crowded her head, crushed her confidence. No, she had to stop second guessing herself. She fished her ticket from her pocket and crossed the barrier — with only a little fight as the closing gate chomped on her bag.

On the main floor of the busy station, she stopped. The Underground entrance opened before her. People flowed around her as she stood before the gapping maw. She refused to listen to that voice telling her to turn back. *Lazlo needs me.*

The ticket machine mocked her indecisiveness; she had no idea if she was just going to make one stop or a couple. Even if two, the individual tickets would probably be enough, but in the end, and to the accompaniment of the man behind her tutting, she decided to select the Zone 1-2 day ticket. She also decided to take her time with every step of the process thereafter, just to annoy him further. It might be gone three in the afternoon, and maybe she wouldn't get value for money from the ticket, but she got value for the effort when she heard the man huff. She turned to the side as if to walk away, but didn't, taking time to put her change in her purse then her purse in her bag. He sucked air through his nose. She looked at him.

"Less haste, more speed." And walked away smiling.

You're a bad person. She mentally gave a single finger to the voice in her head, it sounded way too much like Jason.

The platform was emptier than expected. Then again, rush hour hadn't exactly started yet. The train pulled in as she walked towards the middle of the platform, doors swishing open. By way of accepting the invitation, Elaine stepped in. The carriage was half empty, so she picked the seat immediately to the left of the door, behind the glass panel, which allowed her to look up at the line diagram to see how many stops she needed. Four. Then change lines and four more.

A plummy voice told passengers to stand clear of the doors before they hissed closed, then with a jolt, their journey through the tunnels began. The train rattled forward, the light occasionally flickered as they buffeted around bends that never showed on the underground map. With nothing better to do, Elaine glanced around the other passengers. None of them were out of the ordinary. They were at roughly half capacity for seating, a mix of genders, a mix of races, a mix of social and economic backgrounds judging from the tattered trainers up to polished handcrafted brogues. She saw a dog collar and a hijab. A string vest — brave lad — and a leather biker jacket. Which, the more she thought about it, struck her as odd on the Underground. *Stop thinking about it.* What really struck her was that not one of them looked happy. There was no meeting of eyes, no general openness.

With a "Mind the Gap" the doors hissed open. Just to prove her wrong about the innate loneliness of the city, a group of three men stepped in. Shouts of "Dave", greetings of "Mate!" rang out. The group all wore combat trousers, two in tee-shirts and thick padded shirts, the other two in big baggy hoodies with oversized, overpriced brands scrawled across them. She checked their feet. Sturdy footwear, bovver boots, the type she remembered from her youth. The type she'd seen stomp too hard on too much flesh. She closed her eyes and pushed the memories away.

The train moved off again, three more stops. She looked down at her suitcase, absently drumming her fingers and trying to drown out the voices in her head telling her she couldn't possibly help and should just go home. It took a few moments to realise that the bovver-boys were muttering, and the mutterings were growing louder, less pleasant.

Elaine remembered a day back in school, the day she finally hit back at the bullies. This was how that started. Eleven years old and...

Stop it. Forget it. Ignore it.

That was what she had done for years. She'd ignored the comments and the taunts, the pushes and the 'oh sorry I didn't mean to tread on your toes' when obviously they had.

One of the men moved within the group, the one originally on the train — the one they'd called Dave. Though still with his mates, he stood proud from them.

"Why don't you just go home?"

She asked herself the same question. Then realised he wasn't talking to her. He was talking down to the young woman in the hijab sitting a few seats from her. The young woman glanced at the men, then turned away without a word. Elaine glanced at the girl. In all likelihood, she was home. As the abuse continued, Elaine wished the racists would all bugger off, but they were probably home too.

"We don't what your type here, Paki!"

Elaine blinked. That level of stupidity said it all. What also spoke volumes as they came to an unexpected halt in the tunnel was that no one acted to help the girl. Smart leather-shod man looked the other way, probably didn't want to mess up his perfect do. String vest man hung his head, as if ashamed of his inaction which as something she supposed. The young man with the Marley headphones and the dreads kept his eyes closed, mouthing the words to the song, and bobbing his head in time to music. Elaine doubted he was listening to it. The priest had turned away. A girl at the far end of the carriage, behind the men held her phone up. *Dear God, she's videoing it. So much for intervention.*

"Does your husband force you to wear that scarf?"

Even as Elaine shrunk back, memories of Jason's taunts cowing her, the inaccuracy of the man's statement, the inaction of other to defend, all annoyed her. Hijab, not scarf. A glance at the woman's hand proved she wasn't married. Did Muslim wives wear rings or was that a Christian thing? Elaine had no idea. As the insults continued, Elaine remembered just how awful it is to be on the wrong end of such barbs. She'd snapped at last, stood up and punched her bully in the face. Of course, that was when the headmaster turned up. She had been expelled for bullying, vilified, and shamed, and no amount of truth had wiped that clean. She'd gone from quiet A-grade student to hanging out with a very wrong crowd. She'd started drinking, sleeping around, and a lot worse. Life was different now; she didn't have the teenage belief in her own immortality anymore. Instead she had twenty-three years of being beaten down by her husband to teach her the truth. She knew if she confronted these bullies the situation would escalate, and she'd likely end up being the one punched. She didn't fancy that.

"Your lot don't fucking even belong here. We dunt wan' your Sharia Law. We're Christian, we are."

So much for Christian tolerance and charity.

Another tube rushed past, embarrassed to be near this behaviour. Their train lurched as the man threatened gang rape.

"Coming over here with your backpack bombs-"

Elaine shot to her feet. The girl's bag was the same as the laptop bag she'd been provided with by work. The squareness of this bag suggested it held a laptop and a lever-arch file. She couldn't take on the bullies, she wasn't big enough or strong enough, but she could stand up and be counted. Jason had kept her down, a bigoted stranger wouldn't. Her case dragged behind, she stood, grabbing the upright brown pole, putting her back to the men and getting between them and the girl. She looked down at the woman in the hijab.

"Hi." No response. Her heart hammered harder than the engines. "Hi!" She had to talk loudly over the noise of the moving train. The young woman turned to look up at her and for the first time Elaine was struck by quite how beautiful the girl was. *Girl? She's well into her twenties, she's a woman, stop being so ageist just because you're old.* "Great weather for using the Tube today. It was pouring down as I came into London." The insults and jeering continued from behind her, whilst ahead of her she saw another passenger hold up a phone, recording again. Elaine had no idea what she was saying, just said anything that came to mind. She didn't try to engage the woman in conversation. "Don't even look, dear," she said as the girl's eyes darted to the men still hurling senseless insults. Elaine sensed they had moved closer. "Your dignity's worth more than them." She talked about the weather, their journey, things to see in London. The men grew louder, laughed about how fat old birds were only worth killing and tearing apart, not even worth ''aving'.

Marley's Rasta glared across at the men for a second before he stood up to put his back to them and leant against the pole next to Elaine. Behind her a greying man in a suit turned shiny by use, stood up, she saw him in the window reflection. He grabbed the overhead rail, also putting his back to the gang too. They formed a human wall shielding the young woman. Elaine kept talking, aware of the mundanity of her words even though she was being filmed, front and back. More importantly she knew another station lay ahead and aggression from behind had calmed to general insults and mutterings again.

She carried on talking, asked the woman if this was her stop, the woman shook her head. The doors opened with the usual announcement and Elaine privately wished those men wouldn't mind the gap well enough. Thankfully, they got off, throwing indecent gestures at her, hurling abuse from behind the safety of the glass. As the doors closed Elaine raised her left hand and indicated a five-knuckle shuffle towards them as the train pulled off.

As they moved away from the idiots, the whole carriage started cheering and the two men at her side clapped, patted her on the shoulder.

"Sweet, Mon, sweet!"

Elaine shook, hot and cold washing through her. Suddenly nauseated. Blurred vision. She sat down and the carriage returned to some semblance of normalcy as they moved towards the next station.

"Are you okay?"

Was she? Yes. It was a surprise, but yes, she was fine. Elaine faced the young woman, whose accent wasn't British. "Pretty sure that I should be asking you that. I'm so sorry you have to put up with that rubbish, it's really not the way most Brits feel."

She was rewarded by a genuine smile that lit the woman's face. Perfect symmetry with a clear dusky skin tone and delicious looking eyes made her possibly the most incredibly beautiful woman Elaine had ever seen. "Thankfully, most of the rest of the world actually knows that."

They were pulling into the station now. "I'm glad you're okay," Elaine said as she stood. "And I hope you don't have to experience anything else like that while you're here." She nodded and smiled at the younger woman as she stepped from the train.

* * *

Mac stalked the house; Elaine was long gone. As was her passport. There hadn't been any money in the house, so he assumed that would be in Elaine's purse. Only that wouldn't have been much in the way of cash, not for going abroad. He assumed she was heading out of the UK or why take her passport?

He stood in the lounge and looked round. The missing picture was obvious. The bucket stood outside with the ruined remains. He'd gone through it, just in case. Last night's cold weather hadn't allowed too much to burn, leaving a horrible oily mess that told him nothing. Other than that Elaine was capable of emotional outbursts.

It bothered him that the car remained on the drive. Would she leave without the car? Public transport was regular if not frequent, a train could be easier than a drive. It was altogether possible that if he'd missed her leaving, she'd taken public transport. A bus, not a taxi, he'd have heard that call.

He saw the computer bag tucked in behind the sofa, empty now she'd thrown the actual laptop against the wall. He glanced at the wall. A little filler, a dab of paint, no one would ever know it happened. If she'd gone with a case, she wasn't planning to come back for a few days. That meant she needed money. That meant she would be using her cards.

He left the house, locking up on the way and jogged across to the car. He'd need his laptop to check the use of her bank account, but he needed his laptop which was out of charge. *Damn it!*

He fetched it back to the house, plugged in. As it booted up, he considered his next move. Without silent running, he could put out an APB and get her stopped, but that wouldn't help solve the case. Though if she had the evidence on her, it would stop it going overseas. Of course, if she was travelling to fetch the evidence, it wouldn't help them at all.

He figured that Elaine must know Lazlo lived in Paris, so if she was going anywhere, it would make sense go there. Would she travel from Cardiff airport? He searched to find out.

CHAPTER FIFTEEN

Madison sat at her desk, double checking diagrams for the weekly report and making sure that she had everything ready in case of developments over the weekend.

She had Alan Bromstad's personal phone number in her pocket. It was a good sign, but a worrying one too. Play this one right and it could only be good for her future career. Only this time, she was actually less concerned for her career than she was for her mom. Whatever Elaine was going through right now, she was going through it alone. She'd call as soon as she finished work.

When her phone rang, she answered without checking caller ID.

"Madison, hi."

"Mom!" The last thing she had expected was a call from her mother now.

"Are you free for dinner?"

For a moment Madison was lost for words. A dinner with Elaine would give her plenty of time to ask all those delicate questions. But it was a little impractical. "Mom, I love you, but I can't just drop everything and drive two hours to Cardiff to come have dinner with you." Though with Bromstad's interest, they probably wouldn't mind if she did.

"I understand," Elaine said. There was an odd note in her voice that Madison didn't recognise. "You remember how you once told me you can look out of your office and see the steps of St Paul's?"

"Yeah?" Madison's voice echoed with uncertainty.

"Still in the same office?"

This was just about the oddest conversation Madison had ever had with Elaine. "I am."

"Well," Elaine sighed. "Look out of your window at the steps of St Paul's."

With no idea what was going on, Madison did just that. Just as well she had the window seat so was still sitting down. Elaine was sitting on the steps of St Pauls! "Oh my gosh!"

Elaine chucked. "Do you know quite how American you sound despite twenty years in the UK?"

"Mom, what are you doing in London?"

"Well, I need to speak to you and want to do it face to face. If you've got plans…"

Plans? Only to call her, but this had to be better. "Well… I…" she thought about it. "No, nothing I can't blow off," said added quickly.

"You sure?"

"It wasn't exactly a night at the opera." Madison's voice tried for a laugh, not sure she pulled it off. "Okay, give me a few minutes. I'll be down as soon as I can."

"I'll wait right here."

Madison looked to her neighbour.

"More stress?" he asked.

"Possibly the relief." She stood and grabbed her coat and bag even as she began typing a text to Bromstad.

* * *

The phone switched off, Elaine slipped it into the pocket of the light jacket she wore and looked around her. People striding around, all too busy to connect with anything but their phones. Perhaps that was unfair, she didn't know them or life in the capital. She didn't really want to, but she must move forward. She'd survived the train journey. She'd survived the much riskier Tube journey. Now she just had to make sure she helped Lazlo. She wasn't going to let her son down again.

How long had she been treading water only to have fallen so far behind? She dropped her head and scrubbed her face with her hands. Lazlo needed her. Jason too, she supposed, but so what? He'd been helping himself to things that were important to her for years. She had the thing from the lagging, which she supposed was the evidence everyone else wanted, though it made little sense to her. Without knowing what the cypher meant, it meant only that she had it, not what to do with it or where to start. Perhaps Madison was smart enough to help her with that. If she managed to explain any of it.

"Mom?"

Elaine looked up; Madison rushed towards her, trying to pull on a three-quarter length mackintosh as she speed-walked. Her sensible low heels still clicking on the pavement. Elaine forced a smile, stood, happily accepted, and returned the greeting hug.

She envied Madison's physicality. The American dream. Tall, shapely, blonde with perfect teeth and excellent poise. And such a nice person; happy, generous, honest, free. Elaine's exact opposite.

"I need to talk to you, but not over the phone."

Madison looked concerned. "Okay, we'll go somewhere, talk over dinner."

Elaine sighed. "Alcohol and privacy would be good right now."

This time Madison's brows rose, her smile dimmed, and she leaned back a little. "Is everything okay?"

"No," Elaine admitted.

"We'll go to mine and order in."

"Okay," Elaine agreed, wheeling her bag, and walking with Madison. "Wait up. When I said dinner, I meant lunch." Though a check of her watch told her it was gone two so a little late for lunch really. "Don't you have to get back to work?"

"The hours I've been doing of late? They can give me a free pass for the remains of the day." Madison took her arm and started her walking again.

"In that case, can we stop to pick up a couple of bottles of wine on the way?"

"No need." Madison offered a small smile. "I keep a cooler stocked."

Twenty minutes later, Elaine looked into a wine cooler with an embarrassment of riches. Her eyes ran over the Pinot, Chardonnay, Cava, Prosecco, Sancerre; spotting a Liebfraumilch in the mix surprised her. "Wow, you weren't kidding, were you?"

"Nope." Madison's laugh echoed in her voice.

Madison took glasses from a nearby cupboard as Elaine selected a Sancerre. They poured generous measures and moved to the seating area of the open plan flat. Though not a fan of open plan, Elaine liked the space, it made her home seem rather enclosed. The floor to ceiling tinted windows looked out over the Thames. This converted warehouse had been gentrified beyond the wildest dreams of the original architect. She guessed Madison's inheritance had come into its own to get this place. Or she was earning a hell of a lot more than Elaine realised.

Madison sipped her wine and looked directly at Elaine. "So, what did you want to say?"

Elaine hadn't realised until that moment just how much she didn't want to have this conversation, but that wouldn't stop her. "Put your glass down."

"Why?"

"Because you have hardwood floors and I'd hate to see you spill that wine all over. Or break a glass." She'd had enough of finding tiny shards of the broken laptop screen.

Madison took a long frowning look at her, a scrutiny Elaine met evenly. Finally, Madison put the glass down.

"Last week, Tuesday afternoon, just before I left the office, I took a call from the British Embassy in the Czech Republic. Jason and Steve Southgate had been reported missing."

Madison sat forward. "Jason's missing?"

Why did it only now occurred to Elaine that the difference existed? Madison called her 'Mom' and Jason, 'Jason'. She should have noticed but hadn't. Numb. She guessed those pictures explained a lot. They had certainly cleared her vision more effectively than the best cataract surgery.

"I'm not finished," Elaine said. "On Friday, I was told Jason was dead. I've even got his death certificate."

Madison slumped back. "Oh my God."

"Still not finished. Yesterday I got a call from Lazlo."

"The Russian kid you took in for a few weeks when I was in uni?"

"Two years and he's Latvian, but yeah. He called me yesterday evening. He claims Jason is still alive." A dry throat brought Elaine to a halt, so she took a sip of the wine. Then another full mouthful that she held onto before she swallowed. "Lazlo sounded distressed. He told me that he and Jason are in trouble, that they are under threat and that if I give the people who are threatening them something that Jason left in our house, then their captors will let them go."

Madison leaned forward. "I don't understand, is Jason dead or alive?"

"Officially he's dead. Hence the death certificate, but what Lazlo said indicates he's alive. So, I really can't be sure one way or the other."

"Have you told the others?"

Elaine understood that Madison meant the other foster children. "No one but you."

"Fair enough. So, what did he leave?"

Elaine's breath shuddered as she pulled it in. "Evidence. But I don't know what of, or in what format." She hated lying to Madison but considered it the best option. If Madison didn't know, she couldn't say. "What's worse is that the agency Jason worked for has already searched our house looking for whatever the evidence is. The house feels…" How to describe it. "Actually, it doesn't feel that different, which now I think of it, is a godawful reaction. The only difference is that it feels like I'm being watched all the time. And oddly, not just in the house. That's why I couldn't call and tell you. In case they're listening."

"Oh my God." Madison reached out for her wine and took a long drink.

"Now I've said it out loud, it sounds really paranoid." Elaine wondered if that was a problem. Or was it a case of it's not paranoia if they really are after you? Paranoia, she decided.

"But you don't know what the evidence is of?"

"The word treachery came up, but otherwise, no."

"What did the people who searched the house find?"

"Nothing they told me about." Except some really damning photos and a hidden reference in a picture, which they might not have known about.

"What did they say when you told them about the phone call?"

"I haven't told them."

"Why not?"

Elaine shrugged. "I have no way to get in touch with them. It's not like they left a number or anything."

Madison stood, wine in one hand, the other around her waist, hugging herself. Her heels clicked on the floor as she paced to the window. Elaine immediately thought that the heels would make a terrible mess of the wood flooring, then she looked closer at the shoes. They looked almost brand new; the wide plastic heel wouldn't mark. And unlike Elaine, Madison would not wait until the shank showed to get a new heel piece put in, the floors were safe. More importantly, she recognised this as Madison's way of thinking. She had to let the younger woman process.

"Do you even know what agency you're dealing with?" Madison asked over her shoulder.

"No. But I'm guessing MI6."

Madison turned from the window and frowned at her mother. "Why them?"

"Because I'm fairly sure MI5 deals with internal or domestic threats and MI6 with international threats. Since Jason and Steve went missing in the Czech Republic and they both work overseas a lot, allegedly as IT consultants, I'm guessing they dealt with international threats and information gathering type stuff, therefore MI6. Of course, I have absolutely bugger all proof, and I'm not familiar with the remit of the government's various agencies so it's more than likely I'm wrong."

"So even if you did find something, you wouldn't be able to contact them?"

Elaine shook her head. "If they bugged the house or my phone, they already know. If necessary, I could probably get Keira to put me in contact. They clearly trust her more than me."

"Why do you say that?"

"Because she's known all along what Jason and Steve really do for a living."

Madison sat back down, crossing her ankles neatly to her right. "So, to sum up, Jason may or may not be dead. Lazlo's definitely in trouble, but at an unknown location. Various people want the evidence Jason allegedly has, but whatever it is, something else we don't know, we know you don't have it. And we're not even sure what agencies are involved."

"Pretty much, yeah."

The silence stretched as Elaine contemplated the scarcity of facts.

"Why did you come to see me?"

A good question, an exceedingly difficult answer. "I wanted to tell you about Jason in person. I wanted to talk to someone who wouldn't talk back like I'm a total idiot."

"I never thought you an idiot."

If she was ever going to challenge anyone, Madison was a good place to start. "Maybe not, but you must think I'm a doormat."

Madison swallowed. Elaine suspected she was weighing truth and consequences.

"I've always thought there must be more to you than timid neat freak."

A million reasons popped into Elaine's head. "I'm not a neat freak."

"Mom, I could barely put a book down without you picking it up and putting it away. You sweep, hover and dust all the time. The bathrooms and kitchen always smell of disinfectant."

"Because if I don't Jason comes in and..."

"And what?"

Elaine looked away, took another long drink of the wine, pushing away the worst of the memories. "He never said anything in front of you or the other kids, but, well, the slightest hint of dirt and he..." she swallowed.

"Mom."

"Usually it was just words, but not always."

Madison looked confused a moment more, then her eyes widened as she realised what wasn't being said. "Oh my God! Why would you put up with that?"

"Because."

"He always told us, he wasn't bothered about such stuff," Madison said. "He said it was you who couldn't stand mess."

"Yeah, well I've discovered Jason was a consummate liar. That's not the full reason I came here though. You know a lot more about communication systems than I do, so I wondered if you could trace the number Lazlo called from? Tell me where the phone was registered, if possible, where the call came from?"

Madison's otherwise smooth brow drew together in the middle. "Because of Jason?"

"Well, twenty-five years is a long time to be with someone."

"You're doing this for love?" The disbelief rang loud.

"Oh, God no. I haven't loved Jason for years. I'm not even sure I ever loved him. I believed him to be a safe, secure choice. He was what I thought I needed. I pretended to be what he seemed to want. The fact is, we both lied. But the truth you're after is that I'm not doing this for Jason. I'm doing it for Lazlo." If she were ever to find her courage, she had to find it now. Elaine considered the incredible woman Madison had grown into and felt a burst of pride. She didn't have much to do with Madison's upbringing, personality tended to be set by the age of seven, Madison had come into her care at eleven. But Elaine was proud of Madison all the same.

"Madison, can I ask you something personal?"

"Sure."

"How old were you when you first had sex with Jason?"

Elaine had never seen Madison at a loss for words before. Her eyes grew wide and her jaw slack. It only lasted a second then she blinked and recovered.

"Whatever made you ask such a thing? I never..."

"Don't lie to me." Elaine blinked back tears of anger, shame, and regret. "I don't blame you; I just need the truth."

Elaine saw Madison searching for a way to explain it all to nothing. That couldn't be allowed to happen.

"I've seen photographs."

Now Madison drew in a breath, held it like a gulp of wine for seconds that stretched out thin. "Fourteen."

The honesty meant a lot to Elaine. It also meant it started some years after Madison first come to live with them.

"That's all I know about what the men found. Photographs," Elaine explained staring into her wine. "On the way out, they passed me pictures, well a pen drive. Jason's pictures. You. Lazlo. Colin. Probably others, but I couldn't stand to look..."

When she glanced up to Madison, she saw their connection undergoing a metamorphosis, less mother and daughter, more equals, possibly friends. She'd like a friend right now.

"Were there others?"

Madison nodded. "Not all of them, but some."

"I'll ask when I'm feeling… more ready to hear it. Promise me, when I do, you'll tell me the truth."

Madison nodded. Relieved, but unable to pick at that scab, Elaine returned her eyes to her drink.

"I know it was child abuse," Madison admitted softly. "But even looking back at it now, I can't see it as so bad. Not for me anyway. Others had it worse, the boys especially, but I… You see, I was fourteen, whatever the law says, I knew what I was doing. I liked what happened. It made me feel… good."

Elaine huffed out a bitter laugh. "I'm glad it wasn't awful for you, but…" she wasn't sure how to ask.

"But what?"

"You do get that what he did was wrong?"

"Yes. Do you get that I enjoyed it? And I'm not sorry it happened."

Elaine sighed. If there was nothing else to be said for Jason, he could almost guarantee an orgasm. "I can believe it. Were you in love with him?"

"Hell no!" The way Madison laughed, the honesty of it was oddly reassuring. "I was never that delusional. It wasn't about love, it was about sex. Utku was with us by then, but I was already fixated on Jason. He was the head of the household, frequently absent, good looking and fit. Man of mystery kind of thing. He had the power in the house, and I think I thought if I could lure him in, I'd have power over him. I didn't, but by God the sex was good."

"Since you mentioned Utku, did you and he…"

Madison shook her head. "Regretfully no. But then again, we were teenagers, so it probably wouldn't have worked between us long term. At least this way, we're still friends. He's as much a brother to me as I could ever get."

Elaine was still trying to readjust her thinking to bring this secure and self-assured woman back into focus. And she had to do that with the truth. "There's something more you need to know," she said. "He's having an affair with Keira too."

"Not surprised." Madison nodded. "It's how he controls people."

Elaine agreed. "That's probably why he stopped being interested in me. He had total control over me, anyway." She turned away struggling to keep back some of the memories she'd hidden under numbness.

"Mom?"

It was too difficult to respond for a second. "I'm sorry. I'm sorry, he used you so young. If I'd known I would have stopped him."

"That's why I didn't tell you. There's probably a million people would say there's something wrong with me psychologically for this, but I enjoyed it. I didn't want it stopped."

With the facts shared, twisted and unpleasant as they were, the past no longer seemed a place of monsters to avoid. Elaine sighed, released the pain and allowed a smile onto her lips. "Well, he always was exceptionally good in the sack. And anywhere else."

"Mom!"

"Had the best cock I've ever seen… or had."

"Oh my god! Mom!"

"What? I was young once. I used to enjoy sex too."

Madison stared at her like this she'd never seen her before. In a way she hadn't.

Suddenly Elaine found herself smiling. Jason was the past, he didn't matter anymore, this lovely young woman did. Madison started smiling back. The odd new relationship started with a small, shared laugh. Madison stood up and moved across to sit next to Elaine, hugging her hard.

It felt so good. The sense of freedom was so new, something she didn't remember feeling before. Perhaps she hadn't felt it before. One didn't appreciate freedom until after it was lost. She moved to take a sip of wine but found the glass empty. Madison fetched the bottle, topped them both up, then sat back down, the bottle at hand.

"I can't believe we can laugh about it."

Elaine shrugged as they rested back against the sofa. "I can. It's easier when you realise that, in this context, all Jason really was, for either of us, was a good fuck."

"Mom!"

They laughed again.

"Well, it's not like Jason was my first."

Madison's eyebrows went higher. "What?"

"You think fourteen was bad?" Elaine said.

"Well, no, not really." Madison countered.

"Oh, okay. I was twelve my first time. Met the guy in a pub."

"What were you doing in a pub at twelve?"

"Getting drunk." A bitter smile twist Elaine's mouth as she took another sip. "Wasn't my first time for that either."

"Seriously? You were a bad girl?"

Elaine grinned and rolled her eyes. "Oh, you have no idea."

And Madison didn't. She couldn't have. Elaine was the only one who knew all of what had happened. Even back then… No, now wasn't the time.

Grown more serious, Elaine looked at Madison. Suddenly she looked so much like the innocent young girl she first met. Even then Madison had looked older than eleven, more sophisticated, but just under the surface was the naïve little innocent Elaine heard crying in bed that first night. Elaine remembered going in, checking on Madison. Madison had thrown her arms around Elaine, sobbing. Eventually, she'd cried herself to sleep. Elaine had gently lain her down and stayed sitting on the bed to watch over her for an hour. When she'd returned to bed Jason asked why she had been so long. She'd never forgot what Jason said. *I'd rather sleep with her too.*

That took the pleasure from her memory. *Oh God. I knew – I just pretended I didn't.*

* * *

By the time he was done, he was halfway through his second coffee. He figured Elaine wouldn't miss it, though he missed milk. Elaine's bank came up, he'd already decrypted all her passwords and security pass codes, so was soon looking at her statement.

£500,000?

He blinked and checked again, just to be sure he'd read that right. He had. But half a million? Where the hell had that come from?

He saw the withdrawal of £10k cash, followed by a draft for £450k. Elaine certainly had enough money to go wherever now. He leaned back in his seat, sipped the lukewarm coffee.

What did it mean though? It made sense to take cash, but to take such a large banker's draft suggested she had somewhere else to put that money. Only searching her computer and the deeper searches he had access to hadn't shown any additional accounts.

His fingers ran through his hair.

So, if the agency had given her money, they must want to see what she would do with it. That had to be the rationale for putting him on silent running to follow her. Great job he was doing of it, too.

Was Elaine part of the problem?

If so, why hadn't they picked up on that before? She'd been vetted before Jason married her. Jason reported her as no risk. Steve and Keira said the same. In fact, from the files he'd read, Elaine seemed the archetypal upright citizen doing no wrong. There was nothing untoward in her work dealings or computer use – that had been checked as a matter of course.

He had been told to tail Elaine, get the evidence, ergo, they must think she had something. What?

He remembered that rip in the lagging. She'd dared him to frisk her. He hadn't because he couldn't think why she'd do that unless there was nothing to hide. Had she double-bluffed him? Had he been so blinded by assumptions that he'd missed something vital? The curse word rent the silence.

Was she selling the evidence? That was a dangerous game to play. It could get her killed.

What was Elaine Blake playing at?

"Not so boring after all."

* * *

He ditched the car on wasteland just outside Newport, well not wasteland exactly, but a road so notorious it virtually guaranteed the car wouldn't stay there long. Once long away, he'd report the vehicle stolen and the rental company just might get something back, likely as an insurance claim or the burnt-out husk.

In the meagre and damp morning light, he stripped the car of anything of value, except for a couple of pounds in change which he left clearly visible to encourage an opportunist.

The walk to the train station was nothing compared to army training, but as he hitched the backpack onto his shoulders, he felt every pound of it.

As he walked, he wondered. Elaine wasn't the simple homemaker he'd met at her anniversary party – an internal job to make sure that the wife remained ignorant of her husband's position. She wasn't the emotional and imaginative artist either. Neither was she the drone the deep background suggested.

He just couldn't get a handle on her. His experience suggested Elaine was the problem. A double agent. Only from what he'd seen she wasn't even a single agent.

Best kind of sleeper.

After a working lifetime of espionage, he couldn't believe in Elaine's guilt. He had no explanation for why, only the gut reaction he had always trusted.

That call from Lazlo worried him. Lazlo was manipulating Elaine, wanting the evidence. Why? He pushed worries aside and concentrated on the missing evidence. Current theory was that Elaine had that evidence. He just had to catch up and get it.

Lazlo lived in Paris, so Elaine would likely go there; equally likely was her stopping to see one of her four foster children in London on the way. He should check all of them.

And hope to God she hadn't already moved on.

This would be so much easier without silent running.

A whole different concern.

* * *

Cathartic as the evening had been, Madison was left with ever growing concerns knotting her stomach.

Unable to sleep, she rose and paced the bedroom. Not that that gave her far to go. Living alone for so long, she automatically opened the door to go pace in the living area. This time she didn't make it over the threshold before she spotted Elaine's recumbent form on the sofa.

"What's wrong, love?"

Her mother's voice made her smile, always putting others first. "Sorry I didn't mean to wake you."

"To wake me, I would have had to have been asleep." Elaine shifted to sit up, keeping the blankets over her legs. She patted the seat beside her, and Madison moved over to sit with her.

"I'm not changing my mind," Elaine said. "I have to do this."

"I know." Madison nodded, leaning head on her mom's shoulder. There was so much she wanted to tell Elaine, like the facts that Jason worked for MI6 and she worked for the CIA, only that wasn't an option. When she'd first joined the organisation, she'd said it was because of her parents. Her father had been an agent, that was why the whole family had been in protective custody when her parents had been murdered, that was how she had ended up in the Blake household. What she hadn't said was that it was also because of Elaine, the mother she knew best, the one that quietly carried on, who showed strength and courage in loving and protecting others. She'd found out some time ago that, whether Elaine was aware of it or not, all the children that they had fostered were from families that were somehow connected to agents, or security risks, or cases that they had been investigating. "Do you know that you've been one of the few, sometimes the only, solid reliable touchstones in the lives of the children you've fostered."

"I've tried. Every child who came to us had issues, they'd all been through some trauma or other. I didn't know what. I didn't ask. I just tried to let you all know that I was there if you needed me. I never worried about their pasts, only their presents, their futures. Those were the things I could affect. I tried to be a better parent to you lot than my parents were to me. Not that that would be hard. But there again, that's why I'm doing what I'm doing."

"I don't think Lazlo's worth it but, I know, that's not my call to make. If there's anything I can do to help. I will. I'm good with computers, I can keep trying to locate Lazlo."

"Thanks, love. I appreciate that."

Madison was glad, she meant it. "I just want you safe."

Elaine sighed. "Madison, safe is all well and good, but physical safety and emotional safety aren't the same thing. Besides, being safe hasn't made me happy."

That was no surprise. Madison had learned a lot about Elaine tonight, and felt she understood the woman much better than before. Their home had been full of secrets, and she did believe Elaine hadn't known about Jason's abusive behaviour towards the children, at least not consciously. She also believed that Jason had done all the things Elaine claimed, including the beatings. She had had some experience of that, but also enough gumption to stop it before it got out of hand. Like most bullies, Jason had quickly backed down when confronted. That was why she wasn't going to even try to stop Elaine.

"I get that, but going to make an exchange, when you don't have the thing to be exchanged…"

Elaine hugged Madison and kissed her hair. "I know it's a risk, trying to do something with nothing, but actually doing nothing, that's not an option. I'll figure something out. Hopefully. Look, if I think I can't safely go on, I'll come home. Okay?"

Though Madison nodded, she wasn't convinced that was necessarily the best option.

"Good. Anyway, for all either of us knows, I might yet turn out to be an adrenalin junky, a thrill seeker. A little danger in my life might just make it worth living. Now, you try to stop worrying and go get some sleep."

Though she hugged and kissed Elaine goodnight, returned to her bed, Madison couldn't stop worrying.

The nagging question was, should she report it to Bromstad?

She wasn't sure she wanted to, but the truth was that she didn't have a choice. A stretch reached the mobile, even so, she held it up, contemplating, debating not making the contact. She had to do it. Her text was simple.

She doesn't have it.

CHAPTER SIXTEEN

"Really? That's it?" Elaine struggled to believe what Madison had just shown her. "It's that easy to get a false mobile number?"

Madison sighed and stretched her back. The two of them worked together at Madison's large desk, Madison showing Elaine the results of all the research she'd managed that morning — the evening having turned into a night of wine and talk, tears and apologies, forgiveness and frankness, plans and, in places, agreements to disagree. All followed by an amazingly good sleep.

"Yep," the younger woman said.

"That's criminal."

Madison laughed. "Actually, it's perfectly legal; it's just used by a lot of criminals." As they looked at each other, Elaine wondered what Madison saw.

"I haven't gone crazy, you know."

"You don't have to do what you're doing."

This was the part they had had to agree to disagree on after a heated discussion through several hours of the night. Elaine wouldn't budge on the point.

"I have to try."

"You don't, but if you must, you don't have to do it alone." Madison tried again.

"Love, I get it, I really do. I get that you're worried about me. *I'm* worried about me. But I'm more worried about Lazlo. I'm terrified I'll fail him, but I'll be failing myself if I don't even try."

"But you don't have what those people want."

"And as long as they don't know that, this will work as well as any other plan we can come up with."

A mobile rang. Automatically Elaine reached for hers, but Madison answered her own and walked away. Elaine moved to the windows. The view looked very different in the morning, the twinkling lights in the cloaking darkness giving way to cold October greys, drab and sad. Even the river reminded Elaine of sludge. Her smile was absent as she realised what Madison was saying.

"No, I told you. She's not."

Elaine's hackles rose. Her phone started ringing. The screen said Lazlo. She snatched it up and answered, keeping her voice down, moving as far from Madison as possible in the open plan area. She had no idea who Madison spoke to, but she figured the two conversations should be kept as far apart as possible.

"Lazlo," she greeted anxiously. "God, are you alright?"

"I'm okay."

He didn't sound it. His voice wobbled and shivered like he held back tears of pain.

"You weren't home when I called. Why aren't you home?"

"I found something. But I had to get out of the house. In case those men came back. I didn't want anyone else getting hold of it, so I figured moving around would be safer."

"Where are you?"

The words froze in her throat. "Doesn't matter," she managed. "I'll be moving on in a minute. Tell me where to meet you and I'll be there."

Bile flavoured her throat as she waited. "Lazlo?"

Silence.

"Lazlo!"

The connection was gone.

"Lazlo!"

"Mom!"

Elaine had her hand over her mouth; her stomach roiled. Doubled over, she fought off tears. Suddenly Madison was with her, holding her tight, holding her upright.

"Oh my God. What have I done? What have I done?"

"I don't know," Madison said. "What have you done?"

Elaine found herself being led back to the lounge area and guided to sit.

"Mom, what's happened?"

Elaine told her. "What if they've hurt him because I didn't say where I was?"

Madison gave her a squeeze.

"What?" Elaine demanded.

"I didn't say anything."

"No." Elaine sat back. "But you're thinking something you think I won't like."

Madison looked away.

"Come on, I thought we reached a new level of honesty last night, don't dump on that now."

Madison faced her again. "I'm sorry, but you really aren't going to like this."

Given how much in life Elaine didn't like, she braced herself for one more thing. "Go on."

"The thing is, if they're that bothered about where you are, you were right not saying anything. This way, you're safer."

"Lazlo might not be."

"No. Maybe not."

Madison looked no happier at that prospect than Elaine.

"But right now, we can't do anything about that," Madison pointed out. "We have to keep you safe because the one thing we do know is that they think you have what they want, and that makes you a target."

Elaine's stomach fell like a stone. Suddenly this was all too real. Excitement was good, but danger was frightening.

"Right, let me check if I can trace where Lazlo was this time."

Inner tremors threatened Elaine's foundations as she watched Madison stand and head for her computer. She dragged air into her lungs for courage, then tried to find her voice.

"Wait a sec." She pushed herself on the couch and stood to face Madison. "You told the person on the phone that I'm not. What am I not?"

Madison stopped and stared at her. It took a very long time for Madison to answer. Then she took a breath.

"Lying. You're not lying."

The worst of that was that Elaine knew she was.

Madison moved back, closer. "Mom. I love you. And I worry. I am particularly worried about what you're going to do, so I spoke to someone I know about how to do the phone thing, double checking actions I was unsure about. He called me back to make sure everything was okay with me. That you weren't coercing me."

"I'm not, am I?"

Madison smiled and hugged her. "No. I just want you to be as well-equipped out there as I can make you."

Elaine considered some of the things in her past. The bovver boots. The fights. The general bad girl stuff that she didn't talk about. Her life could have been so very different. And so much worse.

"Okay. Well, if you can, trace Lazlo's call," she said, looking around for her handbag, "I need to go out and get some air, there's some stuff I have to sort."

She wasn't immune to Madison's look of curiosity, but she needed to go. She was virtually running as she hit the street, but her sensible shoes reminded her that they were shoes, not trainers, and running in them was not a great idea.

* * *

Now Madison was even more worried about Elaine. The conversation with Bromstad hadn't been easy.

All she could do now was find a way to support her mom. As she sat to try and trace Lazlo's call, she found she was dialling that personal number again.

"I'm sorry to call again, but M... Elaine has nipped out, and I thought it best to call now."

"Good timing," Bromstad said. "Feel free to call her mom if that's what you're most comfortable with."

"I am, thank you. Mom's not stupid, but I don't think she has any idea what she's getting into."

"More than likely not."

"I haven't told her anything about my job or the possible things that are above my clearance."

"Which you're guessing at anyway," Bromstad's disembodied voice was oddly warming, like he was proud of her. Which was a ridiculous idea, she was nothing more than a cog in the machine that he could replace at any moment.

"Well, I am good at analysing and projecting. Right now, I'm projecting that she's going to need protection when she's overseas."

"And you know you've been told to leave it."

Madison hung her head and sighed. "Yes, sir."

"And you are sure she's not lying about not finding anything the evidence?"

"Yes, sir. She kept Jason's condition quiet to avoid upsetting me over the phone. She's like that. Considerate. I think it took her a while to come to terms with too. But if she had the whatever it is that I'm not to know about, and she only knows in the roughest terms, she would tell me. I'm sure of it."

The line remained silent as he considered the position.

"I just want to help her, that's all," Madison said.

"I understand that," Bromstad admitted. "However, this is a British situation, involving British agents and a British civilian. The situation is not rated as a US priority. It's a problem for the British intelligence services, it's their business to investigate not ours. You can only help so far."

"Yes, sir. But can't I at least warn her?"

"Warn her of what, Agent Turner? That she's heading into danger? Do you think her a fool that she doesn't realise that?"

"No, sir." Which was one of the worst things. Elaine clearly did know that she was putting her life in danger for a boy that didn't bother with her half as much as he could, or should.

"Your feelings do you credit, Agent Turner, but your obedience will earn you more credit."

The warning was clear. "Yes, sir."

There didn't seem more to say, and she expected him to put the phone down. Not to pause and then say. "Have you considered that you have a contact in Paris, who might, as a personal favour to you, check in on your family? Just in case."

* * *

131

Elaine had done a fair amount of research on the train via her tab and the in-train free wi-fi. The bank she had selected was fifteen minutes away according to the TFL site; the journey took twenty-eight. Elaine pushed down fear, told herself the sense of being watched was only because the bank had to have security. It was normal. Without an appointment, she was expected to wait. When finally, someone deigned to see her, he sneered at her as if she was something he'd scrape off his Italian leather Oxfords. Helpful was apparently the last thing he wanted to be. She had copped an attitude to poor Hayleigh yesterday, and she wasn't taking attitude from this prick today.

"Do you have a supervisor in the building?"

Tarquin Thorn-Hamilton looked down his turned-up nose at her. "He's busy."

She deliberately looked him up and down, her lip slightly curling. "Well, why don't you call and ask him?" There was a telephone on his desk. No numbers, but she saw the names. The man didn't move. "Let me make this clear, *Tarquin*, I might not recognise who any of those names are, but if you don't call you supervisor right now, I will start hitting those buttons and telling anyone who's prepared to listen what a complete and utter arse you've been."

He didn't move.

"Well, if that's not enough for you," she smiled and leaned forward, "I have so much worse I can do to get you fired and destroy your life. And you don't have to believe me, you can call Peter Smart, Divisional Head in HSBC and ask him what I did to Hayleigh Navarro." She didn't say divisional Head of Wales because she doubted that would impress this little toff. "You'll find the number for his office on the internet, or I have it in my phone if you'd rather and if you ask for him, you'll find out that he's in a meeting until ten, which..." She checked her watch; quarter past. "he should be out of by now."

The fact that Elaine had no idea about what Peter was up to that day was not something she would not dwell on or allow to stop her, she did have his number in her phone, but only because she'd looked it up on the internet herself. The cold certainty with which she pronounced each fact added to the whitening of Tarquin's face. Despite the butterflies not so much flying in her stomach, as stomping around in hobnail boots, she leaned back, forced herself to relax, and smiled at Tarquin's diminishing arrogance.

"Now, who you gonna call?"

Tarquin's supervisor was in the office within three minutes. Within ten minutes, Elaine had everything she wanted, and Tarquin looked more relieved than he'd probably like to know he'd let on. Which Elaine reckoned meant he didn't know his supervisor as well as he should. When all the details were handed over, she found herself in something of a strange position. Relieved not to be carrying a banker's draft but scared as all hell that she's forget the passwords she had just set up and would lose access to all that money, or that somehow, something would go wrong, and she'd never see a penny of it again.

Next stop, an outdoors shop followed by the biggest Primark scrum-pit Elaine had ever had the misfortune to step into. It was almost a forgotten experience—to try on jeans. Looking over her shoulder in the mirror, she understood why with instantly hated the muffin top. She forced herself to look again. She still hated the muffin top, but suddenly remembered just what a good bum she had had as a teenager, and that, it seemed, hadn't changed for being that bit of wider. A baggy top over the jeans and she'd look fine.

She had risked being away for long enough, so got the Tube back to Madison's, stopping at what Madison had told her was the best bakery in the city to pick up Madison's favourite treat – a giant salted pretzel dipped in chocolate – and another for herself.

Elaine stepped into Madison's flat and stopped in shock to see Madison ready to zap her with a taser. The determined and deadly look on Madison's face crumpled in recognition and the electric weapon dropped down. "How did you get in without using the buzzer?"

"One of your neighbours was coming in as I arrived," Elaine explained as she moved inside. "And I borrowed your spare keys." She waggled them before her daughter's face before passing them over. "Apparently, your neighbour knows your tastes." She displayed the bakery's logo. "And says he recognised me from the photograph on your sideboard. Neil Dailey. Seemed like a nice guy. And don't roll your eyes at me like that, you might do a lot worse than a guy like him."

"I agree." Madison smiled as she took the bakery bag. "That's why I've been dating him for the last three months."

Elaine gaped after the younger woman as she headed to the kitchen. She put her other bags down and followed.

"And it's going well?"

"Mom." Madison put the pretzels on plates.

The buzzer rang. Madison went to the internal phone as Elaine saw to the now boiling kettle and made tea. She was taking a chunk of a pretzel when Madison reappeared with a couriered package.

"It only says care of me."

"That's what I asked for." Elaine smiled as she took the slim package, she ripped it open, then tipped it. A letter with a card attached fell out.

Madison frowned. "You had a credit card sent here?"

"Actually, it's a prepaid card," Elaine explained as she pulled the plastic oblong off the card, rolling the sticky goo off the back before she placed all the excess in the bin.

"What do you want that for?"

Elaine shrugged. "Sometimes cash isn't accepted. And I'm terribly suspicious."

"You read too many crime novels."

"We all need our escapes. Besides, these are great for travelling, and this one gave a 24-hour turnaround. Which they just delivered on." Thankfully. "And talking of too much criminal knowledge, which of us exactly knew how to create burner phone numbers?"

Madison looked momentarily uncomfortable, then smiled. "You know, I like this new you."

"New me?"

"Yeah, you've got all sassy. Challenging." Madison tipped her head as she studied Elaine. "Not the timid little tidier. New."

Elaine figured this was less a new her, more the old her. Which was a worry. "That's good. I might just be breaking free." She shrugged. "I don't know. I'm just doing what I feel I should."

"A butterfly emerging from the chrysalis," Madison smiled.

That image made Elaine laugh. "Not sure about that." Though arguably she was spreading her wings. "I'm not as beautiful as a butterfly, a moth perhaps." She saw Madison about to object, so forestalled her with a question. "Anyway, what did you find from the phone contact?"

As Madison told her, they moved to the seating area again, this time with tea and pretzels.

"That's the same as before, isn't it?"

"It is."

"And it's not that far from where Lazlo used to live."

"Used to?"

"Yeah, he said something about moving. He moves around a lot."

Madison frowned at her. "What does he do for a living?"

Elaine opened her mouth to answer, then realised that she couldn't. She was so grateful that Lazlo kept in touch at all that she'd accepted whatever scraps of information he gave, which wasn't much. "I'm not sure. I'm not even sure what industry he's in. He's always worked, but I've never really pinned down what at." In fact, he'd always side-stepped the topic. Nothing too obvious, but now she looked back, she noticed his answers had been generalised, enjoying his work, liking his colleagues, appreciating the opportunity to travel, but nothing specific. He'd always carefully steered the conversation to other topics, and she'd never noticed. "I really have been sleepwalking through life. Time to wake up."

CHAPTER SEVENTEEN

Wide awake didn't cover it. Adrenalin coursed through Elaine's body, she kept swallowing more than she should, blinking less than she needed. Her eyes and throat were dry, she wasn't sure if she wanted to throw up, or down a ton of Tequila. She glanced across at the bar as the ferry rocked. She could have a drink, but decided against it. Things were risky enough without alcoholic befuddlement.

Nerves stretched like drum skins by passing through customs, had yet to relax. She'd been terrified she'd be stopped at the border. Guilt flooded her, even though she had done nothing. It wasn't like she had used a false passport, an idea Madison suggested, to help keep her route hidden. Madison said she even knew where to get one, but it would take more time than Elaine was prepared to lose. Deception wasn't something she was good at.

You fooled Tarquin Double-Barrelled-Up-Himself.

She had.

You've fooled everyone for twenty-five years about "that thing."

Also true, but neither point was about to get her arrested – travelling under false documentation could. At this point, she didn't really need to hide herself, and once she got Lazlo free, this was over. She would go home, go back to being boring again. Sleepwalk through the remains of her days.

No. She'd go home, but not right away, and not to that job. It was time to start living.

A young girl came to the bar. Elaine watched her in the mirror as she ordered, figured she was probably in her early twenties, her hair wasn't natural – no one grew bright pink hair – but it was beautifully done. There was a ring in her nose, one through her lip and two through her right eyebrow. Her skin was so universally pale that it had to be good makeup.

Suddenly, Elaine was assailed by seasickness. Black hair, pale skin, black lips, ripped clothing. Seventeen and watching death come crawling…

"What?"

Apparently, Elaine had stared too long. This time she focused on the girl, blinking from the reflection to the reality. Beneath all that war paint and obvious distrust, Elaine saw a pretty young thing, and understood all too well.

"Don't surrender."

The girl's lip curled. "What are you drinking?"

Elaine smiled and looked at the glass. "Only cola." She turned back to the girl and smiled a sad smile. "What I meant is don't let anyone tell you you have to conform. It's a hard life. Don't make it harder. If you bow to convention, it might seem to make your life easier, but you'll never be happy." This time she peered into the glass again. "And suddenly I wish this was something more interesting than cola." She sighed and drank it all the same.

"That what happened to you?"

The sneer told Elaine that the girl didn't really understand at all. She wouldn't, not for another twenty or more years.

"Yep. So let me be a warning to you. Conformity will turn you into yet another middle-aged drone silently screaming in desperation with nowhere to turn."

The girl looked at her, the thick eye liner marks drew together, all but blacking out her eyes. "What are you doing here? Running away?"

Suddenly, Elaine's smile grew wider. Perhaps the girl understood after all. "Pretty much."

"Never give up, huh?"

This time Elaine did laugh. "Never give up. Never surrender."

The girl frowned at her.

"It's a line from a film. Good film, actually. Galaxy Quest. Ironically funny." Elaine said. "Unlike my life, which has moments of irony and not so many laughs."

"You should get a better husband."

She glanced at her left hand; she was still wearing her wedding ring. "I suppose that's possible now. My husband died a short while ago." A small evasion, but saying Jason died just a few days ago opened up too many new questions.

"I'm sorry."

What else was there to say?

"I'm not." Elaine saw the surprise on the younger face. "Yes, that's harsh, and part of me hates me for it, but it's true."

"Yeah, well…" With a shrug, the girl walked away with her drink.

Elaine stared at her ring. A simple slim gold band that had shackled her for years. The symbolism hung heavy. It would be the simplest thing in the world to pull the ring off, throw it over the side of the ship. A smile tugged at the corners of her mouth. That would be fabulous. Her moment. Only she didn't know what the future would bring, and after more than twenty years of never taking the ring off, losing her it would feel worse than losing Jason. Not that that would be difficult.

The image of a tired, middle-aged woman caught her attention, and she stared at the reflection. When had that happened? When had she got old? *That's what life in a penal colony does to you.* No, she had to stop thinking of herself as a victim.

Who was she? Who might she be?

Whoever you want to be.

That surprised her, but simple truths often did. She only had to cast off the bindings, take off the mask, hatch from the chrysalis. She had to decide what kind of butterfly she was going to be.

A dragon.

She sneered at herself, looked away from her reflection in time to catch the eye of a man the other side of the room. For a second, they seemed linked. He seemed familiar, but she couldn't say why. The engines of the ferry changed note and she glanced away, when she looked back the man was gone. Another nobody in the crowd.

She yanked up the handle on the holdall at her side and headed out to the deck. Some fresh air would do her good.

* * *

Damn it!

The luck he had enjoyed earlier in the day slipped away.

Once seen, he ducked out of the bar easy enough, being average was a virtual cloak of invisibility. Only he hadn't been invisible, he'd been seen and by — of all people — Elaine!

It was such a rookie mistake to let a mark spot you.

Am I losing my touch? Maybe getting too old for the game?

Or was she just that good?

She'd spotted the wig when he'd been to her house, even the guy who'd he'd been with hadn't seen that, only checking after Elaine mentioned it. She'd been so damn normal, he'd almost forgot that she was, potentially at least, the traitor they hunted.

No, that doesn't fit either.

He just couldn't get a fix on her. Couldn't see the real Elaine Blake.

Luckily, he did spot her as she left the bar and walked the decks. He maintained a discrete distance. Eyes on at all times.

He'd found her easily enough in London. The more he'd thought about things on the train the more he'd become convinced that Elaine would go to Madison. Good fortune had it that he'd spotted Elaine coming out of a patisserie near Madison's flat.

Changes in her were obvious. Not only the clothes, which looked brand new, they certainly hadn't been in her wardrobe when he'd searched, not even the massive amount of shopping she had carried. She wore a smile. A genuine smile, a million-watt smile. And the people she smiled at, smiled in return. He'd scanned the bags. Clothes and sports shops. Nothing high end, so not exactly splurging. He'd kept an eye on the flat for a couple of hours, then followed her to Charring Cross and the train to Dover Priory. From there to the Calais ferry, border control had been longer than it used to be, but they both got through easily enough.

He'd nearly lost her on board. By the time he'd been checked through she had disappeared. He'd been surprised to find her in the bar. Now, she headed for the duty free, he stayed outside.

She browsed. Looked long and hard at the wine selection but came out empty handed. That surprised him. He'd seen her recycling; it showed her preference for white wine. She wandered on deck, moving as far forward as permitted. The decks were sparsely populated – something to do with the lashing rain and freezing air no doubt.

The boat slammed up one wave and down the next.

The sound of splattering puke drew his attention behind him, that poor lad was having a bad day, and his girlfriend had just learnt not to stand down wind of the ill. A turn back showed Elaine stumble over the shifting deck, but she kept her footing and moved to the leeward side of the vessel. In the minimal shelter of the bulkhead, he zipped his jacket to the chin and watched Elaine pull up the hood on her new Gortex. She even used the toggles to tighten it. She leant on the rail and looked out to sea at the white cliffs on the way into Calais.

For someone who claimed not to be a good traveller, she was doing pretty damn well from what he could see.

When they docked and the worst of the rolling seas calmed in the shelter of the port, only then did Elaine return inside. Like the rest of the flock, they had to head out, and this time, he found himself ahead of her. The option to linger and drop back was out, she'd almost definitely notice him, so he set foot in France ahead of her.

Once there, signposts led to the train to Paris. Only Elaine looked unsure now. The information board in English was crowded around with big-bellied men smelling of beer and prejudice. The way they sneered at the locals and comments made to passing women fulfilled the worst stereotypes of Brits on a beer run. Elaine wisely detoured around them, but he observed with surprise that she moved to the boards in German to check times and platforms.

Background checks said she did GCSE German, got an A* even, but that had been a long time ago, he doubted she remained proficient in a language she never used. Still, she found the information she needed, purchased a ticket, then turned around looking for where to go. He brought his own ticket, he headed directly to the right platform. There he pulled a thin rain shell from his bag and put it on over his jacket. With some relief he saw Elaine arrive a few moments before departure.

CHAPTER EIGHTEEN

The train ride to Paris did nothing to calm Elaine's nerves. Thoughts swirled in her head on an endless loop questioning if she was doing the right thing. Paranoia fought to win and her confidence as taking a battering.

On looking out the train window, made mirror-like by the hour and the gathering cloud, she saw the reflection of another passenger further back in the carriage. For one dreadful moment, he looked like the man from the ferry bar. Then she blinked and realised that guy had been wearing a green jacket, this one had on a yellow raincoat of some type—it was difficult to see clearly with him being sat down.

She calmed her racing heart and told herself not to be a fool. No one was following her. And even if that was the same guy, which it wasn't, being on the same ferry and train meant nothing. This was a well-used route to Paris, there were probably any number of people on this train who had been on that ferry. They wouldn't all be following her.

Not all, but one could.

She told the paranoia to shut up.

Probably.

No, definitely not. She'd been panicking since before she'd left the house, the newness of action and activity, of stepping outside her comfort zone. The unusual practice was as unnerving as Lazlo's calls. Was this normal? Did people usually feel this stressed out because they travelled? Jason always said she was a bad traveller, he told her...

She pulled herself up short.

Jason had told her she was a bad traveller. He had nagged her so much, she'd become a bad traveller. But she'd got herself this far on her own, no mishaps. Admittedly, she hadn't reached Paris yet, but what could go wrong now? Not knowing that answer didn't help, but if something unexpected happened, well, she'd deal.

Like she dealt with everything all her life. The desire to scream and shout and punch out was great, but she kept it contained. She hadn't been able to do that when she was younger, and it, plus the dreadful fight that had ensued, had nearly derailed her life.

By the time they pulled into Gare du Nord, cramp and tension had knotted her body. Now, with the late hour and encroaching fatigue, she needed to find a hotel. She suspected hotels nearest the station would be expensive, being so convenient, she headed south into the city, crossed a couple of large roads and following Madison's advice, she turned lots of corners, but tried to avoid dark alleys. Eventually, she realised, she was simply lost, couldn't tell east from west, north from south.

The bag proved too heavy, so she took it from her shoulder and wheeled it. The noise grated on her nerves, the thing twisted her wrist as it bounced off pavements, but she lacked the energy to carry it further. It did, however, allow her to test her theory about being followed, it made so much noise that she stopped suddenly, turned around, and spotted no one jumping to hide, no one lingering in the long street. At least no one that didn't look entirely like they belonged there. And no one in a yellow raincoat.

Paranoia be quiet.

The cobbled back street reverberated with every step. Dragging the pack set up such a vibration in her arm, she feared it might fall out of the socket. So, she stopped and looked around. Hôtel.

That'll do.

The room, when she finally got to it, was bijou to say the least, and out-dated, the 1970s resonated unpleasantly, but it was clean. The en suite comprised a toilet and hand basin, the bathroom itself was on another floor. The guy on reception had been such an arse about her staying only one night, but he'd been happy to take her cash. Buying one thousand Euros in London was the last transaction she would make on her old cards.

Tomorrow, she would find somewhere else to stay, but tonight, this would do.

The door locked, she used the limited facilities to lighten the load and freshen up. She slumped to sit on the bed and checked her phone. 45% power. That would do. She huffed out her lack of… whatever it was she lacked. Oomph, she supposed.

She really wanted to let Madison know all was well, but they had agreed calls and texts were to be kept to an absolute minimum. If anyone was looking for Elaine, then her phone was likely to be the first thing they checked, so best to keep off that as much as possible. Besides, she wanted the phone free in case Lazlo called. She checked her phone again, still 45% power, but saw she had only one bar of signal. That wouldn't do. She took her smallest bag filled it with essentials and headed out to find better phone reception.

And food, please.

Her stomach gave the timely reminder.

The narrow streets stood ominously over her as Elaine looked again at her phone – stronger signal already. The cobbles quickly gave way to wider pavements as she headed south, and it didn't take long before she saw the dark ribbon, almost black but sparkling as it reflected the evening lights. The River Seine.

She took her life in her hands, to run across the road where no driver seemed inclined to slow despite the pedestrian crossing. On the river side, she looked across at the Eiffel Tower. Her breath caught. A place she'd always wanted to visit, she'd read that the views over the city were incredible from up there. Like a moth drawn to the flame of the tower's lights, she found a footbridge to move her closer to the iconic site. For a moment Elaine stopped in the centre, the river sparkled and danced below. The city pulsed with life, its heartbeat pounding in passing cars, people talking, the river running.

For one moment she only cared that she was somewhere new, somewhere different. The past disappeared; the future was put on hold. She enjoyed the now. A smile pulled across her face, and as it widened, she looked around, the world carrying on. She caught sight of a man on the bank; as their eyes clashed, he looked away, turned his face. She'd embarrassed him just by looking, and why she found that so funny was anyone's guess, but the chuckle bubbled from her. The laughter died as her ringtone ramped up.

"Hello?" Even she heard the sudden anxiety in her answer.

"Mum?"

"Lazlo, thank God. Are you alright?"

"I'm fine. Where are you?"

"Paris."

"What? Why?"

The question surprised here. "The last address you gave me is here. I've been trying to find it. Find you." It was also the area that Madison had told her his call had come from, but she wasn't saying that. She wasn't sure why, it wasn't that she didn't trust Lazlo, more that she realised that his captors would be listening and the less they knew, the better.

"I'm not in Paris."

Elaine frowned. "Okay. Where are you?"

"You have what I'm looking for, haven't you?"

She stared into the dark river the twisting Styx ready to drag her to Hades. "Yes. I brought it here to make that easier. Where are you?"

Her stomach flip-flopped to her feet when the phone went dead.

* * *

Expertise or complete incompetence? He wondered if his struggle to follow Elaine Blake were because she took random paths deliberately well or if she simply got lost? He was damn sure he wasn't losing his touch.

He really couldn't figure her out. And why wasn't she sleeping? Their journey had exhausted him, why not her? She showed no sign of fatigue as she answered her phone. Then she looked terrified.

A brief conversation. Though unable to hear her from where he stood, it looked much like she called the name Lazlo a few times before she acknowledged that the call was over, then and slipped it into her bag. She ran a hand back through her hair, turned this way and that. A woman on the edge. Finally, she stepped back to the bridge wall, both hands on it, she leaned towards the water and for one awful moment, he thought she might jump.

Then she took a deep breath and fished her phone back out of her bag and tapped the screen several times. She looked about her, moved the phone in different directions. Eyes moving frequently back to the phone, she first walked south to finish crossing the bridge, then turned sharply and came north, back the way she had come, towards him. He moved out of the way as she marched, with surprisingly long strides, right past him without seeing him. At least he got a glimpse of the phone. She was following an online map.

As he followed her, she took a couple of wrong turns and had to double back, but as he processed the route, he had a sinking premonition of where she was heading.

This being central Paris, the lights stayed on, places stayed open, and people wandered the streets. Not many, but enough. Elaine looked up at the very building he'd hoped she wouldn't go to. The yellowish stone was deeply carved with horizontal lines for the ground and first floors, though above it looked smooth but for the prominent carving around the windows that supported Juliette balconies. Those French windows opened inwards, they had to the balconies were a mere 6 inches deep. The traditional double doors to the street were dark wood, and beautifully aged. Elaine stepped up to the door, to the keypad for apartment bells and the names there.

She wouldn't find what she looked for. The name Zakis wouldn't appear, for all this had been Lazlo's address.

She checked her watch, automatically, he checked his. 12:35.

Good God, gone midnight. Would this woman never sleep?

No, she shrugged deeper into her coat and turned away.

Octobers were warmer now than he remembered them in his youth, but at this time of night, it was cold. His hands were frozen and stuffed into his pockets as he moved back to lounge by the wall of a wine bar. A couple of glasses had been left by the wall, he picked one up to look more like he belonged. Couldn't Elaine just give him a break and go back to the hotel? He needed sleep, how did she not?

It looked like she might, only she stopped suddenly. She stared directly ahead, right past where he lurked in the shadows. He looked too, saw the figure walking down towards the buildings. *Oh hell, no.*

CHAPTER NINETEEN

Exhausted physically and emotionally, Elaine headed back to the hotel. She turned from the building and spotted the man walking purposely towards her. With black hair and dusky skin, shadow either side of a prominent nose hid his eyes.

Talek.

No, it couldn't be. Could it?

She stopped in her tracks and stepped out of the way of others on the path, using her phone this time to show her the route back to her hotel. As she watched, the Arab-looking man rushed past on the other side of the street, crossing behind her as she turned to watch. He walked directly to the building she had visited, used a key to get in, slammed the door closed behind him.

Her heart hammered in her throat. That was Talek. And if she hadn't seen that anniversary picture, she would never have remembered him. She drew her bottom lip between her teeth, vacillating between storming over and banging on every door until she found the man, and running away as fast as possible.

As she stood in the dark, her stomach suddenly growled loudly, and she realised she hadn't eaten since Madison had forced her to have a light lunch. Uncertain of what to do next for the best, she noted there was a bar just down the road where people were still milling about outside, and drinks were still being served. Even a pack of peanuts at this point would be welcome.

Crossing to the bar, she looked back at the building Lazlo had lived in. Might still live in. A light had come on at the third-floor level. She couldn't be sure that it identified the right flat, but she was sure that light hadn't been on before.

She popped inside the bar. No customer waited, so she ordered straight away. "Un glas de vin blanc, grande. Danke. Erm," she shook her head trying to remember the right words. "Merci."

"'S'all right love, don't try so hard, I'm English too," the young man behind the bar said with a smile. "One large glass of white wine, which by the way is *un verre de vin blanc*. Pinot or Chardonnay?"

"Which one is better here?"

"This is France, they think all their wines are fabulous."

"But you're English and might be more discriminating."

He smiled at the compliment. "Chardonnay then."

"Great. Any chance of a bar snack?"

A large glass of wine and an apologised-for curling sandwich in hand, Elaine returned outside. There were no tables, but a few milling patrons. She moved to one side, propped herself against the windowsill, using it to hold her glass as she wolfed down the sandwich. She had no idea what the cheese was, it tasted horrible. She took small bites and swallowed without chewing; at least it quieted the belly rumbles.

As she ate, she watched the light on the third floor. Someone moved about inside. The crusts of the sandwiches were too dry to even swallow, so she left them and drank the wonderfully cold wine. After about ten minutes, the light went out. Elaine found herself unable to breathe or move.

The glass hovered halfway to her mouth. That light going out meant one of two things. Either Talek had gone to bed, or he was heading out.

Or it's not his flat and you're imagining it all.

"You done?"

Surprised, she flinched, slopping wine on her hand. The bartender stood at her elbow.

"Almost."

The guy smiled, took the paper plate.

"Have you been around here long?" she asked before he moved off.

He shrugged. "About five years."

Long enough. "Don't suppose you remember a guy call Lazlo Zakis?"

The barman's face tightened; he knew Lazlo alright. "Not a British name, how would you know someone with a name like that?"

"I was his foster mother."

That obviously surprised the bartender. "Sorry, you don't look old enough."

Elaine grinned at that; she knew full well she did look old enough. "Yeah right, Smoothy. You know him, then?"

"Yeah, he used to have a flat up the way. What's your interest?"

"Like I said, I was his foster mother. I lost my husband recently and I'm trying to let the kids know personally, but he's not answering his phone and I couldn't get an answer at his address. I'm worried about him."

"Sorry." The guy failed meet her eye. "For your loss that is." People always became awkward when deaths were mentioned. "But I haven't seen Lazlo in a couple of months."

She kept her eyes on his as she finished the glass.

"I think someone else is in his apartment now. Some Arab bloke." The man looked up the road, frowning. "Actually, come to think of it, I think the Arab might have been there first, then sublet to Zakis."

The wine now finished, and no one having emerged from the flats, Elaine offered the empty glass to the barman. Then looked sadly back to the flats. "Wonder if the Arab'd be able to tell me where Lazlo went."

"You could ask him; he comes in occasionally. You'd probably be best just watching the street. Occasionally he comes in for a drink, afternoons mostly, around two-ish. Though I can't guarantee how often." The young guy smiled. "Fat lot of help I am, I guess."

"You've been more help than you realise." Elaine smiled. "Thanks."

* * *

The only reason he could come up with for Elaine not even noticing him when he stood so close was her concentration on other things. Probably not the curling sandwich, which she sneered at, but ate just the same. He'd known what it was to be so hungry he'd eat anything. Like now. Even the dried crusts she left would be good at this point.

She chatted easily with the bartender, it appeared to be a motherly thing. She was comfortable in herself and nonthreatening, didn't push too hard. And she got more information than she should have done that easily.

Again, she used the mapping app on her phone to guide her back to the hotel. The act an open invitation to the opportunistic thief, but none took a shot. On reaching the hotel, he hung back, let Elaine get in, then after a few minutes, he went in himself.

CHAPTER TWENTY

The hotel offered breakfast, but Elaine took one look at the cold buffet and returned to her room, gathering everything before checking out. She quickly found another hotel, better and cleaner, willing to keep her suitcase aside for when she could check in officially later that day. Unburdened, Elaine wandered into the street and wondered what she to do with the day. First things first, she found somewhere for breakfast: La Bauhinia was open, she walked in.

She ordered the eye-wateringly expensive continental breakfast, but such were the joys of sitting in the Shangri-la Hotel. She wouldn't contemplate what a night here would cost. On the plus side, the hot chocolate was the richest and best she had ever had, and the croissants melted in the mouth, fresh and spectacular.

As she sat and sipped, Elaine looked around. She felt a little out of place in jeans and a sweatshirt, dressed for spending the day in the open while most of the other women looked like they might be spending the day shopping, with personal shoppers and lots of sitting down judging by the height of their heels. Still, the staff were unfailingly polite and attentive, treating her no differently from the others.

"What to do for five hours?"

"You could—"

Elaine jumped at the sound of the voice, stopping the young waiter in his tracks as he collected her empty dishes.

"Sorry." A small laugh covered her embarrassment. "I hadn't realised I'd spoken out loud."

"Oh. My apologies." The waiter spoke with heavily accented, but perfect English.

"No, go on, what would you suggest?"

"It is just that the hotel sells priority tickets for the Eiffel Tower. It would save you waiting in line. And no one should ever visit Paris without visiting the tower."

That sounded like a particularly good suggestion. She thanked the waiter. Elaine left enough cash on the table for the meal and a generous tip, then headed for the reception desk and secured a ticket before leisurely walking towards the tower.

She reached the famous tourist attraction just after ten and, even though the day was bitingly cold, the queues were forming to snake about the plaza. She located the priority line and headed into the west pillar. Though her priority ticket only allowed her to jump the first queue. When it came to the lift, she stood in the same line as the rest. As they waited for the lift to return and take them up, Elaine listened to the surrounding voices. The conversation that drew her ear was a German couple. Apparently, this was their first day in Paris, a treat for their twentieth wedding anniversary, if Elaine translated their conversation correctly. German was the only language she had any level of fluency in, other than English, she couldn't even speak Welsh. Mr Frisse was being extremely romantic, demonstrating over and again how much he loved his wife. Elaine smiled to herself and kept the envy under control.

As they moved into the elevator, Elaine found herself separated from the Germans and next to a young English couple. He was clearly a good few years older than the girl, who looked around eighteen, and not overly happy. Elaine soon saw why, when the guy started going on about structural integrity of the wrought iron girders and how time and rust would decay the safety. When the girl asked him to stop, he pointed out rather snottily that as a structural engineer he knew about such things.

Elaine stood back, thinking the engineer really didn't know as much about things he'd believed. Like, when on a city break with your girlfriend – she caught a glimpse of a small ring as the girl tucked some hair behind her ear – scratch that – when on a city break with your fiancée in the middle of the most romantic city in the world, engineering talk pointing out the inherent and increasing likelihood of structural failure leading to almost certain death, really wasn't the conversation to be having. She watched in increasing horror as the girl sighed and smiled and encouraged him, nonetheless. As they stopped on the second level, the crowd started to move, the tall guy shifting before the younger woman, and Elaine last of all. So, she did something she couldn't hardly credit she had the nerve to do. She reached out and pulled the young girl back.

"Don't do it," she whispered quickly. "He's not good enough for you."

The girl stepped away, her attention called by the man. Elaine moved off in the other direction, looking for the lift to the top viewing tower. This lift seemed to move with the wind and Elaine's stomach knotted, she felt rather grateful not to hear an engineer talking of imminent doom.

At the top, that unsteadiness continued or worsened. Just as on the ferry, she found her sea legs. The swaying of the tower was, she knew, an inevitability of such a high structure, but it was not as pronounced as her queasiness tried to insist.

She moved to the observation deck and filled her lungs with sharp, cold air.

You shouldn't be here. Go home and get real. You're not capable. Jason's voice echoed in her head.

I am not a bad traveller. She gripped on to the caging that kept people from falling — or jumping — from the platform.

I am not a bad traveller. I am a little scared right now, but that's because I am high up and not good with heights, because this is the first time that I have ever been abroad on my own, being scared right now is acceptable.

She sucked a deep breath in, then coughed as the cold air tried to freeze dry her lungs.

Anyway, it's not fear-fear. It's anticipation. It's excitement. Which is probably inappropriate given that I'm here in some half-baked attempt to help a kid I haven't seen in five years, but it is what it is. For the first time in forever I am actually doing something.

She noticed that her index and middle fingers were outstretched on the wire mesh, the other two curled under. Almost like the V for Victory sign Churchill gave. She took it as a sign of her own triumph over adversity – and two fingers up to Jason's controlling.

Like Churchill, I take action this day.

With that silly thought, she laughed, pushed herself away from the rail, walking before she looked and slamming straight into another woman. She was already apologising as they found their balance again. Both had dropped bags and as she straightened, she looked up and realised that the woman was the German lady she had listened to downstairs.

"Entschuldigen sie bitte." She picked up the other woman's handbag and the keys that then slipped from the pocket as the bag rose and passed it to the other woman. "Ich habe nicht darauf geachtet, wo ich hingelaufen bin. Absolut mein Fehler. Es tut mir wirklich leid. Ist alles in Ordnung? Ich habe Sie nicht verletzt, oder?" The apology tumbled with surprising ease from her lips.

The woman smiled taking back the bag. "Nein, mir ist nichts geschehen. Unfälle passieren. Schauen Sie demnächst einfach besser hin, ok?"

She wasn't hurt and the gentle rebuff to look before walking was given good naturedly.

"Werde ich machen. Vielen Dank und noch mal Entschuldigung," Elaine thanked her and apologised again, as the other woman moved away.

Elaine bent and scooped up her own bag suffering the pangs of being a total idiot, then had to bob again to pick up her passport, which she popped straight into her pocket as she plonked the bag back on her shoulder. She really had to stop putting such valuable items in open pockets. Now she turned the corner of the deck and looked out again. The incredible vista of city and the huge Champ de Mars stretched out before her now. The tree-lined paths, the broad grassy -

Wait, I don't put valuable items like passports in open pockets.

Her hand reached to her pocket. Yep, the passport was definitely there. She dragged her bag around, propping it on the rail. She unzipped the long central zip and then the zip for the internal security pocket. There nestled her own passport, the one she'd renewed for no good reason a few years ago. Paranoia showed in the way she looked around, checking no one around paid her any attention, she took the passport from her pocket and looked at it.

German issue.

Oh, Dear Lord, she'd accidentally picked up the other woman's passport.

The identification was jammed back into her pocket, she zipped her bag up as she moved, quickly walking around the observation deck searching for the German couple. She couldn't see them. She looked around inside, even looking in the Champagne Bar, which seemed a suitably romantic place for a celebrating couple to visit. Nothing.

Even as she considered about finding a lost property office or passing the passport into the Police Nationale, she realised that a second passport might yet come in handy. Since Brexit, the English weren't exactly flavour of the month on the continent.

She should do the right thing and hand it in.

She would.

After she'd explored the tower a little while longer. After all, she might see the couple again while she did.

If I look for them.

She hated herself for that thought, but it was the best she could do. Since the second elevator was here, Elaine took the trip to the top.

The glass walls of the lift left her feeling slightly sick. A sensation that wasn't helped she was stepped out and realised that some of the rocking was in fact, the floor under her feet. The Tower was rocking in the wind.

Her hand went to her stomach, this was worse than the ferry. At least on the ferry everything was moving, her brain and her guts could cope with that. Stopping by the rail she held on, closed her eyes and took a deep breath.

"Y'all okay there, ma'am?"

The voice was American, a Texan drawl rounded off by years in Europe she'd guess. Then she opened her eyes, the guy even looked American, though thankfully he wasn't wearing a ten-gallon Stetson. Like being over six foot tall needed those extra few inches.

"Wow, they really do grow 'em bigger in Texas." The words were out of her mouth before she even thought about. Still words were the better thing than that which had threatened ejection a few moments before. And it made him smile, a big all-American overly white-toothed smile.

"Hard to cover my origins sometimes, ma'am, but really are you okay? You're looking at little off colour there."

She offered him a smile. "Wasn't expecting to need my sea legs on dry land, so I'm taking a moment to adjust."

"Well, you adjust away, I'll wait right here to make sure y'all's okay."

"There's no need," she said gently.

"Always a need when a li'l lady's a li'l under the weather."

This time she rolled her eyes, wondering if he could get any more stereotypical. Or if he'd even heard of the #MeToo movement. Still, at this point he didn't seem dangerous, he was keeping a respectful distance, hadn't attempted to touch her. There were still some decent men in the world, she'd give him a little leeway for now. "I'm fine."

"Yes, you really are."

No, she really wasn't, and she gave a look that told him she recognised flannel when she heard it.

"Okay, okay, that was probably a touch too much."

"Definitely, but how too much would depend on what you're attempting to do," Elaine pointed out. "If you're altruistically looking after a stranger, yes it was too much. If you're trying to pull, it was way too much and doomed to failure from the start, anyway."

He looked to her, she raised her left hand.

"Ah, you're married. Is the lucky fella around?"

"The lucky fella died. Recently," Elaine said. "That's why I'm here. Visiting one of the places we never got to." It was only a twist of the truth, not a total lie, she told herself.

"Sorry for your loss. But that doesn't mean you can make a new man-friend, does it?"

"It doesn't, as long as you understand that friend is as good as it can get. In honesty, this is likely to be more a case of passing acquaintances."

"Fair play, ma'am. Always good to know the rules of the game." He offered a hand to shake. "Chuck Linklater the Third."

"Chuck?"

He shrugged. "Charles officially, but all my friends call me Chuck."

She smiled. "In that case, Chuck, I'm pleased to meet you, but I don't shake hands. It's not you, it's a me thing."

Again, he shrugged and relaxed against the rail. "So, are you going to tell me your name?"

"Oh, sorry. Yes. It's Elaine."

"Just Elaine? No surname? Like Cher?"

"More like I haven't decided if I still want to be known by my married name or if I'll revert to my maiden name. I realise, of course, that widows usually keep the marital name, but times are different now." She shrugged.

"Well, Elaine the undecided…"

That made her chuckle.

"One thing that hasn't changed, in a very long time, is how lovely Paris is. Let me show you the views now you're up here."

She probably shouldn't, but for now, not feeling stressed to the point to quaking and wanting to scream was a welcome change.

"Good company is always welcome, lead on."

* * *

Un-bloody-believable.

Despite being up before six, checking out and hanging around outside the guest entrance of the hotel, he'd managed to miss Elaine's departure. Bored by eight. Wandering by nine. At ten he returned to the hotel to get management to check. Only the girl at reception didn't have to check, she had seen the English woman leave as she arrived at a quarter to six.

He'd missed Elaine by minutes! And wasted hours waiting.

He'd spent years honing his skills and an amateur, allegedly 'doesn't-travel-well, Elaine Blake', constantly slipped through his fingers like a pro. It was infuriating.

What if she's slipping away like a pro because she is a pro?

No. He couldn't believe it. Every year of her life had been spent in the UK; all movements accounted for. No opportunity to be recruited from outside. The usual place for that was university, but she'd meet Jason there. No way she had been playing both sides that long.

One point remained that he could pride himself on. As often as she slipped away, he caught up to her. As he walked away from the hotel, the question was how to do that this time.

CHAPTER TWENTY-ONE

The drizzle started as Elaine travelled back down on the Eastern pillar of the tower. She had looked for the German couple, but not with any vigour. Chuck had proved a welcome distraction. Similarly, she scanned the area for a lost and found but didn't see one. Chuck had wanted to escort her around more of the city, but she'd demurred, in the end quite strongly. The guilt of actually being with someone who was pleasant and courteous became too sharp. She wasn't here to play or enjoy, she had a mission. Of sorts.

She pulled up the hood of her coat, lengthening the handle of her bag to cross it over her torso more securely. She headed back to the new hotel and checked in. After a shower and a change of clothes, she dried her hair as much as she could be bothered. She looked at herself in the mirror. A mass of curls bounded from her. Jason hated the frizz. Normally she'd drag a brush through to straighten it out, control it. Not today. Her hair was one of the few parts of her she actually liked.

She should never have let Jason control her to such an extent, but she'd feared her own lack of control. Which seemed foolish now. Yes, she was taking chances being here, doing whatever the hell she was doing because she wasn't entirely sure, and her own fear threatened to be her undoing. Every new experience twisted her guts, yet she instinctively knew she was on the right path. Doing a new and exciting thing. She was alive at last.

Maybe it was electrifying, she certainly looked like a cartoon character who'd stuck their fingers in a plug socket. She scraped the front of her hair back and plated it over the rest, she needed to be able to see.

She checked the time. Too early to head to Lazlo's old address, not enough time for more sightseeing. She checked the phone for charge: still 87% since she'd charged it overnight.

Thankfully, this hotel had a bar, so she decided to go for a drink. Too early for strong liquor, but lunch and a beer wouldn't hurt.

The bar was sparsely populated; three couples, two businessmen together, four other men alone – one fixated on his phone, one reading a paper and one with a notebook, staring out of the window, and one in jeans and a thick top who studied a map while referring a tab. The air carried the low buzz of conversation in French, none of which Elaine understood.

She found a quiet table and sat down to look over the menu. The impressive selection left her in a quandary that was solved when the waiter came up and she said the item her eyes landed on first, she added a bottled beer and a glass of water.

When her phone rang, she wasn't the only one who jumped.

Embarrassed at having forgotten to reduce the volume after upping it while she showered, she fumbled the mobile out of her pocket to answer.

The name on caller ID nearly made her decline the call, but she had better manners than that.

"Hi Keira," she said as she answered, she looked up and realised she the guy across the room was frowning at her; as soon as she caught his gaze, he hid himself behind his French newspaper.

"What the hell are you doing?"

Elaine scowled her response. "Really? That's how you greet me now?"

"Well, what are you doing?"

"Doing all right, actually. Thanks for asking. I just ordered lunch. How are you doing?"

"Are you kidding me?"

"No. I'm having grilled fish." She stopped to thank the waiter as he served an ice-cold beer with a glass and the water she had requested. "With a cold beer."

"Why are you in Paris?"

"How do you know I'm in Paris?"

Keira prevaricated.

"Oh, so this is what your promise not to lie to me is worth?" Elaine asked.

Keira didn't answer.

"You know what? Never mind. Really not interested. Here's the thing. I love you, you are my best friend, but after over years, I am free to do whatever I want. I've always wanted to come to Paris. So, I have. I arrived last night, I spent this morning visiting the Eiffel Tower, great views by the way, and now I'm having lunch. Later I'll go for a walk, soak up some atmosphere. I might visit the Louvre, Notre Dame, wherever. This might not be your way to behave after losing a husband, but it's mine. If you and your secretive mates don't like it, tough. I don't care." Only as she said it did she realise the truth of the statement. "Turns out my marriage was a sham, my best friend lied to me, and my home has been violated. All that's, left me unwelcome in the one place where I expect to be most comfortable, so I decided to do something I expected to feel uncomfortable doing. I've decided to do a bit of travelling. And, despite expectations, it's not uncomfortable. If you've got a problem with that, that's your problem, I ain't making it mine." Elaine wasn't sure exactly when she'd started channelling her inner East End Emo, but she hadn't said that last sentence since being in her teens. It felt good, true.

"The problem is, you took their money."

"Actually, once it was in my account, it became my money. And it was hush money. I've kept schtum, so I'm at liberty to take that money and do what I want with it. Morally it's mine. Legally too probably, not that we have a contract that would stand up in court or anything. Not that the people we're talking about worry too much about things like court cases."

She listened as Keira dragged in a breath and considered her response. "You're different."

Elaine wondered what she was going to say next. "Yes, I am. I've changed hugely. In only seven days. And I like it. I'm not going to be the subservient little mouse anymore. I'm going to be…" she lost momentum. "Actually, I have no idea who I'm going to be. Me, I guess. I'm not sure who that is right now. You decide if you like me enough to continue to be my friend, or if you have to pretend that I'm dead like Jason and Steve. What's it going to be?"

Her heart hammered. She so wanted Keira to say the change didn't matter. Heat welled in her eyes. *Please Keira, please care about me.*

She heard something from Keira's end of the line. A man's voice?

The line cut dead.

* * *

Silent running meant he couldn't contact the agency, but that didn't mean he was without resources. Keira wasn't employed by the agency, and she was Elaine's friend. While it was ethically questionable to use her, he had to do something.

He had heard every word Elaine had said. Even over two phone lines she sounded honest. If that were even possible. That Keira couldn't figure out who Elaine Blake was right now, was oddly reassuring. If neither Elaine nor Keira knew, he had little hope figuring it out.

Had Elaine really spent the morning as a simple tourist? Was it possible that this was, as she'd claimed, just her acting out, a reaction to Jason's death? Was she touring sights her husband denied her?

The sites she had mentioned were all here in central Paris, if he kept scouting, he would find her.

Unless she's lying.

Why would she lie to Keira?

She had lied, he realised. Lied by omission. She hadn't mentioned Lazlo.

Oh! Idiot!

She'd been to Lazlo's address, seen the man she called Talek, and gathered from the barman that he sometimes turned up around two in the afternoon.

CHAPTER TWENTY-TWO

The bass tasted divine, but the more Elaine considered Keira's call, the more the fish turned sour in her mouth.

Jason's employers were not mucking around. They wanted something they thought she possessed. Something Lazlo thought she had too. She should be worried. She was less caught between a rock and a hard place than she was between warring factions.

That voice nagged in her head to go home. The thought of Lazlo in trouble glued her to the spot.

Given the way Keira put the phone down, it seemed unlikely she'd phoned of her own free will. Acting under orders?

The last time Elaine felt like this, she had been a teenager. Back when she'd been with Eric. Eric ate through life. Every moment had to be filled with enjoyment. A hedonist. She knew the term now if not then. He always said that life was to be tasted in all its glory and savoured. Then the day they ran over the weir. His life had been consumed quickly enough, and she'd barely dared taste hers since.

The big fear was not that she'd be eaten but chewed up and spat out. Or left dead in a gutter somewhere.

She moved the plate to one side and checked her phone. Charge and signal. Lazlo might call at any time. If he called again. Again, she found her bottom lip between her teeth. Had she messed up, coming to Paris? Uncertainty gnawed at her. Had he lied about not being in Paris? Or had Madison?

Madison.

No, she would not believe Madison had lied to her. This situation seemed important enough, she lifted the phone and called London.

"Mom, what are you doing calling me?"

"Calm down, Madison. I took a call from Keira a few minutes ago. She knows I'm in Paris and I never mentioned it, so someone is already watching, already knows where I am."

"Who? How?"

"Jason's employers, probably. I didn't try to hide the fact that I was coming to France, and it doesn't take much to check a credit card spend or a passport control list."

"But we can't be sure who is actually after you?"

"No, but that's my problem; I'll worry about that." She already was worrying about it. "Well actually, I won't. From here on in there will be no electronic trace."

"You're on the second SIM?"

"Not only am I on a second SIM, I brought a new phone."

"Where did you leave your old one?"

"In your spare bedroom. Plugged in and on auto-divert, but now it's diverted, you can turn it off. Look sorry to be pushy, but I was wondering if you could work your magic for me again? I had another call from Lazlo earlier. He said he wasn't in Paris. I need to know if he's lying."

You have what I'm looking for though?

As Elaine spoke with Madison, giving details of timing and conversation, she realised what Lazlo had said. *What I'm looking for.* Previously, he'd used the anonymous *they.* What if there was no *they?* Did that mean there was no threat? Was Jason alive or dead? What else was Lazlo lying to her about?

"Mom? What's wrong?"

Trust Madison to pick up on her concerns. "Do you know how proud I am that you're so smart? I realise it's nothing to do with me, I don't have a right—"

"Mom, shut up." The voice down the line sounded close to tears. "You're the one I call Mom and you're the one who let me grow up to be all I could be. You're the one that supported me through Uni even when officially I was nothing more to do with you. You always went above and beyond for me and every other kid you ever looked after. Which is probably why the idea that one of us is lying to you hurts so much. But I'll do what I can and call you when I have something."

"If you find it after half past, do me a favour and don't call, text."

She could almost hear Madison thinking in the pause that followed.

"I so want to ask why but have a feeling I might regret it. You just make sure you're careful, stay safe."

Elaine smiled. "Who exactly is the parent here?"

* * *

Madison put down the phone and fretted. Chuck had already called to say that he'd made contact, that Elaine seemed like a sweet lady, but not a threat, and not in any particular danger from what he could see. He'd followed her despite her request not to, and he'd been much more aware of any possibility of a tail than she had, but he'd neither seen nor sensed one.

That was what worried Madison. If someone with Chuck's training couldn't see a tail, but Elaine was getting calls from the

UK knowing she was in Paris, then someone had to be following her. They must be. If it was an electronic tail, as Elaine had supposed, then that would only get them to a city, not to Elaine. As long as she wasn't using her own credit card, but that pre-paid card she'd had under the name Hyde. Or better yet, cash. But even the same city was too close for Madison's comfort.

Madison slipped out of the office to make another phone call.

"Hello?"

"Mrs Southgate, hi, it's Madison. I'm not sure if you remember me, I was fostered by Jason and Elaine for some years."

"Of course, I remember. Elaine talks of you often."

"That's nice to know." And it was. If Elaine spoke of her, it reinforced the bond between them.

"How are you, given the dreadful news?"

"Still processing." Which was true. She really didn't quite know how to cope with all that she had learned.

"Yes," Keira sighed. "It's not easy."

"No, it's not. And it seems to have hit Mom particularly hard."

"True," Keira sighed. "She does rather seem to have gone off the rails."

"Really?" Madison asked. "I'd have said she's been knocked back on the rails myself. After all, she hasn't said anything to you about the fact that you were sleeping with her husband, has she? No, she's treated you with respect and kindness despite knowing that you've been lying to her, that you betrayed her."

"I..."

"No, no, don't bother denying it. I know mom, she wouldn't have told me those things without knowing it was true. Of course, that fact that she found photographic evidence made not knowing, kinda impossible."

She was pleased to hear a stunned silence.

"So, let's get to the point, Mrs Southgate. I have those pictures and if you don't tell me what I want to know, I will have them posted on every form of social media with your name and address, telling any man who wants to fuck a whore to call on you. Understand."

"That's blackmail."

"That's right," Madison said easily.

"You bitch."

"Rather takes one to know one," Madison said. "Mom told me all about you and what you do. She said you told her that you don't know the men who searched her home. Unlike my mother, I wouldn't trust you as far as I could throw you, which right now would preferably be down a very deep well. One with hungry eels. So, tell me who were they?"

"I don't know." The depressed tone came back.

"Really, Mrs Southgate? You need to do better than that unless you want to be the next best thing on the web."

"I swear, I don't know."

There was something too pat about that statement.

"One more try, Mrs Southgate. Either you give me their names now or I press send and post your prostitute pic—"

"Letterman. Cormac Letterman." The tone was dejected, and it deserved to be. "He was one of them. I honestly don't know who the other one was."

Madison paused, gave the woman to worry.

"I mean it Madison. I know one was Cormac Letterman, but the other I didn't see, didn't speak to."

"Fine. I'll take you at your word for now, Mrs Southgate. But if I find out your lying..."

"You know I lost my husband too. Elaine isn't the only one suffering."

"She is the only one I care about, though."

Madison ended the call.

* * *

The cold bit hard as Elaine stepped out onto the street. Under the grey sky she zipped up her coat and ambled along. She would reach the river far too quickly even at this speed, but she needed to think. Implicitly trusting Lazlo being the biggest weight. Of course she trusted him; he was her boy. One of them. She'd do anything for those kids – any of them. Even the ones that didn't call any more. Hell, she'd just travelled abroad for the first time in years on the off chance she might be able to do some good.

Fat chance.

Stopping by the wall separating the street from the lower walkway by the river, she looked over the broad flow of the Seine and wondered what it would be like to be that free and why the hell she'd let herself be chained all these years?

She shifted to moved off, to head for that other bar when her phone started ringing. "Hello?"

"Mum, it's Lazlo."

"Sweetheart, are you alright?"

"I'm okay, for now. You've got the evidence, yeah?"

She swallowed the lie. "Yes."

"The Jardins du Trocadéro, there's a large open square at the north end, and there's a waffle stand there."

"Waffle stand on the square at the north end of Jardins du Trocadéro. I'll find it."

"Be there with the evidence tomorrow at noon."

The line disconnected as soon as he'd finished. She slipped the phone back into her pocket and moved along down the Avenue de New York. *Well, that isn't going to go well.*

And it would go even worse if she turned up to that meeting without the evidence. Which she had to. On account of not having it.

* * *

Without any better option, he headed to the wine bar opposite the apartment where Lazlo had lived and hoped Elaine would turn up. He selected a table with an easy view of the door and the outside area.

She walked in at 13:53, moved straight to the bar and ordered a small Chardonnay. The bartender was not the man from last night, and she didn't try to strike up a conversation with this one. She paid and found a table near the window.

As it grew colder outside, and the shadow of the buildings either side kept the street in gloom, he was glad she hadn't chosen to sit outside. He didn't fancy standing out in the rain.

Instead, she sat diagonally on the bench seat to watch the road and the flat.

Though she sipped the wine, she didn't seem to be enjoying it. Her expression was tight, contemplative, worried. She should be bloody worried. He still had no idea what the evidence was, and he wasn't convinced she had it, but if others thought she did, her life could be forfeit. Did she have the vaguest idea of what that meant?

The way she sighed and slumped forward, putting her forehead on the table would suggest that maybe she did have an inkling.

A frown furrowed her brow, suggested problems as she pulled her phone from her pocket. What she saw didn't seem to please her, and her hand trembled as she reached for her glass.

The Arab she came looking for stepped in as she took a sip from the wine. There was no attempt to mask her surprise, though she avoided choking on the drink. With a paper under his arm, it only took a wave of the man's hand to order a beer.

He slunk back against the wall, not wanting to be spotted by either Elaine or the Arab.

CHAPTER TWENTY-THREE

The dark sky and cold air were unpleasant and just about perfect for the meeting Madison was going to. The earlier rain had left the city damp and depressing, no clean sweep this time, but that matched her mood too. The tiny tapas bar was a hidden gem in the back alleys of the City of London. It had opened two months ago, and the trendy crowd had yet to find it, which was just as well, it could only handle a dozen covers at a time and Madison would meet with her contact as privately as possible.

The woman she had come to see was obvious the second she arrived. The table was the only one so far back that was occupied. The front two tables were full, but they were also busy talking, so absorbed in their own world and the food that they were unlikely to even notice that they had company.

Madison nodded to the waiter and headed straight to the woman. Her birdlike features were only sharpened by the fact that she didn't have a spare ounce of body fat. A result, Madison knew, of a rather serious illness she had yet to recover from fully.

She slipped into the chair opposite Number Two, still finding it odd that it was easier to think of the woman that way rather than by her real, and rather boring, name of Sarah Smith. There was many a joke about her handle being an excellent description of the woman, but the English tended to enjoy an off-colour toilet-based joke. Their greetings were, as usual, cool and perfunctory. But they were business acquaintances, not friends.

"So how can I help you?" Number Two said as she took a slice of sourdough from the mixed offering on the table to her own plate, then drizzled olive oil with herbs and garlic over the fresh bread.

"I want to know everything about Cormac Letterman."

The drizzling stopped. One last drop of oil plummeting to the open texture before Number Two return the bottle to its holder.

"I doubt that you do," she said easily as she broke a small chunk of bread off and popped it in her mouth.

Again, direct questioning might not be the right track. She'd try something else. "Then tell my why you're known as Number Two. It's hardly an official MI6 designation."

She blinked at Madison. "No one's asked that for years."

"Off limits?"

Number Two considered for a long moment before she shook her head. "It was an insult. Back when I was a fairly new intelligence officer. Someone, even I can't remember who, used it to call me a shit. However, over the years, those who don't know have assumed it was because I was higher up the hierarchy. Ultimately, it's been useful to me, helped me climb the ladder."

Madison blinked, surprised by the admission, and needing to readjust her view on the woman. "What's Letterman working on?"

Number Two shrugged.

"Now is not the time to block me. You know what's going on. You know my connection to it."

Number Two simply regarded her. "And you know I'm under absolutely no obligation –"

"Chatham Wren." Madison had no idea what that meant, but it was Bromstad's suggestion that she use the key phrase should she need it.

Number Two went even more still and pale. "You do realise we both work for supposedly secret services?"

"You do know that we all use whatever tools we can."

"Tools or weapons?"

Madison was screaming on the inside, but she had to stay cool. "I don't care what you call them. As long as they're effective."

That effectiveness was uncertain as she waited for Number Two to speak again. She counted six heartbeats.

"All I can say is that he's on silent running. He is not to contact me or anyone else in the organisation until he has achieved his given aim."

"Which is what?"

Number Two shrugged her shoulders, a skeleton with skin on.

"I know he's in Paris," Madison said.

"Then you know more than I do." Number Two stated.

Madison took a moment. "He was assigned to searching the Blake home."

"You mean your home?"

"Former home, I live here in the city." Though in many ways she did still think of that house in Cardiff as home. It was where she felt most loved. Not because of Jason, but because of Elaine, and some of the other foster children she'd got to know. Utku Solak mostly. They had become good friends as teenagers and stayed close, brought together in some ways by both Jason's treatment and Elaine's love. They remained friends even now, though distantly, what with his having returned to his native Turkey. Clearly, Elaine had hoped something more would grow between them, and it might well have, had Jason not got in the way.

"Were you afraid they might find something embarrassing?"

Madison didn't react, though God knew Keira wasn't the only one Jason had on film, or pixel or — it didn't matter. "Absolutely not. I've nothing to be ashamed of." And she didn't. "Given Jason's recent death, why is my mother targeted for no reason?"

The woman broke another piece of bread. She ate like a bird. "What if there is reason to target her?"

Madison didn't frown at the woman, though she wanted to. Poker face was important. "What reason could there possibly be for you to investigate a woman who is, unfortunately, little more than a suburban housewife and a mom with an overactive need to clean?"

"Is that why you've nothing to worry about regarding the past? You think she would have cleaned up all the evidence?"

Madison didn't react, but she did wonder. Mom has said she'd seen the pictures, but not what she'd done with them. "To be entirely honest, I'm not sure if she would. She might, but I don't worry because I've nothing to be ashamed of."

"I've got some pictures that might make you think otherwise."

Madison suspected as much. "And you'll see more in most underwear catalogues. If those images were really dangerous to me, Chatham Wren wouldn't have bothered you."

It was a standoff. Who was going to blink first? Madison didn't think that the moment was worth winning. "So why are you targeting her?"

"I'm not."

"Then what was the search for?"

"Didn't she tell you?"

"She doesn't know."

Number Two watched her for a while, ate another tiny piece of bread, then pushed the plate aside as if she'd eaten enough already. She washed the last of the bread away with a slow drink of sparkling water. "Tell me, if Elaine Blake is merely a suburban housewife and a mom with an overactive need to clean, why has she disappeared?"

"She hasn't disappeared," Madison argued. "She's taking some time out, gone away to think. I believe she's in shock after Jason's death."

"I see," Number Two allowed.

"Assuming Jason is dead."

"Mrs Blake doesn't think so?"

"She does. After all, she's got his death certificate. I, however, am better acquainted with how this game works. How things are rarely all they seem. This is my mom we are talking about. I need to know what's going on."

Number Two's gaze raked over her. "First, you tell me something that went on. There are rumours, never substantiated."

The way the other woman paused, Madison was fairly sure that she knew what Number Two didn't want to say, but was going to have to. But she would have to let the woman say it.

"One of the children sent to the Blakes, Liam Donovan, claimed that Jason had tried to…"

It wasn't like Number Two to hesitate even on such a sensitive subject. Liam Donovan had been six years ago.

"He claimed Jason encouraged him to commit certain lewd acts. Several times, Liam claimed. He also said that others had been involved. Other children that is."

But if she was asking, and they had still sent children to the Blakes, then there was an issue. "Why didn't you believe Liam?"

Again, the pause before an answer came. "Liam came from an abusive situation. It was known that his father was a paedophile. It was equally known that Liam made other claims which were demonstrably wrong. Call him a liar, a fantasist, or just a mixed-up kid, whatever, he was unreliable as a source. There was no actual evidence, and Blake was pulled in, questioned. He was aghast at the suggestion. Suggested that Liam was projecting his father's actions on the next available father figure."

"And you believed Jason?"

"Not entirely. Not personally anyway." Number Two said.

"Was that why you stopped sending foster children to them? Because of the allegation?"

The constant pausing was evidence to Madison that this openness wasn't easy for Number Two. Sharing dirty linen never was. "In part," she admitted at last. "But I also kept Jason out of any case where I thought a child might be in danger, so the opportunities dried up for him."

Madison nodded, but she also had more she needed to know. "Why did it start?"

"Jason's abuse?"

"No," Madison thought Number Two was being deliberated obtuse. "Why was Jason even allowed to start fostering children?"

The way Number Two drew in a breath seemed like a smoker drawing in nicotine, only Number Two didn't smoke. Not anymore, anyway. "I don't know that either. The decision was made above my pay grade back then, and I have never asked. I doubt that I'd get an answer if I did ask. Now, can you confirm or deny Liam's claims?"

"Neither. I wasn't with the Blakes when Liam was."

That cold gaze bored into Madison, but she'd faced worst.

"Did Jason ever do anything to you?"

"Not against my will."

Now a frown crowned that gaze.

"Are you aware of his doing anything against the will or reason of other children sent into his household?"

Madison paused. Did she really want to say anything? Did she want to be in the mire to which that would inevitably take her. *Truth, justice.* If she really believed in those concepts, she had to truly uphold them. "Yes."

The one clearly spoken word hung between them. Madison didn't know what Number Two would do with that.

"Was Elaine Blake part of it?"

"Good God no!" Madison was horrified by the idea. "Elaine would never. She's just not like that."

"Are you sure?"

"Absolutely." And she was. Madison sighed. "I think there's a lot more to Mom that anyone realises, but she would never hurt a child. And using sex for control, that was Jason's schtick."

"Elaine took the money."

"You were fool enough to give it to her. I think she's taken it more to be bloody minded than anything else. Now, will you just tell me what you know?"

Number Two took a breath. "Cormac Letterman is a seasoned agent. Trustworthy."

There was a great deal behind that statement but Madison wasn't sure how much could be read into it. In truth, she had

had the pleasure of meeting Letterman once or twice. He had seemed nice enough, but then most spies did, it was part of their job to fit in. To be acceptable to people. But there was something more in the way it was said. Number Two was just too monotonous. Until the catch of that last word. "You have feelings for the man."

Number Two maintained eye contact, but the slight swallow said everything. "It was a long time ago."

"So was my going to live with Mom, but it still has emotional power over me."

Again, the suspended moments when no one spoke. Over ten years, different nationalities, and supposedly friendly organisations stood between these two women.

"Is that it?" Madison asked. "Does Letterman somehow have emotional power over you?"

"No one has emotional power over me."

That didn't surprise Madison much. This woman was rather the head over heart type, she wouldn't give anyone the opportunity to hurt her.

"Then there shouldn't be an issue with telling me the truth," Madison spoke softly. "I love Elaine Blake, and I'm worried about her. I need to know what kind of man is on her tail."

The poker face didn't entirely drop, but the older woman was considering her response. "Love will put you in danger, get you hurt."

Number Two surprised Madison with her words.

Again, the British agent took time to think before speaking. "Once upon a time I believed myself to be in love. It was convenient at the time, but it wasn't real. He loved field work and had no ambition to climb the ladder. I wanted promotion. He would have held me back. I put the job first."

"It seems to have worked out for you." Everyone who knew Number Two respected her, even though she wasn't greatly loved, she was always the coolest head in the room. Many said she was also the coldest heart, though this turn in the conversation suggested there was still a heart beating in there somewhere.

She shrugged. "I cannot tell you where Mac is, or what he's doing. Because I honestly do not know. All I can say is that he's off grid. Silent running."

"Because of the danger or the sensitivity of the issue?"

For a moment Madison didn't expect Number Two to answer that.

"Both."

"Is he following Mom, I mean Elaine Blake?"

"You mean 'Mom', and I respect that. Just as you have to respect the fact that I can't tell you."

It was a fact Madison couldn't respect, but that she'd have to live with. Just as she knew she would have to endure with the frustration and the worry. But there was one thing she needed to know. "Is Jason dead?"

"As far as this agency and government is concerned, yes."

That was it. That was the difference she'd just made. Jason must officially be considered dead, or Elaine wouldn't have a death certificate. But that didn't necessarily equate to Jason actually being dead. People could be moved on, given new identities. But after telling this woman what Jason really was, it seemed she had ensured that that wouldn't happen. If Jason wasn't already dead, his way back to the United Kingdom was blocked. He was cut off, alone. Without identity and without support, without a way home.

It was what he deserved.

With a quiet nod of understanding, she moved to stand.

"I can tell you this, however."

Madison sank back in the chair.

"We are questioning if we trusted the wrong wife."

* * *

When Elaine sat up and looked around, she saw him.

Seven years since she had seen this man, but she was sure he was the same man. It helped that Ladderman had shown her the anniversary party picture, reminded her.

Talek. Though the longer she considered about it, the less she was convinced by that name. She just couldn't be sure. The man's name was less important than his possible link to Lazlo.

But what to do?

Talek crossed his long legs, the open paper hiding his face. She watched him. He held the edges of the paper with long, relaxed fingers. The beige trousers had a sharp crease and the brown suede shoes were marked with used worn soles. She suspected they'd been bought for style but used for comfort. That was definitely Talek. He must have walked in while she had her head on the table. It was unlikely he remembered her. She'd spent two decades acting like the wallpaper, why would he remember her?

Carefully, she picked up her glass and stood, moving to his table. She sat opposite him without invitation. He remained still.

"Hello," she said as he appeared around the paper.

He looked like he was trying to look confused. "Pardonnez-moi?"

"It's been a few years, hasn't it?"

He looked at her through narrowed eyes. "Je ne parle pas anglais."

"My fifteenth wedding anniversary. The last time we met."

"Nous n'avons jamais rencontré, madame."

Body language. Typically languid, typically French. Except that the typical – perhaps stereotypical – Frenchman would have simply gone back to his paper, this man hadn't. She'd seen the recognition in his eyes. His words said more than he meant them too. She wasn't good at French but rencontré was close enough to reconnoitre and rendezvous for her to guess.

"If you don't understand English, how do you know I referred to a meeting?"

He paused and swallowed.

"Je ne vous connais pas."

"Whatever." She realised he was denying something but had no idea what. "Look, you can lie as much as you like. But here's the thing. I know you, and I know you know me. You also know Lazlo Zakis. You're living where he used to live. All I want is to know where he is now."

"Je ne sais pas."

"Don't tell me you don't know; I don't believe you."

"Je ne sais pas."

Suddenly she felt all the anger welling up, another memory too. She grabbed him by the front of his jumper and pulled him across the table.

"Don't give me your rubber neck, boy. I am sick to fucking death of being lied to, Tannek." She'd suddenly remembered the right name. "Now where is Lazlo? Where's my son?"

He looked pale, and the sudden silence in the room told her she was making a scene. *Sod making a scene, I don't care what anyone else thinks of me now.*

His hand wrapped around her wrists, his fingers like steel bands, and the tips crushed her bones. All pretence slipped from his expression until the only fury remained. He twisted her wrists too now, pain spreading from hands to elbows.

"Play with fire, Mrs Blake and you will get burned."

* * *

"Tannek! Calm down." Mac himself was calmer now he knew where Elaine was staying tonight. All he had to worry about right now was Tannek's reaction.

"Calm down!" Tannek paced the small room, in an absolute fury. "She remembered my name!"

"You should never have used your real one."

"It was one hour – years ago."

"And someone photographed it." Cormac Letterman sat on the sofa; there was barely enough room for one person to pace. "Things aren't that bad."

"No?" Tannek swung on him. "And who recently showed her that photograph?"

Mac might be guilty as charged but couldn't let that stop him. He'd agreed that that probably was why Elaine recognised Tannek, but he'd not expected her travel to Paris and look the man up.

They hadn't found anything in the Blakes' house, but perhaps Elaine had. That ripped lagging, her being in Paris, it was too coincidental. Though in truth, Keira made a good case for Elaine acting out. Elaine had been kept under the thumb for many years. Jason had always described her as a doormat, a mouse, but Mac had realised on first meeting her that mouse would one day roar and then Jason could look out.

"You could at least have warned me," Tannek spat.

"I shouldn't even be talking to you. I'm supposed to be on silent running." He'd be in trouble if Number Two found out he'd spoken to Tannek. Mind you, that was the good thing about the silence — it worked both ways.

"What has Lazlo got to do with any of this anyway?"

"Not sure." It was a lie, but the less Tannek knew the better. "When did you last see him?"

Mac watched Tannek stop, turn, and scowl at him. "Why? What is going on?"

"You do understand that we work for a secret service?"

"What about Number Two? Can she tell me?" In typical Arab fashion, Tannek was animated, spoke with his arms, his dark skin flushing with anger. "Perhaps I should call her and tell her what happened tonight."

"That wouldn't be a good move for any of us." Mac didn't move, but Tannek seemed to shrink back as if he'd been threatened. Perhaps it wasn't Mac, more likely it was the shadow of Tannek's memory and the times he had seen Mac kill without compunction. "Tannek, in our line nothing is clear cut, we wade in muddy waters. Now, tell me what you know about Lazlo and maybe I can figure out what Mrs Blake is up to."

Tannek sighed and leaned against the door. "Lazlo has been working some girl from the Russian Embassy, nothing useful has come of it yet. If there was anything to come of it other than Lazlo getting laid; apparently, the girl is very attractive."

And pillow talk was as good a way as any to get answers. There again, Lazlo was in his early twenties, he was probably just as interested in getting his leg over as protecting the state.

"These last two weeks I've hardly seen him. He popped back a couple of days ago for more clothes but said nothing."

Mac nodded. The action was hardly odd for an agent. "Did he take his passport?"

"Both." Tannek nodded.

Both. Meaning British and Latvian passports. That seemed odd, but again, not totally out of place given their circumstances.

"And he didn't say anything?" Mac asked. "Didn't mention his family, anything?"

"He's an orphan, what family is there to mention? I know he stayed with the Blakes, and Mrs Blake referred to him as her son, but that woman is screwed up about not having had kids of her own. Is that what this is all about? I heard Jason's dead. So, is she just hunting for her lost kids?"

"It's possible." Mac carefully breathed in. "She visited one of the girls they took in before she left the UK, but if she's on a tour to see her 'babies,' then there are more of them in the UK than out of it."

"What am I supposed to do now?"

Mac shrugged. "Whatever it is you were doing before. One little altercation with an Englishwoman shouldn't change anything much."

"As long as it stays one little altercation. There's no guarantee she won't come back."

"There's no guarantee she will." Mac's brief was a watching one only, but he might be able to do something. "Look, if she thinks you're a dead end, there's no reason for her to come back. For now, all I can suggest you keep your head down and concentrate on your own case. Blake is my problem."

Mac left, returning to the hotel. On route he started wondering about just how much of a problem Elaine Blake would turn out to be.

* * *

Madison had never had a case chew up her insides this way before. There again, she'd never had such a personal connection to a case before. Not being able to see the best course of action wasn't a sensation she enjoyed.

It wasn't so much keeping secrets from Elaine that was the problem, she'd been doing that for years. But this new Elaine was different, wilder, stronger than the woman she had thought she'd known. Still as loving and generous, but the mouse was a tiger now, and roaring away. Only Elaine had dived headlong into a world of sharks, and even a tiger could drown, sharks or no. For a foolish moment, Madison imagined Elaine as some hybrid shark tiger, a stupid cartoon image she had to shake from her head.

The situation was already dangerous, and Elaine knew that, but she was coping. Even as she walking the tightrope, did she really need to know that there were spears fixed under the safety net, or possibly no safety net at all if Letterman lost her or decided she was disposable?

If she didn't know, then she couldn't be prepared. Madison would have to tell Elaine.

No.

Elaine had coped well enough so far. Madison hoped that might be a good indicator she would carry on coping. But with the past no indicator to the future, the additional fear of knowing the extent of the combatants she was facing, could just as easily push Elaine over the edge to a foolish mistake.

If Cormac Letterman was as good as the rumours said, he'd stay on track and he'd save Elaine if she needed saving. The best thing Madison could do was support her as she asked and not overburden her.

She hoped.

Madison lay back in bed, listening to Neil breathing beside her and grateful for the comfort he'd given by just being with her that afternoon. She turned on her side and snuggled again him, smooth warm skin she loved to caress. She welcomed the movement when he shifted to lay on his back and pull her against him, kissing the top of her head.

"Whatever it is, sweetheart, you'll work it out."

CHAPTER TWENTY-FOUR

Elaine rubbed her wrist. It didn't hurt, but the memory did. Way out of her depth already, she had to push the nausea down again. Embarrassed and ashamed, she mooched around her hotel room. The idea of meeting someone in the Trocadéro tomorrow quaked inside her; she didn't even have what they wanted so couldn't expect a straight swap.

She pulled out her notebook, the handwritten transcription of the cypher. Watch Tower, Godiva, and North Gate Spell. It made no sense!

She'd made a huge mistake in contacting Tannek. Bad enough he'd been no help, what happened if he decided to hinder her? Perhaps she should have found another way to approach him, something quieter, not that she meant to be loud in the pub.

With nothing else to do, she made the only call she could. "Hi Madison."

"Thank God you called," Madison sounded out of breath. "I've been worried sick."

Elaine frowned. "Why? What's happened? Are you okay?" Suddenly she realised England was an hour ahead of France time wise. "Oh, please tell me I didn't just disturb you with Neil."

The small huff of a laugh came was a relief to listen. "Actually, Mom, yes, you did, but it's fine. Your timing was perfect. We were… Hold on."

Elaine heard movement, guessing Madison was getting out of the bed she shouldn't have been disturbed from. She checked her watch. A little afternoon delight. She was almost jealous. Neil seemed a nice guy. And attractive. Probably good in... things she really shouldn't be thinking about. "Well, yes. I'm fine, I'm not the one who ran headlong across the channel on some hair-brained mission."

Given that her confidence had already fallen through the floor, that only served to sink her further.

"Am I doing the wrong thing?" she asked. "Should I just turn back, go home?"

Madison didn't answer immediately. Tears pricked at Elaine's eyes.

"Oh God, I've made everything so much worse!"

"Mom?"

She sniffed. "Yeah."

"Shut up."

Madison's instruction surprised her.

"What was it you used to say to us? Don't be a daft a-hole."

That was so wrong Elaine laughed. "Apeth. It's don't be a daft apeth."

"Whatever," Madison said. "There's a big part of me that wants you home, wants you safe. But honestly, Mom, you're doing the right thing. Don't underplay the danger, you have to be careful, be watchful, take care of yourself. But you have to keep going. You can do whatever you need to. I believe in you."

Her chin wobbled; her eyes prickled. Elaine blinked the emotion away. "Thank you. I needed to hear that."

"Yeah, well, you need to hear this too," Madison sounded serious and worried. "I tried to get a location on Lazlo's call, but it bounced all over the place, no way to trace it like I traced the others."

The technicality made no sense to Elaine. "Why would that change?"

"I don't know, but it would seem reasonable that, since you travelled to Paris for no indication other than that that's where the calls might have come from, they may be worried you have a way of tracing the calls so they made sure you couldn't."

"Hmm." Elaine worried. "Good to think they might be crediting me with more smarts than I have. Especially when I told them I came to Paris as the last address I had for Lazlo."

"Maybe, but when you think about it, they weren't wrong. You do have a way of tracing calls."

"*You* have a way."

"And you have me. You used a tool, so ultimately it's the same thing."

"You're a lot more to me than a tool, love. But we should keep these conversations short, so thanks for trying."

"Sure, but wait, there's more." Madison called her attention as she moved to end the call. "When I couldn't trace the call, I tried to trace Lazlo. I found two tickets purchased in his name. One heading for Frankfurt, the other Geneva. I've got no idea which one he's going to use." She rattled off the details and Elaine scrabbled to write them down.

"Okay." Elaine didn't know what to think. "That's… odd." She'd have to try to work out why Lazlo would do that. "Thanks. Look, I'm going to try not to call you again. I don't want to drag you into this any deeper. I really appreciate all the help you've given me, and I want you to know that I love you."

Madison returned the affection, and they ended the call. Elaine turned off the phone, even turned it over to take off the back and remove the battery, without power she was pretty sure the phone was untraceable.

Frankfurt or Geneva.

Jason had gone missing in Prague, what did Frankfurt or Geneva have to do with anything?

Unable to stay still, she stood up and paced.

There was something about Frankfurt that she knew and couldn't bring to mind. The city name resonated in her head. There wasn't much space in the hotel, she felt like it was a single step and turn, it was five steps and turn, but there was still too much turning. Her head was spinning, just like it did when Jason started talking about his job and why he was going to be gone so long this time. Just like when he was telling her what the six-week absence was all about. All those lies.

What if they weren't all lies?

She stopped and thought about it. Yes, Jason had said three weeks in Prague, which he'd later refined to nineteen days. Then the run of conferences in Germany. *Starting in Frankfurt!*

The passport she'd acquired sat on the table beside the TV. She opened it and looked at the woman's picture. Since the introduction of biometrics, using another person's passport was incredibly problematic, but EU citizens travelled in the EU without borders, she should be okay. She reviewed the visible details. She and the woman were roughly the same age and height. She looked over the picture, A bit of make-up, shadow and highlight the right places and they were easily mistakable. The only real difference was an easy change.

CHAPTER TWENTY-FIVE

One of the hardest parts of maintaining surveillance on a subject was keeping eyes on. This was particularly difficult when working alone. Especially when he'd had to check in with Tannek. As Mac returned to the hotel, he hoped Elaine hadn't slipped away again. He'd have to do something to check. Perhaps he could send her room service and see if she answered. Only he didn't know what room she was in.

He turned the corner and saw the entrance, just in time to shift back as Elaine stepped out, looking both ways, before turning away from him. That was a relief, and he'd have to maintain pursuit. He had no idea where she was going. Though she had her outsized handbag over her shoulder, she didn't have her holdall, what should indicate that she wasn't leaving the city—at least he hoped it did.

When she headed down the metro, he ran to catch up. It didn't take long to see her struggling with the ticket machine. As he hung back, using other travellers as a shield, she finally picked a destination, he clocked the position of the button and once she took her ticket and headed down, he quickly moved up to the machine and realised she was heading to Charles de Gaulle Airport.

Now Mac was worried. If she got on a plane out of the county, he was going to fall at the first hurdle, he wasn't carrying a passport.

On the metro, he entered the carriage at the opposite end from Elaine. He managed to get a seat, though she didn't, that gave him the benefit of being able to watch her unseen.

Elaine got a seat a few minutes later and as she sat, she pulled something from her bag, a spiral-bound book she opened as a solid block, and then she started sketching. He knew she'd kept her hand in over years, but he was surprised by this move. She kept looking up as her pencil moved over the page, he assumed she was drawing the scene opposite her, a young couple with sun bleached dreadlocks, patchwork clothes, walking sandals and more piercing than he could see, not to mention big back packs that would sustain them indefinitely. The couple caught her looking at one point and there was a friendly looking exchange that he couldn't hear. As they were approaching their final stop, Elaine showed them the work, and the girl took out her phone and photographed it.

Another smiled exchange and Elaine exited the carriage as the two swung those big packs on. Mac followed her, his guts twisting as she walked smartly to the check-in lounge. As always there were plenty of people milling about, some check-in desks trailing lines, and even the terminals for online check in were surrounded by people trying the technology.

He watched as Elaine searched the overhead boards that declared which flights were being called for check in. She took some time to read through, if she was looking for a particular flight, she didn't find it quickly. The way her body relaxed, he guessed she was pleased with what she saw. Then she stepped back and away, looking through the crowd.

If the way she moved and looked around her was anything to go by, he judged she expected to see or spot someone she knew. But this was the departure point, not arrivals. Was she waiting for someone? Here to meet Lazlo? What if she was planning to make the exchange here?

At least with the number of people around, he had the chance to move closer, though again, the way she was monitoring the crowd didn't make that easy. He moved behind a board and slipped off his jacket, holding it so the lining was outermost, effectively changing its colour.

Elaine had moved to the edge of the hall, found a place to prop herself against the external wall, and she brought out that sketch pad again, her pencil working over the page even though she kept looking up and looking around. Several people glanced at her, but they didn't bother her. The idea of an artist drawing seemed to make her as ordinary and invisible as everyone else.

Then she looked up and saw that the check in boards had changed. She looked for the desk number and moved her position. It was on.

Only it wasn't. She had looked out the desk, which he realised was for a flight to Frankfurt. A fact that rung warning bells in Mac's head. Frankfurt had been one of the destinations on Jason's itinerary when he'd gone missing.

But Elaine didn't get in line.

She watched the line, and checked the self-check-in area.

Searching for someone.

An hour later the line was down to the last few passengers. Elaine was still on the side lines, still sketching, still repeatedly looking up and around, and generally getting ignored. Which was better than he was doing. One of the security guards was starting to take way too much notice of him.

The check-in desk closed.

The sketchbook went away.

Elaine looked annoyed. She checked around one last time. Whatever she'd been hoping for, whoever she'd wanted to see, that person wasn't here.

Shoulders slumped she headed out of the hall, and Mac was unusually happy to follow her. Back to the metro, back to the hustle and bustle of the city—which was where he lost her again.

The damn annoying woman was as slippery as an eel!

* * *

The airport had been a bust. She wasn't sure what to make of that. Was Lazlo going to Geneva while she'd looked for the Frankfurt connection? Had Madison unwittingly fed her false information? She had to believe that it was an unwitting act, because she wanted someone on her side, and she needed Madison to be that person.

Of course, it all added to the paranoia. It dripped poison into her ear. Like Chinese torture. She'd started this to save Lazlo—clearly, she had over inflated ideas of her abilities. But now she wasn't entirely sure he even needed saving.

Be prepared.

While no Boy Scout, or even Girl Guide, she definitely remembered one of the more annoying lecturers in university often repeating the phrase: 'Failure to prepare is preparation to fail.'

She had to be ready, and there were a million and one possibilities, more she was sure than she would ever think of, and many that she had thought of that were too wild to be of any real probability. But she was going to go with some of her ideas. If nothing else, it gave her something to do.

On the Metro she thought about the first step, she'd need to find a chemist, and though her very meagre French wouldn't allow her to remember what the French word for that was, she was reasonably sure that over here they were identified with a green cross for a sign.

The journey back felt like forever, and when she did get into Paris, the crowds were gathering, like the darkness. The evenings were drawing in far too fast and far too cold. She was grateful it wasn't raining. Which was when she felt the first drops of the light shower. With a tut she looked up at the heavens and wondered if God was listening after all and trying to annoy her.

Thankfully he might actually have been trying to help her, because that was when she spotted a shop with a green cross lighted up in front. She ducked under an opening umbrella and ran for the shop. A glance up told her what the place was.

Pharmacie.

Well, of course! Stupid of her not to have remembered that. There again, it was so close to the English word it was little wonder her brain hadn't registered the difference. Inside the clear signage wasn't much help, she couldn't read French any better than she could speak it. Probably not even that well. She was just grateful to find one open after five on a week day.

Still there were some things that were universal, so a brisk walk around the aisles and she soon saw what she thought was what she needed. She recognised the brand name and, on checking, found the instructions were in pictorial form as well as French. That would do. Seemed fairly pricy at the checkout, but she was willing to pay. Didn't have much choice.

The walk back to the hotel was cold, and she missed a couple of turns as she had to keep her hands and phone in her pockets. She really needed to buy a decent pair of gloves.

She considered what she was doing. Was she really prepared to give away secrets that could undermine the UK state? The answer really should have been a simple no. But that wasn't her reaction, a worry in and of itself. She was balancing the life of one person that she cared about, her son Lazlo, and the lives of people who signed up to be spies, so they knew the risks they were taking.

And what about all the innocent lives back home that those spies might inadvertently expose to danger.

Paranoia or conscience?

Either way, she pushed the voice aside as she stepped into the foyer and felt relieved to be out of the wind chill. She also noticed the sign for the dining room, which was just as well since she was starving. Under that, she noticed the signs for gym, sauna, and pool. A nice relax in a sauna would be very welcome. Only she didn't have a swimming costume with her. And she might not be able to come down to dinner.

She moved over to the reception desk, and the young girl there greeted here with a smile.

"Sprechen sie Englisch?" Even as she finished saying it, she hung her head, shaking it, muttering under her breath. "Great asking if you speak English in German when you're France. There's brilliant for you."

"Pardon?"

She looked up as the confused young woman, smiled and tried again. "Parle vous anglaise?"

"It's 'parlez-vous anglais,'" a man said from behind her. The Texan drawl gave him away.

Elaine turned to see Chuck Linklater III standing behind her, grinning. "Thanks."

"Pardonnez-moi, madame," the receptionist said. "Ne parlez pas anglais."

Great. She vaguely understood the no, GCSE French had taught her a little. Now she was stuck.

"What did you want to know?" Chuck asked again.

"Right now, I want to know why you're here. Are you following me?"

"Now, while that's an appealing idea, my darlin' Elaine, I just happen to be staying here tonight too."

The coincidence seemed too much, she also got the impression that Chuck lived in Paris, so there was no obvious reason for him to be staying at the hotel at all. "Okay." She'd believe him for now. "In that case, I was wondering if they do room service, as in bring a meal to the room, not service the room."

His grin was broad. "Oh, can't I tempt you to join me for dinner tonight? I'm sure the dining room can accommodate us both."

"I'm sure it could, and that's a generous offer, Chuck. But I've got a load of things I want to get done this evening, so dinner alone in my room is what's in store."

"Oh, I am broken hearted," Chuck said leaning closer. "What's your room number?"

She paused before giving it, feeling so awkward. But there again, she was highly unlikely to be subject to overbearing interest. As Jason was often wont to tell her, she was short, fat and ugly, no man could want to be with her. "Why?"

"So I can advise this lovely young lady," his head tipped to the receptionist. "And so that I know what room to ask for if I feel the desperate need to call you tonight and tell you all the magical things I want to do to you, only to hear those lyrical Welsh tones turn me down again."

For all she rolled her eyes and shook her head, she couldn't help herself grinning, as she gave her room number.

The man spoke to the receptionist in French and the young girl rattled away with her answer. She probably said more than was necessary given that Chuck returned to English to tell Elaine, yes, they did room service, but only after seven, ring extension 12 from the room to order, and there was a five Euro surcharge on the delivery. She thanked him, and the receptionist, but her cheeks burned at the suggestions that lingered in her mind.

Her cheeks were still hot as she closed the door safely behind her. She flopped on to the bed. What was she doing here? If she couldn't even have a decent conversation with a receptionist, she was in no fit state to be travelling.

Though in fairness, travelling wasn't really the issue here, making an exchange for Lazlo was.

Of course, the whole thing depended on her being able to exchange the evidence that they wanted, for the son she wanted. Jason was beside the point. She really didn't care about him.

The fly in the ointment was that she didn't have the evidence. It seemed to her now that there was a question over how honest Lazlo was being with her, so she felt slightly less worried about lying to him. If he wasn't lying, she didn't have any compunction whatsoever about lying to his captors.

But if he wasn't lying and he was at risk without the evidence, what was she going to hand over? Without the real evidence, she'd have to fake something.

What?

She couldn't give them the cypher or the key that she had found. That might not be handing over the evidence, but it was handing over the route to the evidence, and she couldn't do that.

She looked back at her bag. The pen drive. She had no problem giving them the pictures Ladderman had given her, most of them anyway. Lazlo's youthful behaviour had happened. He'd have to live with the results if that came out. But there was one picture she didn't want them to see, the one with more cryptic clues, even if she didn't know what to. She also had qualms about handing over some of the pictures of Madison, though again, she might have to live with the consequences of that too. She was well aware that deleting a file actually only deleted the recording of where that file was stored on the disk. If someone really wanted to, there was software that could bring a deleted file back. She just had to hope that they didn't have that kind of software.

With an adapter, she linked the drive to her tab and opened the picture of her anniversary party. The tab had come with some free image manipulation software installed, using that she zoomed in and overwrote the area of the picture that held the numbers. She saved the file, reopened to check it. Then she deleted it. Hopefully now, even if they did retrieve the file, there was nothing left to find.

It was easier to look at the pictures now. Not only had she seen them before, so the shock was gone, she felt differently now. The fault lay entirely with Jason. He had been the adult. He had been the abuser. No one to blame but him. The young men and women in the images had only done what they had been persuaded, groomed to do. They hadn't, despite what Madison had said, actually been mature enough to really understand what they were doing or consent to it. Looking at some of the facial expressions, she thought they might have been under the influence of drink or drugs.

She found the images of Madison, again opening the files and blanking out details. Well, blanking out everything actually. They were all made into big black squares. Again, she saved, reopened to check, and then deleted.

She huffed out, that at least was one thing she could hand over.

The thing was, if they did have Jason, he might have told them what they were looking for. She copied the style of the cypher into her own notebook, making sure that when they decoded it, it wouldn't say what Jason had left. The first five letters she left the same, to ensure that they looked like they had the right codes, but after that it was all different. She considered making the rest a rude message but decided working it out would be too much trouble, she only needed to fool them for a few minutes to make the exchange. The rest she simply filled randomly. Given that the other sheet of paper had been folded and yellowed by the heat of the tank, she had to do something to mimic that. She whacked the temperature gauge right up, folded the torn page and hooked it over the slat in the air con. She didn't know how successful that would be in colouring the paper, but she had to try something and lighting a candle in a hotel room wasn't a wise move given the sprinkler system.

The other item of course, was a key. She wasn't sure what to do about that. Handing over the real key wasn't an option, but she would have to give them something. She hadn't seen anything that looked vaguely like a locksmith while walking around the city, but then again, she hadn't been looking.

What she did know, was that most gyms had lockers. And though she didn't have any proper fitness gear with her, she had a pair of trainers, some leggings, and a t-shirt. It would do.

To reach the gym felt like a trek to the bowels of the earth, but she found it and she was glad to see two things: that there were indeed lockers, and she was the only one there. The lockers required a one-euro coin, and she happily paid that to get the key.

* * *

Mac hung back in the reception and seethed to see Charles Linklater the bloody turd, smarm up to Elaine. It would seem that the smooth American was already acquainted with Elaine, and Mac wondered how. Had they previously met in the UK? Was Madison, another American, the mutual acquaintance? He couldn't credit that it was just coincidence. And Elaine looked way too cute when she blushed. That Linklater made her blush, crawled like ants under his skin. When Elaine had left and got in the lift, Linklater had merely turned to him, given a sarcastic wink, and then gone on to chat in fluent French with the receptionist. That took Mac's irritation to a whole new level.

More annoying still, Linklater was in fact, booking a room for that night. At least Mac now had Elaine's room number. Assuming she'd not lied. The way she had hesitated told him she hadn't keen to share, but had she had the sense to lie? There was one way to find out.

He made his way up to the floor she was on and wandered along the corridor. Not up to anything, just looking like he was going to or from a room. At the far end of the hall, before the turn into the fire escape, there was a window he was going to sit and wait there, but he heard a door unlock, begin to open, and realised that it was the room Elaine claimed to be using. He opened the door into the fire escape and stepped in, the large glass pane would allow him to see through. It was indeed Elaine stepping from room 310, he moved out of sight and waited. On the count of fifteen he looked out again. Elaine was at the lift, wearing what seemed to be an exercise outfit. Was she going to the gym? It didn't really matter. As long as she was out of the room, that was all he needed.

He kept the fire escape door open a crack, he heard the arrival of the lift and the footsteps of people getting out. He waited, expecting the other guests to move quickly into a room. Only the voices, the giggles and exchanges carried on.

Get in the room already!

He was impatient for the chance to try Elaine's room, but he really didn't want an audience. He considered stepping out, perhaps his presence would encourage them into a room, but again, he didn't wish to be seen. The minutes ticked by and the sound of a thump and the way that a woman moaned made his brows raise. They weren't really doing it in the hall were they?

He shifted position, put his head out of the door, quickly pulling it back.

Great, a couple having sex in the hotel corridor. Now he really couldn't go down there, the interruption would be too memorable.

Given how their thrust rhythm sped up, soon followed by the mans grunted exclamation, Mac realised he wasn't in for a long wait. Not an impressive performance, he judged, but each to their own. There was a little more giggling, then the sound of a door being opened and closed. With a sigh of relief, he opened the door and stepped into the corridor, heading to Room 310. The card reader door controls weren't the easiest to bypass, but he had his ways.

Another minute and he stopped, glaring at the door. His ways weren't working today.

And just to be really helpful, the lift binged to announce its arrival on the floor. Given that the lift was closer than the fire escape, he moved that way and stood to the side. The side one was less likely to look when getting out.

Thankfully, Elaine didn't look. She was obviously worrying about something, given the way she was chewing on her bottom lip. What the hell was she doing back so quickly? After she'd gone, to make it look good, he stepped into the lift, ordered it to go one floor up, which it did, and then to come one floor down again.

When he stepped out of the lift, he half expected Elaine to be walking back towards it, having collected whatever she must have forgotten. But she wasn't. Again, he moved to the window at the far end of the corridor. Propping himself against the ledge to sit and wait and watch.

And wait and watch he did. And nothing to see.

When he heard heavy footfalls on the stairs, he saw the shape of a man coming down, in jeans and a button-down shirt. The height gave the game away as much as anything else.

Linklater pulled open the door but stopped in surprise to see Mac standing there facing him.

"English."

"Yank."

"Get it right 'old boy'," the fake British accent grated. "I'm from Texas, the Confederate South. Biggest and best state."

"Alaska is twice the size of Texas."

"Great, well you go freeze with the bears, I'll stick with the warmth of the Lone Star state."

"Then why are you here?"

"Well, just maybe I can persuade li'l honey bear Elaine to join me for dinner." Then Linklater grinned. It was way too triumphant for Mac's comfort. "I'd wager I'd have more luck than you, or you wouldn't be cooling them there heels of yourn at this end of the corridor while the lovely lady is down yonder."

There wasn't much Mac could say to that, since it was true. And Linklater was already moving down the corridor at quite a swagger.

"You won't win." He hadn't meant to say it out loud, but it stopped Linklater in his tracks. The man stepped back.

"Sounds like I already did," he laughed, a look of smug self-satisfaction on his face. "What's that matter? You already struck out? Is that why you're skulking in corridors?"

Mac fell on cold superiority for an answer. "Despite the impression James Bond might give, we Brits don't take advantage of vulnerable woman for sexual or political advantage. But at least I know how good a kisser she is." The memory of how she felt pressed between him and that wall warmed him every time.

"Maybe she doesn't think you're as good a kisser."

Mac met the other man's eye with cold hauteur. Remembering too late that a gentleman doesn't kiss and tell. Wondering if Linklater had a point.

Linklater's look turned serious, he said quietly, "I saw the look you gave me in reception. I've never seen you angry before. It's unprofessional, and unlike you. If this case is getting to you, if she's getting to you, you should request reassignment."

Mac's hackles rose. "I've a job to do, and I'm not the one who gives up when the going gets tough."

The other man's eyes slipped away, but only for a moment. "I was following orders. You'd have done the same."

There was some truth in that, but it didn't make the death of a colleague and a civilian any easier to think on. "If you think Elaine's going to fall for your smarm, you don't know her as well as you think."

Linklater shrugged. "Given what I've heard, what I've seen from you, I don't think anyone knows her as well as they think." Linklater sauntered away. "Not even you."

Mac felt his ire rising. He wanted to tell the damn man how wrong he was, but he wasn't that kind of liar. Elaine was getting to him, was putting him off his game. In other circumstances requesting reassignment would be the right thing to do. Unlikely to be granted, but the right thing to do. Here he didn't have that option, not on silent running.

Stopping at 310, Linklater threw him another wink and knocked gently on the door.

It didn't open.

Linklater knocked again, then frowned over to Mac, who could only shrug. Surely Elaine hadn't gotten away again.

"Chuck?"

The voice came without the door being opened. Clearly the spyhole had been used. Mac had to strain to hear, but he heard.

"Hiya, darlin', just came to renew that offer of dinner."

"I was in the bloody bath!"

Mac heard that clear as a bell, and he grinned at Linklater.

"Well now, let me in and I'll be most happy to scrub your back for you."

"I don't think you want to know what you can scrub with that idea," Elaine's indignant voice came through.

Mac grinned at Linklater, who for the first time, possibly ever, wasn't looking quite so sure of himself.

"Darlin'—"

"Don't you darlin' me," Elaine said.

Then she must have said something that Linklater could hear, but Mac couldn't. Linklater moved to lean his forehead against the door, Mac could see that something was said, but couldn't hear what. The exchange continued, though not for long. Then Linklater stood upright and said, deliberately loudly enough for Mac to hear, "I'll look forward to it, darlin'."

Then the tall American strolled casually away, towards the lift at the other end of the corridor.

Mac considered following and demanding Linklater tell him what he would look forward to, but Mac was willing to bet that all he'd get from that gigantic ego was guff and nonsense. Besides, Elaine was his target, and she'd sent the man away. Thankfully.

Roughly an hour and a half passed before one of the hotel staff arrived with a tray at 20:15. Elaine came to the door wrapped in a robe and her hair in a towel, the waiter passed her the tray, left and she closed the door. That suggested she was settled in for the night.

Great.

CHAPTER TWENTY-SIX

The cold felt worse because Elaine still had wet hair. Even if it was under a fleece hat. There wasn't a drier in the room, but she needed to do this. She had to be sure, wet hair notwithstanding.

On reaching Tannek's address, she had intended to check the bar first, but as she approached, the man himself stepped from the bar. He glanced her way, hesitated on seeing her, then quickly moved toward the apartment building. Elaine broke into a run, thankfully the sprint was short before she stopped in front of him, stopping him.

"One question," she gasped, breathing harder than she should. "Just one and with the right answer I'll go away and never bother you again."

The Arab glared down at her. "This is not a game, Mrs Blake," he grated the words as he looked around him.

A game was exactly what this seemed to be to her. A deadly one, but still a game. She wondered who he had looked for, but that wasn't the question she needed to ask.

"When was the last time you saw Lazlo Zakis?"

His attention was back on her, then he pulled her over to the shadowed edge of the street.

"Does it matter?"

She nodded. "To me it matters hugely. Please. When did you last see him?"

"Three days ago."

"Shit." He seemed surprised by the expletive, she automatically apologised. Three days ago, that was when Lazlo started calling her. "And he wasn't under any duress at that time? He didn't look beat up or anything?"

"You said one question, and you'd go."

"I said I'd go with the right answer."

"I gave you the correct answer."

Good to know. "But it wasn't the right one. I need to know if he was free of duress three days ago."

Tannek frowned down at her, curiosity warring with annoyance. "Why should I answer your questions?"

Good question. She swallowed and tried for a persuasive answer. "Because men like you have all the power. I'm just bumbling around like an idiot. Well, I am an idiot. But I'm an idiot caught up in this now, and I can't just stop. Lazlo is my son and I love him, and I need to be certain that all this is real, and I'm not just being manipulated. Please, you can help me, and you all have to do is say yes or no to his being free from duress. Then I go away forever."

Again, he searched her face, looming over her. The tremble started in her belly, but soon overtook her limbs in a way that was obviously more than shivers from the cold. She felt herself trying to crawl back inside her own skin. This was how she felt when Jason had started hitting her. Jason at least had pulled back. Tannek wouldn't feel any such constraint.

"Yes."

The word was a much as blow as a punch would have been. She sagged against the wall, then he moved away. She called a thank you after him and pushed herself to her feet. Her knees felt like jelly as she started away, heading for the bar. She really needed a drink.

* * *

Mac caught up with Linklater in the hotel bar. The guy had the gall to be chatting up some other piece of skirt. One Mac sent scurrying away with a few well-chosen words.

"Thank you so much."

"You're welcome," Mac said as he took the suddenly vacated bar stool and ordered a coffee. "What's your interest in Elaine?"

"What's yours?"

"She's a British citizen, her welfare is a part of my remit."

"And my business is none of yours."

"Is that what this is? Business?"

"Oh, my dear boy, a woman like Elaine would be an absolute pleasure, the fat bottomed girls often are. They're so grateful for the attention."

Mac wanted to punch that smug face, but his phone rang. There was only one man he'd given this number to and Tannek's call was not a joy to take.

Mac left the hotel as soon as he understood what was going on. As he moved, he did his best to calm his old friend down, though in truth, Tannek's concerns did not seem as major as they might. He was already calmer than when Mac had visited earlier.

"You said you wouldn't let her out of your sight."

The accusation cut deep with Mac. He'd done his level best, but after seeing her take her dinner in her room, and that she had obviously been in the bath, he hadn't expected her to leave the hotel again tonight.

"That woman's slipperier that a greased-up eel." Mac was on the street and striding towards Tannek's place.

"Well, it rather looks like she's getting tanked up now."

"What?" Mac had no idea what Tannek was on about.

"She's gone to the bar, the woman might be smart enough to lose you, but she's fool enough to take a window seat in a public place."

"Something to be grateful for," Mac said starting to move at a jog.

"Are you sure she's not an agent for some other side?"

It was a question he kept asking himself. "Nothing I've found suggests so. Besides would an agent behave as she has today?"

"No, but it does suggest you're losing your touch."

Several insults came to mind, but now wasn't the time to use them. "It also suggests you're not as well hidden in Paris as you should be."

"No, and believe me, I will be relocating."

"As long as you don't cite any of this as the reason."

"Wouldn't dare," Tannek said. "Now get your girl — or should I say, old lady? And keep her the hell away from me."

As soon as Tannek ended the call, Mac rammed the phone into his pocket and moved the jog into a run. He nearly slipped rounding the corner into Tannek's street. The rain wasn't hard, but it hadn't stopped for hours, so the pavements were slick. Lactose burning in his calf and sucking wind, Mac looked to the bar, the light from inside showed him a woman with her back to the window, the lilac hat was one he'd seen in the pocket of her coat on the ferry. She had a large glass of white wine again. But her head was on the table.

The question was, what to do now?

Thus far, he'd been keeping back from her, but if she were willing to contact Tannek, maybe he should approach her. Seduction as a route to search wouldn't be original, but it was a classic that worked.

The risk of course was, that he'd already met Elaine, and he had no idea how she'd react to him. After all, he knew how she'd reacted to the photographs he'd given her. She's destroyed a laptop, would she try destroying him?

As he approached, he saw another man move towards Elaine. She sat up, and Mac hung back. He couldn't hear what was said, but a head shake was a no in any language.

The man sat down anyway.

Mac moved to the bar window, the tables were still out, but no one was standing outside in this rain, he zipped his coat and pulled up the hood to look closer. He didn't recognise the man. Though the sloppy lack of control in his movement and the way he didn't take no for an answer suggested ignorant ape or drunken bum, Mac couldn't make out which from here.

A flash of anger zipped through Mac as the other man put his hand on Elaine's shoulder. She tried to sweep it off, but the man kept hold. The man said something, moved closer, Elaine tried to move away, but was stopped by the end of the bench seat.

His tap on the window was more of a punch, the man and Elaine looked up, startled. He hoped the hood shaded his face well enough that she wouldn't recognise him. The man flipped him the finger and leaned, leaned right into where Elaine was holding her glass of wine and she threw it in his face.

The startled man reared, roared and stood, but as he wiped stinging alcohol out of his eyes, Elaine was already on her feet and rushing out. She saw Mac, threw a 'merci' in his direction, clearly not recognising him, as she rushed away. The wine-soaked man came after her, Mac stepped into the way, understanding a fair amount of the insults. When the man tried to get past him, reeking of alcohol, Mac pushed him back. When he tried again, Mac realised that the man wasn't going to give up. So, he took the opportunity to vent his current general frustration and punched the guy so hard in the face, his knuckles cracked. The pain was worth it when he heard the unmistakable sound of a nose breaking and the man falling back on his arse on the wet ground, blood pouring from his nose. Mac sauntered away, reminding himself not to whistle, then the urge disappeared as he imaged Linklater laughing, proving his point.

* * *

Why did some men assume that a woman drinking alone was available to anyone? She had no interest in any man, especially one who spoke a language she didn't understand. How difficult was the word 'no' to understand? It was pretty similar in all languages. She'd wanted to punch him. She wished she had.

If that guy outside hadn't slapped on the window, she'd have stayed totally petrified. Literally petrified as in turned to stone and unable to move. Then that bang had scared the bejeezus out of her, she'd thought she was looking up at the hooded figure of death. Then she found some courage or had gone crazy and thrown that glass of wine over the guy.

At least it hadn't been a good wine.

The odd thought actually made her laugh out loud as she turned into the street of the hotel. She got some odd looks, coming back late, clearly soaked from the rain, and laughing to herself. Still, what did she care? She wasn't likely to see any of these people again.

Back in her room, she sat down and wondered what the hell she could possibly do to prepare for what was ahead.

She had to meet Lazlo's contact at the Trocadéro tomorrow at noon, even though she did not know why.

She needed to make it make sense, and the fact that it was gone midnight didn't make a difference.

Think it through.

Okay.

Three days ago, Lazlo had called and said he was in danger. Well, him and Jason. And they want the evidence.

Evidence I don't have.

Shut up. I've faked it.

Then Madison said Lazlo had transport to either Frankfurt or Geneva. So, she'd gone to the Frankfurt flight, only Lazlo hadn't. Did that mean he'd gone to Geneva?

Tannek said he'd seen Lazlo three days ago, and he had not seemed under duress. So, was that before or after Lazlo had called her? The only way to find out would be to ask Tannek. Only she couldn't do that, because she'd promised not to. Which was a shit reason. It was fairly important, and worth breaking a promise for. Only she got the distinct impression that if she went anywhere near Tannek again, he'd hurt her. Possibly kill her. Her getting dead wouldn't help Lazlo.

None of it helped.

Maybe her brain was overheating.

She grabbed the hat off her head and threw it across the room. Grabbing handfuls of hair, she shook it out. The very back, where it had been bunched was still damp. She'd have to put a towel over the pillow to sleep tonight.

Since she was going into the bathroom anyway, she saw to her ablutions.

The big question, as she returned to the bed, wrapped the pillow in the big towel, and stripped off her clothes, and got in, was: what difference did it make?

Lazlo might be lying, he might not.

Lazlo might be in danger, he might not.

Lazlo could have gone to Frankfurt, or Geneva.

She didn't have the evidence.

They didn't know that.

Jason — well there she just didn't care either way.

And the truth was, she couldn't afford to care about the rest of it.

Because whatever else was true or false, she would be in the Jardins du Trocadéro at noon tomorrow.

Today.

If she got any sleep.

CHAPTER TWENTY-SEVEN

Despite all the activity yesterday, and the late night, Elaine had stayed awake worrying long into the night. Which was then followed by nightmares recalling fights she'd rather not have had, injuries she'd rather not have received or inflicted. The nightmares of her youth. Eric has left her with so many scars she doubted she could ever be free of.

Getting up held no attraction. Only she had no choice. There was much had to be done today. She lounged in bed till eight when her back nagged for being horizontal too long and she realised she still had to prepare herself for the day ahead.

So, she got up, dressed and dragged her hair up, still not sure about the change, but at least it was dry now. She shoved it under her fleece hat again. She hoped no one asked why, then she headed down for breakfast. Her stomach growled to remind her that while she had ordered dinner to her room, she had only been able to pick at it. The steak had been overdone to the point of cremation and the seasonal vegetables must have been last season's given how limp and tasteless they'd been. Not eating was not like her. She had never been one to skip meals, food being one of the few comforts in her life. Which explained why she'd stopped being a perfect ten more years ago than she wanted to think about. At least the large glass of house white had been sufficiently cool.

She dressed for the cold as best she could and made sure she was ready for the day ahead. Ready to move out of Paris as soon as she was able.

As she waited to order breakfast, she considered the idea of Belgian waffles, but decided they sounded sticky and over sweet. She filled up on a continental breakfast and worry. There was the man behind his paper again – if it was the same man. She hadn't looked that closely before.

You should start.

She really should make an effort to be more observant. She didn't know what she was doing, but Keira's call suggested she was being watched, so she should watch for watchers. Was that what Linklater was? Was he a plant? Was that why he's tried to schmooze her? Come to her room? Had he been sent to… She didn't want to think about what he'd been sent to do.

Until now she was probably being tracked electronically, use of her credit card in London, use of her passport to reach France, calls to Madison to reach Paris. Physically being followed was unlikely. Why would they? She had nothing of value.

That was, she had nothing of any actual value, but Lazlo believed she did, logically, whoever had him must believe it too. The threat to her son made her stomach clench. Her appetite evaporated, but she must eat. Failing for lack of nutrition would be stupid at this point.

As she ate, she tried to study the man behind the paper. It wasn't Tannek. And it wasn't the guy from yesterday, there was a difference in the way he sat. A blocked view didn't stop her imagination. She filled in the blanks, reckoned he was in the high five-foot range, but under six foot. His casual black slacks had been pressed well, and his shoes were…

she shifted slightly. Well-polished Doc Martins, soles gently rounded by use. The only thing missing was the yellow stitches, but there again, they were highly polished but not patent leather, use of black boot polish would, over time, recolour the yellow thread. She had a similar pair in her bag, she'd owned them about twenty-eight years, worn in, but not worn out. They were comfortable, all-day everyday wearable. More so than the new walking shoes in fact.

She saw the bottom edge of his casual jacket. She couldn't identify exactly what type of jacket, certainly not a traditional suit jacket. She supposed it was some kind of sports jacket, though not tweed, which she thought sports jackets were meant to be. She saw no shirt cuff at his wrist. His nails were neatly manicured, at least on his left hand which was the only hand she could see. He wore no wedding ring, though that didn't necessarily indicate.

She'd been watching him for a while when she realised, she hadn't yet seen him turn the page in the paper. Was he really reading or hiding?

Was that normal or was she paranoid?

It's not paranoia if they really are after you.

He moved the two sheets together to turn the page. As he appeared from behind the broadsheet, she got a quick glimpse before the paper got between them again. She didn't get enough of a look to be able to describe him, but there was dark hair, a clean-shaven jaw and she got the impression of intelligent, sharp eyes. She also spotted a high-necked sweater shirt – which explained the lack of cuffs.

She smiled as she sipped orange juice, remembering avant-garde movies and the cool cat Frenchmen in their polo necks. There were times when she liked the free flow way her brain made odd connections, she kept them inside precisely because they were free flowing and if they flowed out of her mouth, she'd get the worst for it.

* * *

What was she smiling about?

After yesterday morning's hanging around for nothing, Mac had been up at 5am, and paid the night porter to confirm Elaine Blake hadn't checked out. Just after six he'd had to check again and been forced to flirt with the receptionist as well as pay for her trouble only to learn that Mrs Blake was still in her room. Mind you, at his age, he should be glad women still considered him attractive enough to flirt with. 47 wasn't old, but he felt every year.

Confident he wouldn't be left behind today, he sat in the breakfast room, and waited. There was only so much coffee a man could drink, so he grabbed one of the complementary papers and started reading. The barrier proved useful when he saw Elaine Blake come in, waited as she ate, then he wondered what on earth she had to grin about?

"Good mornin', darlin'."

The grin slipped from Elaine's face as Linklater slid into the frame. Mac pushed down the emotional reaction, as he watched the American invite himself to join her at the table and sat down. It was galling that another agent had called him out for unprofessional behaviour, and been right. Punching that man last night has been the worst. He had to get a grip and do his job. He ordered and was quickly served coffee. Mac was glad to see Elaine carry on with her cooked breakfast and avoid many of Linklater's questions, refusing his offers of company.

"Thank you, but I really don't want to take up your time, besides, I'm going to the Louvre, they have these walking tours you wear headphones for, so it's not like I'd be able to listen and converse with you. Like I told you last night, my being in Paris is for me, I want to be alone. I need to come to terms with all that's happened. Besides, I took your card yesterday, if I change my mind, I'll call you."

Annoyingly, she kissed his cheek as she left, but that was only a farewell. Then, she disappeared up to her room, which meant Mac still had to wait some more.

The waiter brought Linklater his breakfast and threw Mac a dark look for taking up space for so little custom. Mac left money on the table and stood, not even pausing on the way out as he walked past Linklater.

"Strike two."

Mac left the hotel, bag in hand, to wait on the opposite side of the street for Elaine to appear.

He'd spent the night wondering about her and the last few days. Not an agent, not trained. So far, she'd been lucky. Though pissing Tannek off was a potentially fatal mistake.

It was clear that she was a talented amateur, but some of the errors she'd made could get her killed. If faced with the wrong people, her luck would run out and so would her time on Earth. She'd never survive an encounter with some of the people he'd had to deal with in his time. He needed to get the evidence away from her and get her out of the game as soon as possible. He'd keep eyes on her today and formulate a plan to search her and her belongs tonight. Seduction was an option, though getting a glass of wine thrown in his face was less welcome. As was getting a flea in his ear like Linklater. Still, it wasn't such a bad idea. The memory of how she'd felt when he'd pushed her against the wall flooded his blood south.

Stop it.

Job to do.

CHAPTER TWENTY-EIGHT

The Jardins du Trocadéro stood in beautiful peace as Mac approached, trailing Elaine, checking his watch. 09:53. Elaine had a long stride, and she had been pushing the pace. Now she had reached the gardens, she looked around and…

What was she up to? She seemed to be looking for someone or something. Did she have a meeting? If so, it made sense to check out the location first. It was the sensible thing to do. A professional thing to do. Again, that uncertainty arose again as to whether she was good at what she did or was just smart enough to follow some basic safety precautions. Of course, the problem with this particular precaution was that in all likelihood, the enemy was taking it too, and there could already be enemy agents staking the place out.

As she walked up the stairs on the west side of the gardens, along the array of fountains and towards the various museum buildings that hugged the northern edge, Mac took the matching east steps.

At the top, another nine steps waited and he took them up to the Plaza. Elaine appeared a moment later, the way she rubbed her thigh suggested that her legs ached after all those steps. To reduce the risk of her seeing him, he carried on walking. He'd lost count of the number of times he'd walked right by her the last few days and she hadn't noticed. *Definitely not a professional.*

While he lurked in the Plaza, she just stood, looking around. Searching for someone? Who did she expect?

Lazlo?

The younger man was the only person he could think…

Another man caught his attention. He was looking for someone too.

Damn it, out of time.

Elaine hadn't been spotted. He had to move now. He raced towards her, before she would appear in the other man's eye-line. He grabbed Elaine by the upper arm, trying to turn her away.

She swung, her knuckles connected with his jaw. It hurt. She didn't scream. He didn't loosen his grip.

He glared at her as she looked up with fear. No, not fear, utter terror. For the first time in this whole mess, her fear response finally matched the level of danger. Though she shouldn't be as afraid of him as she should the man who'd he'd spotted.

"Votre fils n'est pas ici, il ne sera pas."

She blinked at him stunned. "What?"

French had been automatic because they were in Paris. He had forgotten that Elaine didn't speak it. He forced himself not to give into the throbbing pain in his thickening split lip.

"Your son isn't here," he said. "Nor will he be."

"Mademoiselle?"

They both turned her to the voice. A young man in street clothes. He was black, big, and tough-looking. He also looked concerned and potentially a threat for all the right reasons.

"C'est personnel, entre ma femme et moi," Mac told him.

He could feel Elaine's tension under his hand. She looked at the man, her head hung, turned slightly towards Mac, as if into his protection. Then she slumped and raised her left hand and pointed to her wedding ring.

"Pardonnez-moi."

The young man scowled at Mac.

Mac spoke fluently. The man shrugged, nodded, and moved away.

"What did you say?" Elaine hissed.

"That while his actions weren't necessary, he did the right thing."

"Oh."

Did she sound impressed? It didn't matter, as he tried to pull Elaine away, she pulled back and turned to him.

"Don't make a scene," he told her between clenched teeth.

"I'll fucking scream my head off if you don't let go." The harsh hiss stayed low enough not to carry beyond them, but she clearly meant every syllable.

He stopped trying to pull her away but didn't let go; she pulled in an obvious breath as if to start screaming. Was she crazy?

"There are some very bad men in this plaza, Mrs Blake, and they're looking for you."

She breathed in. "But—"

"But nothing, Mrs Blake, you need to listen to me. Trust me, that hat is not a good disguise."

"It's not meant to be." As she said it, she pulled the hat off and her untamed curls sprung out, no longer mousy brown, but bright copper.

His brows rose, then he blinked as he looked at the hair. "Better." His compliment seemed to startle her as much as it did him.

A movement out of the corner of his eye gave him some warning. With nowhere to hide, he had to shelter them in plain sight. He grabbed both her upper arms and dragged her to him, pressing his lips to hers, she reared, startled, but for once didn't protest. Her eyes closed, possibly she was long sighted. An old girlfriend had once explained that being long sighted meant a face so close was painful to focus on, so the best option was closed eyes. That at least gave him the opportunity to scout around a little, shifting her to one side to keep her out of view. The man moved on and Mac broke contact though he didn't let Elaine go.

"Who did you see?"

Her question surprised him.

"Your eyes moved over my head, widened, narrowed and then you kissed me. Who did you see?"

"You don't want to know."

"Lazlo or Jason?"

He moved back, and for a moment looked down at her. "Neither."

"Then I'm not interested, Ladderman."

He reared, stung by the name. She tried to pull away, but he wasn't letting go. "Mrs Blake, please, we need to get you out of here."

This time he yanked, and she moved.

"Who are 'we'?"

He glanced at her, then back over her head. "Right now, it's you and me against four of them. Come on."

"What four?"

He wasn't answering that question, just because he'd recognised Ulrich Demko, Illyana Kuznetsov and two thugs who were looking to them for direction didn't mean that he wanted to tell Elaine about them. Their presence here was a huge worry. Both Ulrich and Illyana were mercenaries, highly paid ones, they wouldn't work without significant renumeration. That they were working together, was not a first, but it was an unusual event. And it meant someone with deep pockets was behind all this. The missing evidence must be more than valuable enough to lose another agent over. Figuring out who the money man was, would be his next problem.

"Okay then, how did you get here?"

He wished she'd move faster, stop resisting him. "Followed you."

"Why?"

"For the evidence Jason stashed. I want it." His eyes scanned behind her. "But I don't want either one of us to die for it."

They had reached the wide road. On the far side of the street a statue stood on a plinth, a mounted man looking down towards the Eiffel Tower. The horse's head was down and low, for a second Mac got the impression that Ferdinand Foch scowled specifically at him. Thankfully a taxi quickly pulled over at his raised arm and he bundled Elaine into the back seat.

He heard her grumbling about never getting a taxi so quick, as he instructed the driver as to their destination. As they pulled off, he sat back to find her scrutinising him. Those eyes a little too assessing to be comfortable.

"You didn't answer my question," he said.

She met his eye and ignored his words. "Did that hurt?"

He frowned. "Not getting an answer?"

"Your lip."

"It hurt when you punched me, when it split. For a second." He licked away a little blood that had pooled in the crack. "But I've been hit harder."

"Not then, just now, when you didn't exactly kiss me," she said. "I tasted blood. I hope you're clean."

He reared in affront, then his eyes narrowed, and he looked away. "Kissing you neither hurt nor excited." A small, cruel lie.

"Good. Try it again and I'll bite you."

He turned to her, his brow raised, one side of this mouth twisted up. "I'll look forward to that."

This time she curled her lip and turned her head away.

"Do you have the evidence?" he asked.

"Where are we going?"

His eyes narrowed. "You answer my question, I'll answer yours."

She simply looked at him, meeting his eye. "Not necessary. All I have to do is wait. Wherever you told this guy to go, he'll get there, eventually. He'll give me the answer even if you don't and I won't have to give you any answer to get it."

Her chin tipped up imperiously, and she looked out the side window. This was oddly fun, and there shouldn't be fun with the people who were after her. This was serious. Deadly serious. Her hand remained under his and that was a vulnerable extremity. He didn't like the plan that came to mind, but he would do what was necessary. He pulled her hand onto his lap, took hold of her little finger in one hand the rest in the other, applying pressure to bring the little finger wider than it would naturally go.

"What are you doing?"

Impressively she didn't try to pull away, that would have caused her more pain.

"Testing your staying power." He smiled as the blood drained from her face.

"Really?"

Her jaw clenched; a new tightness appeared around her eyes. There was pain in her expression, but defiance too. Her core was stronger than he'd estimated. She had more staying power than he expected, but everyone had their limits. He increased the pressure on her finger. If he increased it much more, it would break.

"No," she said suddenly.

He frowned. "No?"

"No," she answered. He watched her swallow, her eyes looked wetter now. Finally, a response. Her other hand had grabbed the front of the seat, squeezing the padding as she tried to cope with the pain. "Please," she said, her voice low so the cabbie wouldn't hear. "I'm sorry, I don't have the evidence. I don't even know what the evidence is."

He eased the pressure off her finger. He didn't know what the evidence was either, so he could hardly blame her for her ignorance. "What did you find in that lagging?"

"Nothing."

More pressure. This time her hand came off the seat and tried to force his hands closer, to ease the pressure on her digit.

"Jesus! You'll break my finger if you keep going."

"That's the point, Mrs Blake," he said coldly. "What did you find in that lagging?"

Her eyes watered. He saw her fear again, and the wish to be defiant. She licked her own lips, and that shouldn't make him want to kiss her again, but it did. Without releasing the sideways twist, the easiest way to break a little finger, he pulled a little forward. She gasped and shifted, her lips compressed, then she parted them with a small expulsion of air.

"The photos you gave me, did you give them to your bosses too?"

The question surprised him. He couldn't make out how this woman's mind worked. "Most of them."

"Which did you take out?"

Her eyes studied him, looking for something even as tears of physical pain welled in her eyes.

"The worse ones of Madison," he admitted.

Now her eyes closed slowly as if in relief. "Thank you."

Unbelievable. "I'm in the process of breaking your finger to extract information and you're thanking me?"

As she opened her eyes, a tear dripped from her lashes. "You spared my daughter, that's more important." Her voice wobbled even as she continued. She had a great deal more steel inside than he could ever have imagined. "Besides, the tendons are already overstretched, that break is a millimetre away."

Probably less than that, but he maintained the hold. Only the need to breathe moved anything.

"All right." It was a squeak of pain. "Yes, I found something."

He released the pull if not the twist. "What?"

"A cypher. I didn't know what it was when you were there. I decoded it over the following couple of days. But it doesn't make any sense."

The hold on her hand didn't change. He kept eye contact, searching for a lie. He saw none. "What did it say?"

"Watch tower."

His eyes switched between hers, that gaze held only pain and honesty. He released the pressure on her little finger, she sagged slightly in relief.

"Does it mean something to you?" she asked.

His chin shifted up, turning his pressed lips into an inverted 'u'. "It's the publication of the Jehovah's Witnesses."

"Yeah, that was the first thing I thought of too," she admitted, her tone full of defeat. "I said it didn't make sense."

She shifted away, turned to look forward as any normal passenger would.

"That's it?" Mac asked. "That's all you got?" it wasn't much to work on.

"What were you expecting?"

"Something that made sense would have been nice."

"Doubtless, but I can't make it make sense to you because it doesn't make sense to me. Are you going to keep looking into it?"

He didn't have a choice. That evidence was his only way home. He gave no response.

"What's going to happen now?" she asked. "To Lazlo? To Jason?"

"Jason is dead," he reminded her, though he was having a tough time believing it. "My colleagues are looking for Lazlo." Another lie, Tannek had refused to help without orders, and they both knew those orders wouldn't be coming any time soon.

As she scrutinised him, he saw the little girl lost inside. "Is that meant to reassure me?"

"Elaine, do you have any concept of what the people we are up against would do to you if they discover you don't have the evidence they want?"

The way she swallowed suggested she had a reasonable guess. "But what will they do to Lazlo?"

"Let me worry about that."

She laughed, bitterly. "You think anything could stop me worrying about it?"

No, probably not. She might not be a biological mother, but she was a very real mum. "I understand that this will be difficult for you. But you're playing with fire out here. Go home, stay safe, and if you get any more contacts from Lazlo, let Keira know. She'll contact my people."

She didn't look in the least reassured and he didn't blame her. Keira could get a message to his people, but Number Two wouldn't necessarily give it any credence, or act on it. Given the money that had gone missing.

"All you'll achieve in the field is to get yourself killed."

The light faded from her eyes as she dropped her gaze.

"Take the money, go home. Give it back. You'll be fine." He didn't entirely believe that, but he had no better idea how to keep her safe.

When she spoke again, her voice was dull. "Where are we going?"

"Gare Saint-Lazare."

Now she looked up at him. "Why?"

"It's where you left your case."

"Ho—" Her eyes widened. "Oh." Realisation dawned. "You've been following me."

Finally, she was catching on.

"How long?" Her voice was quaking. "How long have you been following me?"

That information was unlikely to give her any comfort.

"Were you on the ferry?" She was close to tears. "Oh God, you've been right behind me all time?"

He didn't respond.

"You were the guy at the window last night." She looked down at his hand, his right hand, the one where the middle knuckle was red and swollen. "Oh my god, did you punch that creep?"

CHAPTER TWENTY-NINE

"First link?"

Elaine turned to him as she retrieved her holdall from the locker with a sharp tug. She was far too aware of Ladderman next to her, not to mention the ache in her right little finger. She had thought he really would break it. But he'd helped her last night, sort of. Well, he'd helped by slapping on the window. His having punched a creep for her was still unconfirmed. "Eh?"

"You said the Jehovah's Witnesses paper was the first link you considered for the Watch Tower," he pressed.

The black jumper and suit looked good on him, as did his being brown haired rather than the blond she's originally seen on him. Privately she admitted the greying temples added extra appeal.

"I did." He took her arm, leading her out of the station.

"What were the other links?"

She shrugged. "Nothing any more illuminating. I ran through a number of different ideas. Checkpoint Charlie was one. You're probably already aware that that was in Berlin, but I had to research it. Berlin however doesn't match with anything else I know about Jason. Not that I know much, as I recently discovered. I guess you're smarter than me, and have more information, so if you can link watch tower to something, I'd like to hear it."

They went back to the street and again a taxi came immediately to Ladderman's call. The case was stored in the boot, and they sat in the back. He returned his grip to her hand, separating her little finger again.

"Then there's the song," she said rapidly before he started pulling on the already abused digit.

He frowned. "Song?"

"*All Along the Watchtower* by Jimi Hendrix. Jason's a bigger fan than I am, but I am aware of the song. I found a movie on IMDB, which I haven't seen because frankly it struck me as naff. But that was as far as I got. By the way, you've got really hot hands."

October in Paris wasn't warm, certainly not in the wide-open spaces of the station, and without gloves, her hands were freezing. She held up her left hand and waved her fingers at him.

"Couldn't warm this one for me too, could you?"

The way his lips pursed suggested an attempt not to laugh. Which only made her smile more. It would be nice to smile more, but things were awful, so why she felt better around him was anyone's guess. She wondered if she should tell him the rest, but to play this game she had to keep some cards close to her chest – while she still had cards. Or a chest.

"What do you really think is happening with Lazlo?"

His look turned stony cold.

"There's no way I'm not going to worry about it, so you may as well answer. And by the way, there is no right answer. I'm so sick of thinking both sides, flipping from one to the other. I don't know who I can trust." And that most definitely included the man she was with.

His eyes were very serious, as he drew in a breath. "I'm beginning to suspect that he works for the other side."

"Other side of what?" She asked. "Oh yeah." She hung her head in embarrassment. "Stupid question. Wait." She looked back at Ladderman, leaned closer, spoke quieter. "If the evidence is of treachery, do you think it's against him?"

His lack of answer was unhelpful. They arrived at yet another train station. Gare du Nord.

With a sinking feeling, Elaine left the car and retrieved her case as Ladderman paid the driver. This time when he reached for her hand, he hesitated and took the left.

"You really have got cold hands," he said.

"Cold hands, warm heart." She smiled and grabbed the case, wheeled it behind them. "But mostly just no gloves."

As he led inside the station, she noticed the Eurostar sign and realised his plan. She waited as he purchased a ticket, waited and ran everything through her mind. Possible—yes. Doable was more questionable.

"Track 13," she said as he re-joined her.

"Sorry?"

"Well, that," she pointed at the ticket in his hand, "is to send me to London, and the next Eurostar to St Pancras leaves in half an hour. From Track 13. I read the departure boards." She pointed them out. "Track 13 is this way."

She mooched, and he slowed to match her pace.

"You're taking this very well."

She shrugged. "Would screaming and shouting change anything?"

"Only the way you get treated."

She laughed. "Do you always work the whole, 'treat 'em mean, keep 'em keen' methodology?"

His brows arched up aristocratically. "You're not keen and I haven't been that mean."

"You tried to break my finger," she pointed out.

"You punched me."

"True." She smiled. Passport control limited how far Ladderman could go. She joined the queue and let him wait beside her.

The queue moved at a snail's pace. There didn't seem to be anything more worth saying. Which didn't stop things going around in her head. She dragged in a sudden breath and twisted to face him. Only one look at those stoney eyes and the words died in her throat.

"What?" he demanded as she started to deflate.

"Nothing." She straightened to stare directly ahead.

"Elaine." This tone was warning. "Tell me."

"It's stupid."

"Probably, but I'll listen and if it is stupid, I'll tell you."

"A few days ago I was totally clueless about what Jason and Steve really do — did for a living. But Keira always knew."

"So?"

"So, Keira was having a sexual relationship with Jason. Jason who had this evidence that he didn't pass over to his bosses. Jason who didn't tell me anything. What if he was telling Keira? She may be not one of you, but she does have access to at least two of you, one of whom may not really be one of you. Am I being more paranoid than I should be?"

The absolute worst of listening to that suggestion was that it reinforced some of his own suspicions. Now was not the time to admit that. "This is a dangerous game, Elaine."

"Yeah." Like him, she kept her voice down. "That's why it's fun." They moved with the queue.

"It's not fun."

"Spoilsport." She smiled up at him. "And there it is again."

He frowned. "What?"

"The look that questions my sanity." Now next in line, she took her true passport from her bag and took hold of the ticket he had. He didn't let go.

"This is no game for amateurs, so go home, Elaine. At least that way, if I need to, I'll know where to find you."

She shook her head, her mouth twisted in a bitter smile "'Amateur night is over', huh?"

He looked confused.

"It's a quote. From a film. *Jumpin' Jack Flash*." As Passport Control waved her through, she offered a farewell smile. "Goodbye, Ladderman."

CHAPTER THIRTY

Watch Tower.

The words played on Mac's mind as he watched the train pull away. He'd been unable to see Elaine physically onto the train, separated by border control, but she'd been compliant enough. No one remained on the platform once the train departed. With one less thing to worry about he could concentrate on where the clue might lead. Lazlo was on his own. Jason was dead. Though Mac questioned if the report of death might not be premature. It wouldn't be the first official lie told.

Elaine had mentioned two films. He didn't know either, but he knew a man who might. He reached Tannek's apartment, leaning on the bell until he heard the buzz that announced the door had unlocked.

Tannek waited in the doorway, leaning against the jamb. He didn't look happy. "What happened to silent running?"

"I need to pick your brain." Mac stood in front of the man. "Goin' to let me in?"

With a shrug, Tannek pushed himself off the doorway and paced into the flat. The room he walked into, the main one of the flat, was small. A threadbare couch, a flat screen TV and some kind of streaming box. In the corner sat a desk with chair and way more computer equipment than that desk could cope with – so much it overflowed onto the floor.

Tannek slumped down onto one end of the couch, indicated Mac should also sit down with a flick of the wrist. Mac was too wired. His turn to pace.

"Elaine said something tonight that's got me worried," Mac said. "Well, two things actually. But the main one was about Kiera Southgate."

"What about her?"

"Well, we know that she has clearance, Steve could talk to her if he needed to, and she was bound by the Official Secrets Act to talk to no one else about such things, not even their daughter. She was rechecked every year."

"Yes."

Mac stopped at the end of the room and turned to face Tannek. "What if those checks got it wrong? What if she's the traitor in our midst?"

That Tannek didn't just laugh in his face at how ridiculous the idea was, said a great deal. A worrying great deal.

"This is the part where you're supposed to tell me I've been in this game so long and I'm seeing what isn't there."

Mac counted three heart beats before Tannek answered.

"You've been in this game so long, I think you see what is there and the rest of us miss."

Mac needed clarification. "You think it's possible?"

"I've been in this game so long I see many things as possible. What are you going to do about it?"

"I have no idea." Mac's shoulders slumped. "I'm risking my job just talking to you, if I report back without that evidence, I'm fired."

Tannek nodded. "A dilemma. What was the other reason you came here?"

"You're the biggest film buff I know."

Tannek frowned. Films weren't a frequent topic of discussion. They were colleagues not friends, they only met for work, but a month-long stint in a safe house some years ago had familiarised each to the other's penchants.

"You ever heard of a film called *Watchtower*?" Mac asked.

Tannek glowered at him. "There are a few, none particularly good. There's an Iranian one I couldn't make head nor tail of; a serial killing in Oregon, and one soul searching in Turkey. I have a feeling there's a zombie one too – *Dead Rising Watchtower*? Haven't seen that one. Why?"

Mac didn't have any better idea now than when he'd been running up the stairs.

"What about *Jumpin' Jack Flash*? You ever seen that?"

"Several times."

Mac stopped and frowned. "Does it say anything about amateur night being over?"

Tannek nodded. "That's one of my favourite lines."

"It is?"

"Mr Lincoln, some undeclared agency member, probably CIA, says to the hero of the piece, played by Whoopi Goldberg, 'Amateur night, Miss Doolittle, is over. Get off the stage before you get carried off.'"

Not quite what had been said, but close enough. "Sounds threatening."

Tannek shrugged. "That was the intention. Not that she listened, but hey, that's amateurs for you. What's your point?"

She didn't listen.

"Bollocks!"

Elaine never intended doing what I told her.

He ran back down the stairs, had a moment's struggle with the door and ran onto the street. He reached the Seine before he realised, cursed in various languages, turned full circle and ran his hands through his hair.

She got off the train.

"I should have physically put her on the damn train! Gone with her."

He fought the urge to punch something, he clenched fists and jaw as he stalked back to the Gare Saint-Lazare. He carried emergency supplies with him, but when Elaine stowed her bag, he'd felt secure in stowing his. He had no idea what she was up to now, but he needed to be ready for it and all his supplies were in that bag.

He had to work out what Elaine did instead of getting on that train.

* * *

Through the simple expedient of going into the ladies, putting a bobble hat over her newly bright hair, and reversing her coat, Elaine had effectively made herself invisible before calmly walking off the platform and away from Gard du Nord. A little disappointment crept in that Ladderman didn't stop her, but also an ounce of pride. He'd followed her for days without her spotting him, so her evasion evened the score.

Now Elaine wondered what to do. She didn't want to go home. She hadn't finished what she came here for. Ladderman was right that she was unlikely to survive this, though she'd fight tooth and nail to make sure she did. And if – when – she did, then what? It was unlikely to be a good idea to go home. What she had were clues at best, not the evidence. Until that was recovered, people would be coming after the clues. And it wasn't enough to get rid of the clues, someone would just take that out on her. Physically. Which was likely to be painful.

Thinking of pain brought her back to reality. Her hands were painfully cold, and she jammed them into her pockets. She should buy gloves.

She checked her watch. There was still time.

CHAPTER THIRTY-ONE

More confident on the Metro system today than yesterday, Elaine found the route to Trocadéro easily. En route she made sure she had everything she was prepared to hand over. It might look like it, but it wasn't what Lazlo's captors thought they would be getting. As she stood to take the exit, she put the holdall over her shoulders like a ruck sack. It wasn't the most comfortable, it wasn't designed to be used this way, but it was the most secure for now and left both hands free.

The Metro spilled out on the opposite side of the square from the gardens. Her stomach growled. She wished she had eaten more breakfast.

Across the street was the open area with the mounted man statue. And a great view clear all the way down to the Eiffel Tower. Paris really was rather beautiful. It was such a shame she couldn't enjoy it properly. Around her people were going about their daily lives, Elaine wasn't sure what she was doing, what she hoped to achieve. She wondered why that kid had to keep blowing that bloody whistle. It was so shrill, people were looking. The last thing she wanted right now was to be seen.

Right now.

She stopped as her brain kicked in. She would prefer not to be noticed or to attract attention right now, but she could foresee a time very soon when that might be exactly what she would need to do.

A twist and she spotted the kid with the whistle, actually it was a gang of kids. Kids was probably an unfair description. Teenagers, and they were laughing and joking and blowing that whistle, actually she noticed that there were three with whistles. She couldn't figure out what gender each was, but honestly, she didn't care. Gangs were always dangerous, especially for a short woman who didn't speak their language, still, she had to try.

"Paronnez-moi," she said tapping the one group member on the shoulder.

They all went quiet and looked at her, or glared, there was even a sneer.

Then the whistle blowing one said something to make the others laugh.

"Yeah, you know what kid, I'm English and I couldn't give a stuff if you're insulting me. Your opinion is irrelevant."

"Then what you want, English pig?"

Not the best example of grammar or manners Elaine had ever come across, and an irritating reminder of the need to lose some weight.

"A whistle." She indicated the item in his insulting mate's hand. "I'll buy one off you for ten euro. Dix euro?"

A chitter circled the group, suggesting they all understood perfectly well.

"Vingt," the boy with the whistle said.

She frowned at him. Her French was so bad that she hadn't a clue what he said.

"He says twenty."

Elaine looked at the translator. "And I say no. Ten. Dix." Given that the whistles were usually available for a couple of quid the guy was well in profit. She pulled notes from her pocket, took a ten euro and held it up. "Ten euro. One whistle."

Of course, she was well aware that the whole gang was more interested in the wodge of cash than in the ten euro note. She also reckoned it was a little over two hundred euro. The rest of the money she'd changed was distributed in other pockets and through the bag.

The boy who did the translating looked to his mates. Elaine realised that this was where she could so very easily come unstuck.

"You want this?" she indicated the money. "It's about two hundred euro. You want this, I want more than just a whistle."

"What?" the translator curled his lip and asked.

After carefully putting the tenner back into the money bundle, Elaine explained.

* * *

Cormac Letterman could hardly credit what was happening. He'd mistrusted Jason Blake for years, and never found a scrap of evidence against him. And he'd never had any reason to think much about his mouse of a wife. And here he was struggling to keep up with said mouse.

A lot of sweet talking had been required to get the security guard to let him look at the footage from Track 13 and the Eurostar he'd tried to put Elaine on. He'd needed two run throughs to see it, and three to be sure. Elaine had put on a different hat and reversed her jacket, the very same and simple things he'd done when following her, and he hadn't seen her any better than she'd seen him.

He swore.

The only positive from there was that he saw her going into the Metro station. Not that was much help, this station security didn't have access to the underground CCTV so Mac couldn't follow her progress from there. She could have gone anywhere.

Of course, he'd had to promise the guard an evening out, fine dining, good wine, a hint at more. When he was done, he gave thanks, a quick kiss, and reminded his companion to meet him outside at eight that evening. On the road before the station again, he took a big gasp of the cold air and let it out slowly. He wouldn't be back at eight, possibly never to Paris again, that guard didn't seem the forgiving sort, and while Mac knew he'd win in a fight, the guard was too big a bloke to take on unnecessarily.

* * *

Elaine felt sick. She couldn't really guess how this was going to work out. She had plans for the whistle, but whether it would do any good was debatable. In fact, the longer she sat and waited, the more debatable all her scheming seemed. Stupid even. Doomed to failure.

She shook that one out of her head. Jason's voice could nag in her mind as much as it liked. She wasn't here for him. She was here for Lazlo.

Continuing to sketch she tried to think of the best outcomes. She'd get away with Lazlo, and then they'd go… somewhere. Whatever Jason might have said, even made her believe, she wasn't a bad traveller. Solve the puzzle, just to solve the puzzle, after all if she did find the evidence, that was her shield. Her safety net. Her ticket back to freedom. Or her death warrant.

The pencil she was sketching with stopped over the page.

Was she here for Lazlo? That was how it had started, yes, but now? Now she had a pretty good impression that there was something screwy about this whole situation and that maybe she couldn't trust her son as much as her maternal instincts wanted to. It didn't matter though, because now she was here for her.

She wanted to do this, realised she might not survive it, but she had to try. This mouse wouldn't roar, but she'd scream in the face of her opponents before she was done. Probably before the day was done. Or the hour was up.

The shrill sound cut the air, that same gang of teens making their way onto the plaza at the top of the Jardin du Trocadéro. Just kids mucking around, all looked normal.

Her stomach twisting and turning, Elaine put the pad back away, she checked her left pocket, everything she wanted was in there. She was about to stand up and move across, then she saw him.

Lazlo was stepping out of a car that had pulled suddenly and quite dangerously to a stop on the left of the open square – far enough back by the museum so anyone on the square itself wouldn't see it. He didn't look under duress, quite relaxed in fact. He wore a half smile as he turned back. Elaine realised that he was helping a woman from the vehicle.

The woman who stood was taller than Lazlo, black hair in a bob under a golden yellow beret, a matching scarf circled her neck, the rest of her clothes were black. As soon as the door was closed the car sped off.

They had arrived dead on time.

Don't even think that word.

From where Elaine sat in the semicircle of benches behind Foch's statue, she saw the way the woman took Lazlo's arm. Proprietorial perhaps, possessive but not controlling. Not the way a captor held a captive.

While she was close enough to recognise her son, she wasn't close enough to see any real detail on the woman, only that she was taller than Lazlo, and she didn't seem to be wearing built-up shoes. What she was wearing was skin-tight black trousers, possibly jeans, and she had strong if skinny legs. Her puffer jacket was short, bulky enough to hide a lot. A pistol for example.

That idea washed cold through Elaine. She didn't know what the gun laws were in France. But if people were prepared to take hostages, they probably wouldn't care too much about breaking gun laws. What if that woman had a pistol in her pocket? What if that was why Lazlo appeared relaxed from a distance, because he was being controlled by a small but lethal weapon?

Elaine sat on the cold stone bench and felt her knees go to jelly. Talk about being out of her league. She dragged a sharp, as yet unused pencil from the pack she'd brought. A 9H. She'd never use a lead that hard for drawing anyway. The current potential of use was probably not a great idea, but she remembered seeing the mess that a boy had made of his hand by jabbing a pencil into it when they had been at school. So, there was a tiny chance that she could do some damage with one.

Oh dear God, she was taking a pencil to a gunfight. *Draw your own conclusions.*

A few deep breaths were needed to avoid hyperventilation. There were things she couldn't control, but for now, she would go with what she could control, which at the moment seemed limited to her own heart rate.

* * *

There was only one place Elaine would go now, Mac realised. The Trocadéro. The place she had scoped out that morning. He cursed himself for not working it out immediately. Something about Elaine Blake was throwing him off at every turn. All he had to do now, was get there, save Elaine, get what she had and send her home. Though that last idea sat like acid in his stomach.

CHAPTER THIRTY-TWO

The vibrating in her pocket took a while to penetrate Elaine's brain, but when she pulled it out, she saw a withheld number, she also saw that doubt had kept her motionless for too long, she was two minutes late for the meeting, and a glance told her that Lazlo was making a call.

She pushed herself away from the bench, moved behind the statue, using it to shield her from the area where she was supposed to be meeting him.

"Hello?"

"Mum?"

"Lazlo, oh thank God!" She had no idea how she should play this. By ear definitely, but poorly was probably her only option.

"What happened? Where are you?"

"I went to that plaza like you asked, and this bloke grabbed me." The best lies always hid within the truth; she couldn't remember who told her that. "I thought he was your guy."

"What did he want?"

"The evidence, same as you. That's why I thought it was your guy." Elaine found the lies tumbling from her lips. She even hit the right note of trembling fear. She was oddly proud of herself, an untapped talent for mummery. "Then he said something that didn't quite gel. But by then, he'd bundled me into a taxi. He looked blank when I mentioned your name. So, when the taxi slowed, I jumped out. I got away from him."

There was a pause, Lazlo trying to take it all in. "So where are you now?"

She took a loud and obviously shaky breath. "I'm on my way back to you." She sniffed. "I think. I'm not even sure where I'm going. I just had to get away from that man." She forced a sob. "I'm coming to you, Lazlo. I promise. I'm coming."

"Did you give the guy anything?" Lazlo demanded.

"No." This time she full-on faked crying. She doubted Lazlo would notice it was fake since he'd never seen her cry before. "Oh Laz, I wouldn't do that to you. I swear. As soon as I realised, he wasn't taking me to you, I got away. I'm on my way to the gardens, I'll be at that plaza on the north end soon." She didn't have to fake the heavy breathing, she was breathless with nerves already. "I'll be there. Wait for me."

She disconnected the phone and wondered what to do. She had to go over there, act like she was the scared little woman that everyone expected her to be. Though in fairness she wasn't that tall, and she was pretty much scared witless right now.

Car horns blared off to her side. Good thing she was off the phone before that happened; hearing that on the phone would have told Lazlo how close she really was. She looked in the direction the sound had come from and saw that the traffic heading that way was slowing to a standstill, she looked the other way and a couple of tour coaches heading towards her.

Who the hell takes a tour of Paris in the winter?

There again, off season, cheaper. And well, it's Paris so why not?

The French certainly weren't shy of using their horns. As the vehicles effectively parked themselves across the five-car wide road between her and the plaza, a plan, probably a foolhardy one came to mind.

Elaine leaned against the plinth of the statue and waited until the traffic was thick enough. She darted from behind the statue and ran towards the coaches. She nipped between them, winding her way between the rows of vehicles to get to the pavement the other side. There she stopped and made a show of panting as she looked around. Lazlo was still with the woman in the golden beret, but now Elaine noticed two other men dressed in black and looking like, well, thugs. That two of them seemed to keep eyeballing Lazlo and his friend only made her more certain.

This wasn't going to be easy or fun.

Standing she looked up to see Lazlo standing watching her. She smiled as best she could and started towards him.

Her heart thumped so hard, she feared it would choke her. Blood rushed in her ears. The five steps she had to take from the wide pavement to the sweep of the plaza resembled Everest. Her thigh muscles were trembling as she took each one carefully. She hoped she looked sufficiently shattered: she was feeling it.

She kept her eyes on Lazlo, though she had good enough peripheral vision to see that two of the thugs were closing in. They were the fit kind, strong but not overly muscled. She also noticed that the woman Lazlo was with stood slightly behind him, what might be a demure, subservient stance, or could be a better way to keep a weapon pressed into his back.

Dear God, let me live through this.

Even while doubting his loyalty to his family and his country, though arguably Britain wasn't his country, she was still loyal to him. He was her son. He was in trouble and she would do what she could to help him. Because she was loyal to all her children. Though if there was anything being a foster mother had taught her, it was that some people just couldn't be helped, and you had to let go.

She stopped about six feet from where Lazlo and the woman stood. It seemed slightly incredible to her that life carried on like normal around them.

"You okay, Laz?" she asked by way of greeting.

Lazlo nodded. Now he wore an expression of fear, but, given how afraid she was, she didn't entirely trust it, it was too textbook, almost comic book, and there wasn't sufficient tension in his body. Now she looked at the woman behind him. The eyebrows didn't match the black hair, so it was more than likely a wig.

"So how do you want to do this?"

The woman looked Elaine up and down. If that was an attempt to make her feel bad, outsized, out classed, it failed dreadfully; Elaine had been feeling all those things for so long it was normal to her.

"You give us want we vant, ve let little Laz here go."

Elaine watched the woman and wondered what accent she was trying for. It was vaguely Eastern bloc, a touch Marlene Dietrich and so obviously manipulated it didn't convince of anything other than that the woman was deliberately trying to hide her natural manner of speaking.

"You let him go and I'll give you what I found," Elaine tried.

"Zis is no time to bargain, Mrs Blake."

"It's hardly a bargain when you've got your two muscle men pretending—very badly I should tell you—not to be interested in what's going on when they clearly are. All I'm asking is for you to show a little faith and let Lazlo take a step away from you."

The woman scoffed. "And zin vot? You shoot me?"

Elaine frowned. "Shoot you? What with? I mean, don't be an idiot. Guns aren't readily available in the UK. I wouldn't know how to fire one even if I had one. Which I don't. In fact, it never even occurred to me to try to get one. Not that I'd know how to do that either." Elaine looked away. "Which was probably an act of stupidity on my part." She shrugged and returned her attention to the woman. "He said that if I could get you what Jason hid, you'd let him go. Well, I've got it, I'm prepared to give it to you, you just have to let him take a single step away from you."

Neither the woman nor Lazlo moved.

Elaine shrugged. "Or I can just walk away, and you can do whatever the hell you want."

"Do you really think I'd let you do that?"

The Marlene touch had slipped from the woman's accent, it was still eastern bloc, but more southern, more... Elaine wasn't entirely sure where it went.

"Nah, not really, but it was worth a punt."

Apparently, that wasn't a phrase the woman understood.

CHAPTER THIRTY-THREE

Blaring horns welcomed Mac as he sprinted up and out of the Metro into the street. The massive roundabout circling the Place du Trocadéro was stacked with unmoving cars. Angry horns blasted and drivers leant out of windows to shout at the drivers in front, none of whom seemed to have any idea what was going on.

The lack of movement was a bonus. He dodged through the cars, sprinted over the road, hurdled the barriers around the green space and ran hell for leather across the grass. He skidded a few inches as he landed on the damp slabs of the area directly behind Foch's statue, but stayed upright. One hand on the rear of the plinth, he stretched up to see over the cars attempting to inch their way forward on the road. Across in the plaza itself, he spotted the lilac hat Elaine had been wearing that morning, and her beneath it. From there, locating Lazlo was easy, he didn't immediately recognise the woman at his side, but that didn't matter. Would Elaine really hand over the evidence to these people? Or even just the key to reaching that evidence, since that was all she had? Would she betray her country? Had she even realised that there were two hired men lurking behind her? Both far bigger and stronger than her.

Shit, she doesn't have a clue.

Worse, he didn't have any idea what to do to help her. And even less when he spotted Ulrich Demko lurking on the side. Ulrich Demko – the hitman.

Shit, neither of us has a hope.

Then, in horror, he watched as Elaine reached out, clearly offering something to the woman.

* * *

The way her left hand was shaking as she reached out, Elaine wasn't certain she could even pass the pen drive across.

"What the hell is this?" the woman asked.

"It's a pen drive," Elaine said, unable to keep the contempt from her tone.

The woman's eyes flicked up to her, sharp as daggers. "What's on it?"

"Don't know, I didn't look. Didn't want to know," Elaine said. "But that's what I found."

"That's not what Jason said you'd find," Lazlo said.

It was getting more and more obvious that Lazlo wasn't scared, suggesting that he was, in fact, working with these people. She was on her own here. "Then maybe you should have told me what he said was there, so I would have known what to look for." She returned her hand to her pocket and pulled out the paper. "Was this what you were expecting?"

The woman slipped the pen drive into her pocket and took the paper – turning the curved and slightly discoloured paper around. "What happened to it?"

"Jason stored it in the lagging around the hot water tank. The heat shaped and yellowed it."

The woman's lip curled as she opened the folded paper to see the code there. "What is this?"

"It's a cypher," Lazlo said. Then he looked at Elaine. "What's the key?"

She pulled the key from her left-hand pocket. "This? I don't know what it is. Other than a key, of course. Kinda looks like a locker key to me."

"What's the key to the cypher?"

"Oh!" Elaine said, as if she was only catching on now. "No idea. I'm not good at cyphers, wouldn't have a clue where to start."

The woman snatched the key and pocketed that too. "Anything else?"

Elaine shook her head. "That's it, that's all I found." The woman glanced to Lazlo, making Elaine wonder who was really in charge. "Of course," she said conversationally, "if you lot have got Jason like you claim, seems to me you should just ask him. Surely, he knows where the evidence itself is." She slipped her hand into her left pocket and the last item there. She curled the whistle into her palm, mouthpiece by her thumb. "After all, unless that pen drive actually contains all the information that you're after. Which would suggest it was never in Jason's possession anyway, and he's lying to all of us. Which really wouldn't be that much of a surprise. Lying is, after all what he does best. And now I'm babbling. I'll shut up."

The woman's eyes hardened. She nodded to the men behind Elaine.

* * *

Horror and disbelief washed through Mac as Elaine handed something over to the woman he now realised was Illyana Kuznetsov under a wig. Were state secrets so easily sold? Of course they were, but he never thought Elaine would turn traitor.

Illyana nodded.

Two men in black moved.

Demko shifted.
Elaine's luck had run out.

* * *

Elaine saw the man coming, he was oddly hunched. Compensating for her lack of height? The metal whistle chilled her lips, hidden by her hand. A vice clamped around her arm, but the first man had moved closer. Jerking forward, Elaine sucked in air. She grabbed the man's top, yanked him forward. She dodged to the side. Her head by his ear. Shrill tones rent air and ear drum.

* * *

The oddity of sounds. The movement of a fight. A new spectator sport. The crowd stopped to watch. An audience standing uninvolved.

* * *

Mac heard the whistle. The man in front of Elaine cried out. His hand clutched his ear. He fell back.

Ulrich Demko moved forward. Mac couldn't allow that. Sneak attacks worked better for Mac against larger opponents. There was no sneaking in this open arena. Without a decisive surprise first strike, he'd be pulverised. But at least Demko wouldn't get to Elaine.

"Demko!"

The rough shout called the big man's attention. And Mac's.

Charles Linklater. Demko froze.

* * *

Another big hand appeared in Elaine's vision. Big, beefy, and looking to clamp over her mouth. The man struggled to reach past the two bags on her back. She hunched her shoulders to make it harder. Spitting out the whistle, she twisted her head. Her teeth clamped down on the flesh between his thumb and forefinger.

* * *

Mac understood why Lazlo stared in disbelief. Elaine should have been a push over. Only she was fighting off two men at once. Who was this woman underneath? It didn't matter in this moment. Lazlo and Illyana backed away, melted into the crowd.

* * *

The pencil slipped out of her sleeve. Elaine jabbed it at the hand on her arm. The bad position had it skidding off, but she had mistakenly used the blunt end. The gang of kids blew on their whistles, moved in.

* * *

Demko turned to Linklater, growled like a beast. They were of comparable size, both bigger than Mac, but his presence would decide the fight.

Mac focused on Demko, whistled sharply.

Like a hunting dog, the Russian responded to the noise. Looking between the two opponents ranged on each side.

He turned to Mac.

"Little man," Demko sneered.

The insult was old, but still rankled. Mac and Linklater stepped closer in concert.

Demko's eyes narrowed. Calculated.

* * *

The crowd found entertainment in the fight. Phones appeared. Videos and photographs. Four kids ran rings around the second man grabbing for Elaine. Move in. Slap. Move out of reach. A rotation of attacks. He couldn't defend and keep hold of the resisting Elaine. Mac heard the earnest tones of an older woman shouting down a phone, demanding the attention of the Police Nationale.

* * *

Blood poured into Elaine's mouth. She drew back her lips, let it flow out through her teeth. The pencil in her hand was reversed. Point uppermost. The first man was recovering. She'd shocked not hurt him. The second man had her, but with her bite, she had control. Curling her spine, she hunkered down, eyes on number one. He moved nearer, raised his hands to grab her. Unleashing coiled muscles, Elaine sprung up, punched out. There was little resistance. The first man screamed again. Grabbed his crotch. Blood pouring through his fingers as he fell to the ground.

* * *

Good girl!

Elaine impressed Mac, but now was not the time for admiration.

Different whistles. Police whistles. Mac saw two uniformed officers run into the square. The crowd did not make way, enjoying their entertainment. The teenagers punched the second man. Two kicked out his knees. The Police pushed through the mass of watchers.

* * *

The scream propelled Demko to look, to reassess. One man down. Another bleeding. Police arriving. Lazlo and Illyana gone.

Demko straightened as he turned to face Linklater and Mac. He threw a mock salute. "Next time, little man." Then he too rushed away.

* * *

Mac faced Linklater as the American joined him.

"Well, that was fun."

"Why are you here?" Mac asked Linklater as they started through the crowd toward Elaine.

"Personal favour to Miss Madison. Nothin' I wouldn't do for that li'l honey."

Mac glanced at Linklater. "She brushed you off too, didn't she?"

Linklater grinned. "Every time. But I like a challenge. Guessing that's why you keep after Elaine, even though you keep losing her."

Reaching the front of the crowd, Mac looked to where Elaine was—had been.

The man with the pencil in his groin lay crumpled on the

floor. Teenagers still surrounded his colleague, and they were blowing whistles, mocking the man as they circled and baited. But Elaine was gone.

The police appeared from the crowd. The teenagers ran.

The watching crowd parted for them.

* * *

Mac hung back, scanning the crowd for a lilac hat, or copper curls, but whatever direction Elaine had taken, she'd done it out of his sight. Linklater was sauntering away, on his phone already. The crowd closed in watching the police take control of the men and the situation.

Mac had to take control of his own situation.

He stepped back, allowing others to flow forward around him. Just another innocent by-stander.

* * *

Madison sat at her desk, trying desperately to make sense of everything.

Someone had live streamed "Trouble in Trocadéro" and Madison's alerts had pinged. She'd watched with an odd mix of terror and pride. Elaine was proving so much more capable than Madison could ever have predicted. Chuck had confirmed that Ulrich Demko and Illyana Kuznetsov were involved, and Lazlo had left with them, apparently voluntarily. Cormac Letterman was still tailing Elaine, for all he seemed to be having trouble keeping up. None of it helped Madison's indigestion.

If she'd worried about telling Elaine that Letterman was on her tail, no way would she tell her about the other two. If she knew she had two mercenary assassins on her tail, Elaine would probably worry herself into inaction. Hell, Madison wasn't even sure how she was coping with that news.

Her only comfort was that Letterman at least appeared to be on Elaine's side. That he had actually attempted to save her.

The sound of the phone made her jump. The voice of Number Two was abrupt and surprising. "We swept the Southgate house. It was clean."

"Of course it was. Unlike Elaine, Kiera had the forewarning of knowing what's been going on."

There was a pause, Madison read that as Number Two considering what if to say anything next. "We didn't hang your mother out to dry," Number Two said carefully. "She'd have been perfectly safe if she'd stayed at home." Number Two put the phone down.

Madison couldn't have disagreed more with that statement. Home would not now be a safe place for Elaine at all.

The bigger question however, was how in the hell could she safely contact Elaine?

Please Mom, please phone home.

* * *

Mac searched the crowd. Nothing. She was gone. He saw now that the crash that had backed up the traffic was being shifted to the curb. The traffic started to flow as he finally walked away down the Avenue du Président Wilson. Should he turn back? Did he have a choice? Did someone just call his name? He stopped and turned. Chuck Linklater III was coming towards him, a phone to his ear.

"Here, you can tell him yourself." Chuck held out the

phone. "She called me."

Mac had rarely been so nervous about taking a proffered phone. "Hello?"

"Ladderman?"

Elaine? He still didn't like that name, but that wasn't important right now.

"What the fuck was that?" Not how he'd intended to start a conversation with her, not that he had any fixed idea of what he'd say, but it encapsulated his feelings succinctly.

There was a pause. Was she considering putting the phone down? "I spotted you and Chuck. Wanted to say thanks for being there."

"Jesus, Elaine, do you realise that you just committed treason?"

CHAPTER THIRTY-FOUR

Implications crashed through Elaine like a tsunami threatening to wash her off her feet. Nauseated, she moved towards the buildings and gratefully sank to a wide stone windowsill.

"No, I didn't," she said, though she sort of felt like she had. "I think what I just committed was fraud." She took a deep breath and stood. She couldn't allow any man to stop her again.

"What?" He sounded confused, and she couldn't blame him. "What did you give them?"

"That pen drive you gave me." She paused to look both ways and cross the road. "Edited down a bit. I took out the picture of my anniversary and the ones of Madison. I left those of Lazlo. I figure he can face whatever happens to him on his own, if he's been lying and using me. Which I think he was, otherwise why would he so easily have arrived and left with that woman? Or I am misinterpreting?"

"Not from where I was standing. But I also saw you gave them more than that."

"Are you following me again?" Automatically, she turned and searched behind her.

"What do you think?"

"I think you and Chuck were still at the plaza when I ran, maybe still there, given how relaxed Chuck was when I called. No, I don't think you're following me right now."

Elaine declared. Then repented. A very little. "But just so you can panic a bit less. I gave them a faked copy of the cypher that I found in the lagging, changed the code so they won't be able to decode it. And I gave them a key to one of the lockers in the gym at last night's hotel. It won't get them anywhere."

The sigh she heard might have been relief, but there was no way she could be sure. "Like I said to them, Jason, who they claimed to have in their control, should know where the evidence is without the cypher. But they don't seem to know. Can't figure that one out. But I will figure out the rest of it. If I'm lucky."

"You have an annoying habit of being lucky. Like you were lucky those kids got in the way of that last guy. He could have carried you off. For all you bit his hand."

"Yeah, but better than a pencil in the testes," she grinned, amazed at and embarrassed by herself for that. "Besides, getting lucky that those kids ran interference cost me over two hundred euro."

Again, the silence as he digested that. "Where are you?"

She laughed. "You're definitely not following me right this second, then?"

There was more pause, she heard as much traffic his end as hers, but it was different enough to assure that he wasn't close.

"No." The admission was grudging.

"Good. But in answer to your question, now I'm here. I've no idea where here is mind. I just got away from the Trocadéro as quick as I could. Other than that, not a scooby."

"A what?"

"A scooby. As in Scooby Do? As in rhyming slang for a clue? Are you sure you're English?"

He didn't immediately answer and sounded miffed when he spoke again. "Where are you going?"

"Don't know."

"Mrs Bla—"

"What happened to calling me Elaine? I mean, I never said you could, but I prefer that to Mrs Blake. Way too formal, all things considered. And I'm not kidding, I don't know where I am or where I'm going, but I do know it won't be back to Cardiff. I'm not going home. At least not yet. Tell you something else, Ladderman." She could hardly believe she was about to say this, but it was true. "Weirdly, I'm going to miss you."

She ended the call.

* * *

Damn and blast!

Mac wanted to swear but had to keep the stiff upper lip in front of Linklater as he returned the phone to the tall American.

"The one got away again, huh?" Linklater said.

"She gets away, I find her." At least that was how it had worked so far. That was how it was going to work this time. It had to.

"And how are you going to manage that?" Linklater asked.

That was the big question. She was going to follow the cypher, which he was now convinced consisted of more than just Watch Tower, clearly there was something that needed a key too. If she'd replaced it with a locker key, it could be anything. Another locker? A box? Safe deposit? How could he ever tell without seeing the key to start with?

It didn't matter, he didn't need to follow the clues, he just needed to follow Elaine. Somehow.

"How am I going to manage that?" He grinned up at Linklater. "Eel net."

* * *

Elaine had told him she didn't know where she was going, and that was true. She hadn't a clue. She turned off her phone and took out the battery. A tip Madison had given her.

It wasn't clear to her what the situation was with Lazlo. He had betrayed her, but did that mean he'd betrayed the UK? Betrayed Jason? What was the truth about Jason? Loyal to his country or a traitor? Dead or alive?

She didn't care. She had his death certificate, that was enough.

The one thing she did know was that she wasn't the same woman who had left home. She hadn't yet worked out who she was, but she would, eventually. If she lived that long.

At another junction, she had to stop to cross the road. For a moment the busy sound of the city receded, and she was alone, not just for now, but forever and she peered around, seeing the world with new eyes. As much as she'd enjoyed her time in Paris, this wasn't where she wanted to be. Her heart suddenly felt as frozen as her hands, even as she rammed them into her pockets. Her right hand touched paper: a perennial and bad habit of jamming receipts in her pockets and forgetting about them. Receipts and paper money. She pulled the paper out. Not a receipt, nor cash. The original cypher.

She had written the resolution in her small notebook. This was Jason's torn page. The odd jumble of letters she now read as Watch Tower, Godiva, and North Gate Spell. It still made no sense.

She tore it into tiny pieces and dropped half in a bin, a couple of bits she gave to the draft from passing traffic, watched them picked up and tossed about like confetti. The rest fell in the next bin.

But it made her think of what she didn't know. Like what the 'evidence' actually was. Not that anyone else seemed to know either. It wasn't just about the cypher, there was also the key and the code. The run of numbers and letters from the picture. She didn't know what either were about, but she wasn't ready to give up on them.

Why didn't the people who claimed to have Jason already know the answers. Surely, he knew what was what. Unless of course, he needed something she had. Like the key. She took the small item from the secure pocket in her bag.

She stopped in the middle of the pavement, thought about the numbers again.

"Nah, can't be that simple," she said as she moved into the lee of a blank wall. "Can it?"

She riffled through her handbag, pulled out her notebook. She had written out both the cypher and the numbers from the anniversary picture. She considered the code. Two letters, two numbers, four letters, fourteen numbers.

"Bloody hell."

Could it be that simple? All UK bank accounts had a unique number and a sort code. But they also had an IBAN number, which she'd found out about when she'd had to send money to one of the foster children in Mexico. From what she could remember, the first two letters indicated the country, she couldn't remember what the two numbers were, but the four letters were a code for the bank and the last digits were the account number and sort code.

The first two letter of this code were CH. Czech Republic? No, she figured, that was CZ. So, what on earth would CH be? China? Chile? Chad? She couldn't be sure, but it couldn't be that hard to find out.

She put her things back in her bag, made sure to zip it all in tight.

Wherever CH was, that was where she was going.

THE END

For all involved, thank you, we'll finish this game later.

Vs lbh pna ernq guvf, cynl gur tnzr naq svaq gur Dhrra fbat
gvgyrf, gurer'f ng yrnfg bar uvqqra va rirel
puncgre.

DIAMOND
CRIME

COMING NEXT
FROM
GB WILLIAMS

PLAY THE GAME

The Second Part
of
The Elaine Blake Series

DIAMOND
BOOKS

DIAMOND
CRIME

Passionate about the crime/mystery/thriller books it publishes

Follow
Facebook:
@diamondcrimepublishing

Instagram
@diamond_crime_publishing

Web
diamondbooks.co.uk